MURDER IN
LA PLAZA DE TOROS

MURDER IN
LA PLAZA DE TOROS

A
MARCO IN SPAIN
MYSTERY

PAULA B. MAYS

To my good friends Cynthia and Jan thank you for all your support

"Her Andalusian bodice and trim basquiña
set off her round form. Her glossy hair was
parted on her forehead and decorated with a
fresh plucked rose, according to the custom
in Spain."

—TALES OF THE ALAHAMBRA,
BY WASHINGTON IRVING

Praise for Murder in La Plaza De Toros

"Paula Mays, president of Sisters in Crime, is launching another delightful mystery set in Southern Spain. It follows her suspenseful whodunnit *Murder in the Parador*. Paula brings her legal background in intellectual property and her healthcare expertise to create an intriguing plot filled with colorful and diverse characters. *Parador* was a page-turner right to the end with its surprise twist. I can't wait to read her new book, *Murder in La Plaza De Toros*."—Catherine Lincoln, Graduate, St Hugh's College, Oxford University, wife of former Minister to Vietnam (deceased), Member of the Lincoln Club

Chapter One

Marco bolted upright. "I'm not wicked," he said, looking around and realizing where he was; he must have finally fallen asleep over the course of the long night. He glanced over at the clock. A hint of sunlight peeked through the window. Sleep being defeated, Marco swung his long legs over the bed and fought his way out from under duvet covers strewn over him where Belen had thrown them as she tossed and turned during the night.

He trudged off to the kitchen and gulped down a cup of rich, dark espresso, a much-needed burst of energy. He'd been up half the night watching Belen practice her dance routine, twirling and counting, 5...6...7...8. She had a big day ahead. Marco had told her she was wonderful and assured her that nothing would go wrong. Though, as he said it, he thought he felt a pang of anxiety, which he dismissed as fatigue. He'd been working late hours for weeks.

Marco had been inundated with requests for his investigation services ever since he'd solved the high-profile case involving the murder of a British scientist on the verge of discovering a cancer cure. He felt good about that case, like he'd done some good for the world. The cancer cure was in the final days of study and was about to get approval for use, so he'd read.

Marco put the coffee cup down and sauntered off to shower. He might as well go to work early and get some work done before meeting Belen at the bull ring in the afternoon. He towel-dried and shook his thick mane of dark hair and got dressed. He grabbed his keys on the table next to the front door and yelled to Belen, who still lingered in the bedroom, that he'd meet her at two-thirty in the bullfighting ring. He decided to drive to work, a departure from his normal walking routine, as he'd need the car later to go to the bullring at the top of the largest hill in Vivirrambla overlooking the azure sea.

Marco parked his car in the garage next to his building and walked over to Alvarez's for his café con leche.

"Buenos dias, Alvarez," he said as he perched on an open bar stool at the end of the counter.

A pudgy bald man smiled and shook Marco's hand. "Como estas, amigo, I haven't seen you for a long time. Where have you been?" Alvarez asked as he went to start the coffee machine.

"I've been really busy. Business really picked up after that John Donne case. I've even been asked to consult with police forces in Madrid," Marco said.

"Ah, that's great. I'm happy for you, amigo," Alvarez said.

Marco smiled. "Un café por favor, y un postre.".

Alvarez nodded. "Si, coming right up," Alvarez said as he pulled out the sweet cinnamon pastry his wife had made earlier that morning.

"Big day for Belen, today, I heard?" Alvarez asked.

Marco nodded his head. "Definitely. I didn't get a bit of sleep. I've never seen her so excited. When I left this morning, she was dancing around the bedroom like a schoolchild in her first play."

Alvarez laughed his jolly belly laugh which made the top of his head turn a crimson color. "It's going to be great for her career," he said.

"I hope so. I really want her to do well. Dancing's important to her," Marco said as he took one last swig of coffee.

Alvarez swooped up the empty cup and wiped the spot where the cup had been. "Tell her good luck for me," he said.

"I will. She'll be pleased you cared," Marco said.

Marco walked the few yards from the coffee shop to his office. His assistant, Eva, sat at her computer typing. She greeted him with her trademark warm smile. He didn't understand how anyone could be so happy first thing in the morning. Marco informed her that he didn't intend to stay at the office long. He'd work a few hours catching up, then the rest of the afternoon he'd dedicate to Belen.

"I'm so excited for her," Eva said. "I can't wait to hear how it turns out."

"I'll tell you all about it tomorrow," Marco said.

"I want to hear it all, not the male capsulized version," Eva said, laughing.

Marco chuckled. He marveled at how well Eva knew him. He shut his office door and tried to concentrate on his work, but his mind wandered. Belen sent him several texts, adding to his distractions. He rifled through some papers, not reading them. He was relieved when his watch said one-thirty, the time he'd decided to leave. He said goodbye to Eva and headed out. He felt excited and scared for some reason, though it wasn't *his* big day.

"She'll do great. Wish her good luck from me," Eva said.

"I will, thanks," Marco said.

Marco arrived at the Vivirrambla bullring as the Spanish sun blazed overhead. He took a seat in the front bleachers with the other privileged few spectators who'd been given special tickets to watch the taping live. He spotted Belen across the stage. She looked fantastic, dressed in a traditional Spanish Flamenco outfit, a multi-colored frilled skirt, her hair in a bun. Large pink earrings hung from her ears. Belen and the other dancers pranced around backstage, shaking off their nerves, waiting for their cue to perform.

Marco had been there twenty minutes when a short, thin man with tan skin and straight dark hair coiffed at the top of his head entered the stage that had been erected in the middle of the bullring. The other performers took their places around him. The taping began at the instruction of the director who yelled commands. Marco watched in awe as they performed. He forgot the uncomfortable heat of the afternoon. Marco had never met a pop star as big as Kijamba. Now his girlfriend was dancing in a video with him. It seemed unreal. Kijamba moved effortlessly across the bullring to the music. The flamenco dancers, including Belen, seemed to twirl at the speed of light, and their costumes formed a rainbow effect around the singer. All those spectators, like Marco sitting on the bleachers, stood for an ovation after the director yelled, *"Cut."* After numerous stops and starts, everyone finally seemed satisfied with the video take. The Director prophesized that it was sure to be a blockbuster hit.

Belen found Marco in the stands and hugged him. Sweat ran down her face. "Wasn't it amazing," she asked?"

"I'm so proud of you. You looked great out there," Marco said.

That evening, Marco, Belen, the other flamenco dancers, and some of the crew and musicians toasted the video's success at the Townhome bar, owned by Marco's friend, Layla, late into the evening. Everyone seemed in a good mood and excited about the upcoming music video release. The other patrons in Townhome treated them like celebrities and bought them rounds of drinks. "You really danced with Kijamba," they all asked Belen.

"I feel like a celebrity," Belen said.

Marco smiled. "You are, darling."

They went onto the dance floor to dance. Layla let the bar stay open later as everyone was having such a good time. It was dusk, and the sky was changing colors before Marco and Belen got home.

Marco arrived at work the next day, droopy-eyed and tired. He grabbed two aspirina and threw them down his throat with a chaser of water. He was getting too old at thirty-nine to celebrate all night and go to work the next day. He rested his hand on his chin and stared blankly at the computer screen. He jumped when Eva flounced unannounced into his office.

"Marco, I need to talk to you right away. You're not going to believe this," she said.

Marco frowned. "Why? What is it, Eva?"

"Have you been listening to the news?" she asked. "I just heard it a few minutes ago."

Marco sat upright at his desk. "News? What news?"

"Kijamba was found dead in his home this morning."

Marco's mouth dropped open. "Kijamba? Are you sure you got that right?" he asked, knowing Eva rarely, if ever, made mistakes.

Eva nodded. "Yes, the police are at his house now."

"I'd better call Belen. She'll be devastated," he said.

Just then, the phone on Marco's desk rang. Eva answered it.

"It's Detective Flores for you, "she said.

CHAPTER ONE

"There was once a fountain, he said, in one of the public squares called Il fuente del toro, the fountain of the bull, because the water gushed from the mouth of a bull's head, carved of stone."

Tales of the Alhambra, Washington Irving

Chapter Two

Shada adjusted her black Chanel gold-rimmed sunglasses and flicked back the mass of curly long hair dangling on her shoulders. She pulled out a decorative fan from her purse, opened it with one adept move and waved it back and forth over her face. The heat was stifling this far up in the hills.

On the weekdays, the place where she now sat operated an active bullring. Despite weekly protests by animal activists, Vivirramba's Las Plaza de Toros was packed most evenings with old-timers, those who had gone to bullfights all their lives, blood-thirsty fanatics, Hemingway fans, tourists, and curiosity seekers who wanted to see a live bullfight. Attendees saw it as an art form. Protestors and reformers saw it as the cruelty killing of animals. Shada had no use for actual bullfighting; she wasn't there for that reason.

She sat in the front row next to a guy who said his girlfriend was one of the dancers. He was quite handsome with arresting dark eyes and jet-black hair. She shifted her attention back to her husband, Kijamba, the American pop artist, about to film a new sensational video. Kijamba looked sexy in the traditional matador costume, *la traje de luces*, suit of lights, red pants, and a gold blazer attached with sequins so that the light shimmered when the camera landed on him. He was not tall; he was small, the size of most bullfighters. The costume fit well and moved with his body as he danced and twirled. She liked his hair better now that he'd cut the large Afro he'd sported for years. His hair, cut close to his head on the sides, gave him a more mature look. He looked as handsome as the day she'd met him.

Shada felt excited to see the taping. The video producers had paid handsomely for Ricardo Ortiz, famed Spanish bullfighter, who donned a black montera hat and waved his muleta red cap to make a cameo appearance in the video. Ortiz fought an imaginary bull and shouted *"Ole"* while Kijamba twirled and spun around him as he sang a mix of American pop and traditional Spanish music, advertised as a blend of Paco Lucia and Prince. Critics said no other artist, except perhaps Carlos Santana, had stretched himself so musically.

It took some time to get the video just right. Stagehands ran around placing things, and make-up people refreshed the faces of Kijamba and the dancers as the scene was redone over and over again. At last, the director was satisfied. "Great job, folks," he said. "We're looking at another Grammy."

Everyone rushed to the middle of the ring. They all took turns hugging and congratulating Kijamba. Shada ran over to hug and kiss her exhausted husband, who looked as if he were about to faint from the heat.

"Are you okay?" she asked.

"I'm fine," Kijamba said. "That was intense; it just took it all out of me."

Shada frowned. It had been an exhausting taping. She helped Kijamba to gather his things and handed him bottled water. "Let's go home," she said.

Kijamba and Shada returned to their villa estate on the Golden Mile hot and exhausted. Shada asked the cook to prepare dinner for just the two of them. She sensed they needed some time alone. They'd been busy nonstop. They'd hosted a pre-release party the week before, where all their friends had come, about 100 people. Their friend, Catherine Taylor, stayed with them off and on for a week. Shada could see fatigue in her husband's brown eyes. The cook prepared a dinner of lamb and chickpeas, Kijamba's favorite. They popped open a bottle of Cava and toasted Kijamba's success. They decided to retire after one glass. Kijamba said he still felt a bit queasy from the heat. Shada agreed it was a good idea to go to bed early. She was concerned he'd gotten heat stroke.

"Don't worry, Shad, I just need a good night's sleep. I have to get up early to sign the licensing agreement for Cipi's music," he said.

Kijamba had purchased one of the songs from a friend and needed to secure protection for the music. It was part of the business aspects that went along with making music. Shada had never taken an interest in the business side of things.

"Okay," she said, "let's go get some rest."

They headed up to the bedroom. Kijamba fell asleep as soon as he positioned himself in bed. Shada watched him sleep for a minute. He looked so peaceful, like a brown angel, but she, too, was tired and fell asleep within minutes. When the alarm went off at seven the next morning, Shada rolled over, and on her way to the bathroom, she whispered to Kijamba to wake up. She expected him to be awake when she returned. But when she emerged after a shower, Kijamba hadn't stirred. "Get up, sleepy head," she said, laughingly.

He didn't move. She stood over him, perplexed. "Kiki, wake up. We've got a busy day ahead. You've got to do the licensing agreement." She frowned. "Kiki, get up." She shoved him. She gasped and put her hand over her mouth. Her pulse quickened. His body felt stiff and ice cold.

Chapter Three

Marco parked his small car on the Golden Mile, the aptly named neighborhood of sweeping homes and expansive villas on the edge of Vivirrambla. The address he sought was a mansion surrounded by large windows and white exterior walls. Its architecture was somewhere between the traditional European villa and modern-day minimalism. The pristine lawn was littered with paparazzi, news reporters, and mourners jockeying for position. A makeshift memorial with flowers had been set up on the street in front of the villa. Hundreds of red roses and other arrangements had already been placed near a marble statue. Marco made his way through the crowds. He showed his credentials to the La Guarda Civil and was escorted into a living room twice as large as his entire apartment.

Marco's eyes scanned the room. The furniture was all white or cream-colored accented with gold except for a couple of the chairs which were dusty rose silk damask. Curtains of rose and gold tied the room together. He noticed a couple of women in uniform on the other side of the room talking to detectives. Marco wondered how many people it took to keep the house clean. He spotted Detective Alberto Flores conferring with other officers from the Malaga police. They all wore blue fabric booties over their shoes to preserve the scene as they dusted for prints and bagged items in paper bags. Marco was handed a pair of the booties, which he slipped on.

Flores gestured to Marco. "Over here," he said, waving Marco to a corner of the room.

Flores retrieved a mint from his pocket and popped it in his mouth. He offered the box to Marco who shook his head.

Flores chomped on the mint. "Some place, huh," he said. "They found the deceased upstairs this morning in his bed. The room's being examined for evidence, so we can't get up there right now."

"Do we have any idea what happened?" Marco asked.

Flores shook his head. "Nope, not yet. The deceased's wife says her husband went right to bed after dinner. When she tried to wake him this morning, he was dead. She's inconsolable. I think they finally gave her a sedative. She's sleeping now. So far, there's no sign of a heart attack or stroke, according to Javier. Though, he said an aneurysm couldn't be ruled out."

"I don't believe it. I saw him just yesterday, alive and dancing. He died sometime during the night or this morning?" Marco asked.

Flores pulled out another mint and stuck it in his mouth. "It seems so. He died sometime last night. The Chief's worried. With the deceased being a famous singer, there's going to be a lot of publicity and scrutiny. Our whole force is on the line. We called you because the wife's Moroccan. It might be sensitive. We need you to make sure things go as smoothly as possible with her," Flores said.

Marco understood. He'd lost his job on the force because some of his colleagues couldn't accept that he was half-Moroccan, and his former partner had set him up. Now, his origin seemed to be an asset to him as a private investigator.

Flores took the vibrating phone out of his plaid jacket pocket and answered it. "Okay," he said to the person on the other end. He turned to Marco, "We can go upstairs now. They've finished dusting the room for prints. Let's go up and see what we find."

Marco followed Flores up a spiral staircase to an oversized bedroom filled with expensive-looking furniture. A large gold comforter lay neatly folded at the edge of the bed. Someone had removed the sheets, and a sturdy mattress was revealed. Flores and Marco looked around the room.

Flores' cheeks turned red as he raised his voice. "Who cleaned the room? I hope they didn't destroy any evidence. Is the cleaning staff still around?"

Flores asked the officer standing next to him.

"The maid, a Senorita Rocio, had already cleaned the bed when we got here. We got what forensics we could. We spoke to her for a couple of hours; then we sent her home. She said she came in at her regular hour to start cleaning. She was downstairs when she heard Kijamba's wife screaming and crying. She ran right upstairs to see what happened and found the deceased's wife shaking and pointing to the bed. She said she saw Kijamba lying there and not moving. Together, they called an ambulance. It was too late by the time it arrived; Kijamba was already dead. She said she cleaned the room because she didn't want Mrs. Smith to see it in that condition," the officer said.

Marco walked over to the bed, picked up the mattress, and examined it along with the surrounding furniture. Then he inspected the carpet. He opened the large walk-in closet. On one side, he saw suits and leather pants, jeans, and formal shirts. On the other side, he saw neatly hung dresses, blouses, pants, and jeans arranged on hangers. Several pairs of shoes were lined up in order on the bottom shelves.

"Did you find anything?" Flores asked.

Marco shrugged. "Just a lot of expensive designer clothes."

When they returned downstairs, they found Shada staring out of a window. She wore a white dressing gown and white slippers with fuzzy balls on the top. Her full hair hung loose and fell past her shoulders. When she looked up at Detective Flores and Marco, her large eyes were red and swollen. She pulled the belt of her white silk robe tighter to her body. Marco thought about the opulence he'd just witnessed and how it had not protected Kijamba from an untimely death or Shada from the pain she suffered.

Shada spoke with a soft voice. "I couldn't get to sleep even with the meds. So, I came back downstairs. I don't really know what to do," she said.

"We know this is a bad time, but we need to ask you a few questions, Mrs. Smith," Flores said.

"How could this have happened?" she asked.

"That's what we intend to find out," Flores said. "Had your husband been ill?"

Her eyes widened. "No, Kik, Kijamba, I call him Kiki, was in great shape. He'd been to the doctor before the shoot started to make sure he was fit, as the video was intense and had a lot of strenuous dancing. He was getting older, and he wanted to make sure he could handle the demands. His doctor gave him complete clearance and said he was in top health."

"How old was your husband?" Flores asked.

"He'd just turned forty-six," she said.

Marco recalled the vigorous dancing he'd seen during the video shoot. Kijamba would have to have been in great shape at his age to perform the way he did. His dancing rivaled that of Michael Jackson.

"Your husband did a video shoot at the bullring yesterday, didn't he?" Flores asked.

"Yes."

Shada looked over at Marco. "He was there too; I believe his girlfriend was dancing in the video."

"That's right," Marco said.

"You saw my husband. He was fine, right? He seemed a little tired, but that was to be expected," Shada said.

"Who all was at the bullring with Kijamba during the filming?" Flores asked.

Shada counted on her fingers. "The only people allowed on set were the crew, the dancers, the videographer, the soundman, the make-up artist and the bullfighter, Ricardo Ortiz, and a couple of friends. My friend Catherine, who was in from out of town, was there."

"What about the crew who worked on the video? Did you know the members of the crew?" Flores asked.

Shada gave a rundown of the behind-the-scenes workers. The soundman, lighting, and all the crew were regulars who worked with Kijamba on most of his videos. Shada said they were all close. Along with Kijamba's business manager, Thomas House, they comprised Kijamba's team.

"Had your husband had any disagreements with any of them recently?" Flores asked.

Shada rubbed her folded arms up and down with her hands as if to assuage her feelings. "No, of course not, we're like family." She paused. "Why are you asking me all these questions? Kiki was so alive and so happy. I don't understand what could have happened." Shada walked over to the window and pulled back the curtain. "It's going to be a mob scene here soon. I don't know if I can deal with all of this."

"We've got police presence lined up. We'll do our best to keep the press away from you as much as possible," Flores said.

"Thank you, detective."

"What did you do after the video shoot?" Flores asked.

"We came home and had dinner and went to bed," Shada said.

"Was anyone at the house last night other than you and Kijamba?" Flores asked.

"No, just us. The cook made us some food; then we sent her home. We wanted to be alone. Some of the video crew went out to celebrate after the shoot, but Kijamba wanted a quiet evening together as he had some paperwork to sign the next day, and he needed to go over some contracts with his lawyers, something about signing over a licensing agreement. I don't really understand those things."

"So, you and Kijamba came home, ate dinner, and didn't go out the rest of the evening?" Flores asked.

"That's right, we had a glass of wine and went straight to bed. When I tried to wake him up, he wouldn't move." She sighed. "I need to go lie down."

"Okay, I understand, Mrs. Smith. We don't need anything else from you right now. We'll keep you posted when we find out anything," Flores said.

"We'll make sure you aren't mobbed by the television crowd as best we can," Marco said.

"Thank you, detectives."

Shada extended her hand to Marco and Flores. "Forgive me for breaking down. I appreciate all you are doing."

Flores handed her a card. "Let me know if you need anything."

Flores spoke first once they were outside. "I don't know what to think. A young man, forties, in good physical shape. It's hard to believe his death was natural. On the other hand, many people have died of undetected heart ailments or unknown diagnosed diseases."

"True, but he'd been fine, well enough to engage in vigorous dancing. It was really hot that day but the coroner hasn't said anything about heatstroke. When I saw him, he looked a bit tired, but nothing else seemed wrong with him. My instinct tells me this wasn't a natural death," Marco said.

"If not, we'll need to look at the widow first. We always start closest to home," Flores said.

"I'll go and see if Bortello has any new information for us yet," Marco said.

Chapter Four

Marco left Flores and went straight to the coroner's office. He walked past the guards to the entrance to the morgue. It wasn't his favorite place to visit, but it was the only place he could talk to Javier Bortello, who rarely left his office. He found Bortello wearing a plastic suit over his clothing, holding an instrument in his hands, leaning over a body that lay still on a metal bed.

Bortello crunched his face when he saw Marco approaching. "What can I do for you, Marco? I don't have much time. As you can see, I'm busy. I'm backed up here."

"I need to talk to you about the death of the singer," Marco said.

"I figured that's what you wanted. Where is Detective Flores? Shouldn't he be here, finding out what happened?" Bortello asked.

Marco shrugged. "I told him I'd come talk to you. What can you tell me so far? Does it look like a natural death?"

Bortello took off the plastic gloves he'd been wearing. "Not much to tell right now until I get into the body. It could have been a hemorrhagic stroke, what we call a brain aneurysm. We found some bleeding on the brain. He didn't show any of the usual symptoms such as droopy eyelids or confusion, but aneurysms can hit without warning."

Bortello pulled open a drawer that contained the body of Kijamba atop a white sheet on a metal bed. Marco looked down at the corpse. Kijamba was shorter than Marco had envisioned when he saw him on stage that day at the bullring when Belen was dancing in his video. He seemed to be about five-foot-seven inches in real life. His light-amber skin, the color of newly milled dark pollen from a bee, was smooth and taut. News columns described him as handsome, almost pretty. He bore a tattoo of music notes on one arm and the name Shada on the other arm. In some ways, he seemed delicate but, at the same time, masculine. His muscular calves testified to his dancing stamina.

Bortello turned the deceased's head to the side to face them. He used a metal tool to point to Kijamba's right ear. "He's got this wound in his inner ear. I'd like to examine the ear canal before I issue the certificate of death. I'm not sure what that is yet. I'll be able to tell you more later," Bortello said, shutting the metal drawer. A hollow sound like death echoed in the room.

Chapter Five

Marco scurried out of the morgue. He needed to escape the smell of formaldehyde, the cold feeling of death and misery. When he got home, he found Belen busy in the kitchen chopping vegetables. Meat boiled in a separate pot. She appeared to be making some sort of stew. The aroma smelled of his Jaddah's house in Morocco. It reminded him of his childhood when he went to visit her, and she'd prepare a feast for her boys, Marco and his cousin, Kareem. She'd whip up a pot of stew with olives and cinnamon in her well-used clay tagine. The entire house would smell of spices and his grandmother's love.

"I thought we both needed some comfort food," she said as Marco approached her.

He put his arms around her waist. "Smells wonderful. You smell good too, like my grandmother," he said, as he kissed her.

Belen laughed and hit Marco's arm. "Thanks, just what I want to smell like, your grandmother."

Marco turned her head and kissed her on the lips. "Belen, I want to talk to you about Kijamba. I know you're still upset about it, but I've been to see the coroner."

Belen put down the spoon she'd been using to stir the stew and sat down at the kitchen table.

She furrowed her brow. "What did the coroner say?"

"He thinks maybe he had a brain aneurysm."

She stood there in silence for a moment. "That's so sad."

"The coroner wants to know if you or anyone saw any signs of anything like dizziness while you were dancing?" Marco asked.

Belen thought for a moment. "No, I don't recall anything. It was hot, so we all stopped for water breaks."

"Did Kijamba seem nauseous?"

"No, not that I saw. By the way, I spoke to Shada. I called to see how she was doing. She's upset that she isn't able to have a funeral and say a final goodbye. It's tearing her apart."

The smell of the stew intensified. Belen got up from the table to give it a stir. "Now that I think of it," Belen said, pursing her lips, "he seemed a little upset when we stopped shooting for a minute so he could read a note one of the crew handed him. No one thought anything about it, though; he was a ball of energy. We had a hard time keeping up with him."

"Yes, I remember that. I could barely see what was happening, but I think he dropped a paper, and someone came and swooped it up," Marco said.

"One of the stagehands," Belen said.

"You bend and twirl a lot during the dance, don't you?" Marco asked.

She resumed her seat at the kitchen table and took a sip of wine from the bottle she'd put out. "Yep, we do. Kijamba's solo, where he danced and twirled with the mike, I still don't know how he did it."

Marco walked over to the stove and smelled the stew. "That smells so good. Is it almost ready? That dance looked amazing. Maybe he had an ear infection or something he ignored to keep the filming going," Marco said.

"That's possible. He was anxious to get it wrapped up. He said he needed to take care of some important business."

When the stew of beef, tomato, and onion had finished cooking, they took the meal onto the patio. After dinner and more wine, they became enraptured from the intoxication. They both felt as if they needed one another. Marco slept well that evening.

Marco woke up refreshed. He decided to walk to work the next day as it was spring, and the temperature felt comfortable. The scents from the naranja, orange trees, and jasmine and the scenery from the purple jacaranda trees and bougainvillea were a joyous way to start the day. He felt lighthearted.

Once he got to work, he phoned the coroner to tell him what Belen had said. Kijamba had seemed to be dizzy for a few seconds, but he'd kept dancing, and no one noticed anything else.

Chapter Six

Flores's ears turned a bright red like he'd had a sudden allergic reaction. It happened when he became agitated. He fumed as he recalled his conversation with Marco. The coroner was refusing to release Kijamba's body until he completed further examination.

Flores screamed on the phone. "What do we do now, just wait? They're calling the station every day asking us to release the body," Flores said.

"Bortello said he'd finish the autopsy as soon as possible," Marco said.

"That's not good enough! The Chief's already hounding me. He's not going to like this delay. I'm going to get demoted; I know it. Did he say when he'd be finished?"

"He didn't say. It's not your fault. Be glad Bortello's thorough, better that we find out something now than the Americans discover something we missed," Marco said.

"Yeah, tell it to the Chief. The wife calls him all the time. She wants closure and to take the body back home. Kijamba's fans call at all hours of the day. The press is eviscerating us. They're saying we're incompetent, and the case should be sent to Madrid.

"Maybe if we went and explained it to his wife in person," Marco said.

Flores's voice lowered an octave. "I guess it couldn't hurt. It's something I can tell the Chief, at least." They agreed to speak to Shada later that afternoon to explain the coroner's findings to her.

Flores picked up Marco on the way. The two rode in Flores' small blue Citroen through the streets of the Golden Mile, tucked in the hills away from the rest of middle-class Spanish society. The grand villas, occupied by wealthy Swedes, Germans, Moroccan royalty, and old Spanish families, varied in design from the traditional villas to Swedish minimalist architecture with square buildings and large windows. The expansive manicured lawns were a light shade of emerald, green. Water sprinklers spouted and turned from all different directions due to the lack of rain. Marco and Flores dodged the spraying water as they walked. Purplish bougainvillea cascaded down the gates and fences of yards, and tall palm trees stood in majestic salute to all who passed.

Shada's house was surrounded by reporters and paparazzi, some of whom camped out on the lawn. Extra security measures had been taken as Shada had received threats after a rag newspaper suggested she had something to do with her husband's death. Police wearing neon green vests guarded the door. They held back aggressive media, begging to get even a glimpse of the grieving widow. Flores showed his credentials to the officers and he and Marco were ushered through the crowd. A small face peered through the door's peephole when Flores rang the bell. He held up his badge, and a tiny young woman with fearful eyes granted them entrance.

Marco and Flores swiped the soles of their shoes on the entrance rug like children coming in from a playdate. The housekeeper led them through into a sitting room with dark hardwood flooring. Marco wrinkled his nose; his olfactory senses felt overwhelmed by the scent of roses, carnations, and a variety of other flowers scattered in vases around the room.

Shada entered the room and greeted them. Her white pantsuit blended well with the colors of the flowers. She was one of the most beautiful women Marco had ever seen. Her heritage a mixture of Moroccan and Black American produced long full dark hair and huge round shaped brown eyes. She had a tiny waist and firm hips. She reminded him of his ex-girlfriend, Amira. A tall, rangy, sandy-haired man appeared at her side. He wore well-creased navy pants and a crisp white shirt. He extended a well-pampered hand with short nails out to Marco and Flores. Flores, wearing his usual tattered brown plaid jacket, shifted on his heels and took his hand. Marco guessed the man, who looked like a Great Gatsby character, was either British or American.

"Good morning," the man said in an American accent. "I'm Thomas House. Please come in," he said, gesturing with his hand.

He had a square jaw and straight white teeth. His blue eyes sat in small sockets.

Shada gestured for them all to sit. Flores glanced at the white sofa and took a seat across the room in a floral chair of damask. Shada and House sat next to one another on the silk rose-colored settee.

"Please make yourselves comfortable," she said.

She looked over at the man sitting next to her. "This is Thomas House. Tom is Kijamba's business manager. He's been a godsend. I don't know what I would have done without him. It's all too much; the phone hasn't stopped ringing. The paparazzi's been out front for days. I can't even leave the house. Tom's been taking care of everything for me," Shada said.

House looked over at Shada and grinned through China-white teeth.

"I knew she couldn't handle all of this by herself. I loved Kijamba like a brother. I had to protect her for his sake."

Shada smiled a half-smile out of the corner of her mouth. "When will my husband's body be released, Detectives? We need to plan his services. We're having a memorial service here in Spain at his adopted home. Then we're taking him back to the U.S., where there will be more services. He's going to be buried in his hometown of Baltimore, Maryland. His parents want him to come back home as soon as possible."

Flores cleared his throat. "That's what we've come to talk to you about. Unfortunately, Mrs. Smith, we can't release your husband's body just yet. I'm afraid we have some questions as to how he died," he said.

Shada looked over at House, "What does he mean? What kind of questions? Why can't his body be released?"

House patted her hand. "Don't worry, I'm sure they're just doing their job. They'll release him to us as soon as they can."

Marco and Flores exchanged glances.

"That's right, Mrs. Smith. We need to do a more complete autopsy. Once you bury Mr. Smith and forgive me for saying this, but once he's gone, we won't be able to find out anything else. The coroner has some questions about his death we need to resolve. I'd rather not go into it now," Flores said.

"Please, call me Shada. You don't think he died of natural causes then?"

Flores hunched his shoulders. "We just don't know yet, Senora."

"Oh God," Shada said.

House patted her hands again. "Don't worry, I'll be here with you. I won't let you go through this alone," he said.

"Mrs. Smith, did Kijamba have any enemies?" Flores asked.

House flashed his full set of white teeth, like a Fuller Brush salesman selling vacuum cleaners to a vulnerable housewife of the 1950s. "No, of course not; he didn't have any enemies. He was an international star. Everyone loved him," he said.

"How long have you been Kijamba's manager?" Marco asked.

House grinned at Marco. "I've been with Kijamba since the beginning of his career. About twenty years, I think. Anything I can do to help you detectives, just let me know."

"Tom takes care of our finances. He's been a great help chasing away negative publicity over the years," Shada said.

"You know how it is with celebrities, detectives. Someone's always out to drag them through the mud. My job is to make sure that doesn't happen to Kijamba… I mean Kijamba's memory."

"So, you keep all of the financial records for the business?" Marco asked.

House nodded his head. "Yes, I look after all of Kijamba's business interests."

"You told us before, Mrs. Smith, that your husband seemed well that night. Is that what you still remember?" Flores asked.

"He was fine. He was in a fantastic mood," the business manager interjected.

"Yes, he was the happiest I'd seen him in a while. The video shoot went well. He seemed excited about the future, about our future. That video was going to launch a worldwide tour for his new album," Shada said.

"Belen said Kijamba seemed full of energy during the shoot," Marco said.

Shada smiled. "He was, Kijamba really liked Belen, you know. He'd considered asking her to go on tour with us later in the year when the video was released."

Marco's eyes widened. "I didn't know that."

Another housekeeper entered the room and walked over to House.

"Can I get you all a drink?" House asked. He snapped his fingers. "Get them whatever they want," he said.

Flores waved his hand. "No thanks. We'll be leaving soon."

House nodded at the housekeeper. "You can go."

The woman backed out of the room with her head bowed.

"When do you think you'll have any answers?" House asked.

"We can't tell you when the coroner will be finished. We'll try to have the final autopsy as soon as possible," Flores said.

Shada sniffled and pulled a tissue out of her pants pocket.

House grumbled. "Can't you see Shada is upset? We need to get her husband home."

"We'll do all we can to get his body released as soon as possible, Senora. In the meantime, if you can think of anything unusual happening to Mr. Smith before he died, give me or Marco a call anytime," Flores said.

"Yes, yes, I will," she said.

"We'll let you know if we need any more information," Flores said.

Marco and Flores rose to leave. Another housekeeper appeared and ushered them out. Marco noticed that Shada had put her head on House's shoulder.

"Did you see that?" he asked.

Flores furrowed his brow.

"What did you think of that business manager, House? He barely let Mrs. Smith speak," Marco said.

"He seemed a little protective. That's understandable. She probably needs someone to protect her right now," Flores said.

Marco shrugged. "I don't know; he seemed *very* anxious to help. I get a bad vibe from him. That toothy smile of his gave me the creeps, like he was hiding something."

Chapter Seven

Marco took an afternoon break and went over to Alvarez's for a café con leche, which he often did when he needed to think. Something about that smooth, velvety substance made his brain operate better. Alvarez was as busy as usual. He stopped cleaning the bar when Marco came in the door.

"We've got fresh crema catalane," Alvarez said.

Marco rubbed his hands together. His mouth watered at the thought of the rich, creamy substance coming off the spoon. "I shouldn't. I just came for a coffee."

"Oh, come on, treat yourself."

"Okay, you're a bad influence, though."

Alvarez went over to the counter, lifted the rounded glass top, and took out a small brown tureen. He pulled out the bowl of white cream custard sprinkled with cinnamon. He placed a portion in front of Marco, along with a spoon. Then he threw his towel over his shoulder and went over to the double espresso machine. He lifted the handle with his stubby fingers and put the small silver pot underneath. The machine started to roar as the roast churned.

Marco looked down at the fresh dessert. "Uhm, this looks delicious."

"It came out good today," Alvarez said. "Hey, what do you know about that singer who died? There are memorials all over the place. People act like their cousin died. Even my daughter was upset. She loved that guy. She listened to his music all the time."

Marco shook his head. "Yeah, Belen's been pretty shaken up about the whole thing. She said he was great to work with and a genuine talent."

Alvarez said. "I must admit I enjoyed his music." He put his index finger to his lips. "Although I'd never want my daughter to know it. She said he had a new track written by an old friend that was going to premier on his new video. It was leaked on TikTok or one of those social media things. My daughter said it was excellent. Young people these days can get a hold of anything."

Marco laughed. "I thought you only liked Spanish music."

"*Claro que si la verdad*, truth. Normally, I do, but Kijamba's music was everywhere; you couldn't escape it. We were all thrilled he wanted to feature Vivarrambla in his video. Any idea what happened to him?"

Marco took another slow bite of crema. "Not yet," he said.

Marco finished his dessert. He felt guilty for indulging in the decadent sweet. He'd have to go running in the evening. He ran three days a week as a routine; he'd have to add an extra mile after such a rich dessert.

Marco walked back to his office and went to his computer, punched up the Google search engine, and scrolled for Thomas House. The search results revealed stories about House and Kijamba, including a smiling House standing beside Kijamba at various events. A biographical search listed House as the CEO of a company called House Management, Inc., described as a talent management agency that represented singers. The company had addresses in California in the US, Puerto Bella, and Malaga, Spain.

As Marco studied each bit of information, Eva buzzed him, breaking his concentration.

"The coroner, Javier Bortello, wants to talk to you about that singer. I still can't believe he's dead. All my friends are big Kijamba fans. We all feel like we've lost a member of the family," she said.

"His death hit a lot of people hard. I nearly choked in that house from the smell of different flowers people sent to his wife," Marco said.

Eva appeared at the door, startling Marco. "That's right, you went to his house. What was that like? What's his wife like? She's gorgeous in all the magazines. Does she look the same in person?"

Marco chuckled. "She's much as you'd expect. She's grieving her husband.

The house was the typical over-the-top mansion," he said. "Did Bortello say what he wanted?"

Eva sighed. "I'd love to see that house. Bortello said he had some questions and some information for you. I've got to leave early to pick up the kid," she said.

"Okay," he said as he watched her walk out of the door.

Once Eva had gone, Marco rang Bortello.

"*Dime*," Bortello said.

"It's Marco. You have some information for me?"

"Yeah, I found something suspicious. I examined the wound in that singer's right ear. It was a fresh wound. I think he got it right before he died. Something else strange. I found a perforation in his ear drum. It looks like a small object pierced his ear and made a hole about twenty centimeters, the size of a pin. My guess is some kind of thin small object injected with vesical botulinum toxin was stuck into his ear. I found botulinum toxin, a lethal amount of Botox—that's a neurotoxic protein— in his system. I think it caused his heart to stop sometime during the night."

"I'm not sure I understand. Are you saying you found Botox in his ear? How is that possible? How would that make his heart stop in the middle of the night?" Marco asked.

"Botulinum toxin impedes neuromuscular transmission, causing muscle weakening. It seeped into his heart, causing a change in the heart rate, causing a myocardial infarction. To put it simply, Botox injected into areas of your body that aren't recommended can lead to death. Many people don't know that Botox is the most dangerous poison in the world if given in the right amounts," Bortello said.

"Really? I had no idea. How could Botox have gotten into Kijamba's ear?"

"Someone must have inserted something into his ear that carried the Botox poison. The poison ran right through his system. At some point in the middle of the night, he became paralyzed, and like I said, his heart stopped."

"How could someone put something in his ear without him knowing?" Marco asked.

"I leave that to you and the police to figure it out. I can only tell you the medical facts. I can tell you that 0.00000001 grams of Botox is enough to be lethal when injected in an inner ear."

"Wow, it's amazing that little is enough to kill?" Marco asked.

"Yep, it's powerful stuff."

"Do you have any idea what time death may have occurred?" Marco asked.

"I can't give you an exact time. Did his wife say anything about him having pain or not sleeping well or waking up in the middle of the night?" Bortello asked.

"She didn't mention it," Marco said.

"Well, anyway, I've finished the exam. I need to know what the police want to do with the body. I need to get it out of the drawer. Flores said he had to speak to the Chief. I need to know. He can't stay here in the drawers forever. I'm getting calls from the media," Bortello said.

Marco cringed at the thought of Kijamba's body lying unmoving in one of the steel drawers. "I'll ask, but I'm not sure I'll have any influence. I don't know when the police will be ready to release the body under the circumstances."

Bortello huffed. "I don't want to be hounded by reporters forever, so they need to come to a decision soon."

"First, we need to tell his wife he was murdered," Marco said.

"Let me know about the body," Bortello said.

Chapter Eight

Flores walked out of his office with an empty refillable bottle to the joint water cooler in the hallway. He put the empty bottle under the cooler, filled it, and went back to his desk. His head pounded. He rubbed his temples. He grabbed a couple of *aspirina* from the bottle in his desk drawer amongst the soy sauce packets, pens, pencils, and paper clips and took a swig of the semi-cold water. How one manages pressure is a test of one's character. Flores's mentor at the academy had told him that when Flores joined the Malaga police force. Flores never forgot those words. He wasn't sure how he was handling pressure from the death of the famous singer, or whether it was handling him.

Flores felt the intense scrutiny from everyone from the Chief to the newspapers to the legions of Kijamba's fans around the globe hounding him daily. It wasn't that it was his first big murder case. He'd worked on the high-profile Donne case. He and Marco, despite their differences, had managed to solve that case. Kijamba, though, an American singer with worldwide recognition seemed even more overwhelming. The Chief had made sure Flores knew how high the stakes were; not solving the case could be career-breaking. His head pounded again. He folded his arms and rested them on his desk for a few minutes as he had to soon get to an appointment.

Feeling revived after fifteen minutes, Flores rose from his desk and grabbed his jacket from the back of his door. The Chief had invited him to lunch. Lunch on the department dime was rare. Flores shut down his computer. He adjusted the tie his wife had picked out for him that morning and headed out. When he arrived at the restaurant, he found the Chief waiting at a table near the back. The large man looked imposing, even seated at a table. Flores noticed his own hands shaking.

"I picked this table so we could talk in private," the Chief said.

Once seated at the popular tapas bar and restaurant, they ate appetizers of ham freshly sliced from the whole bone-in Jamón Ibérico, resting on the spit at the entrance to the restaurant.

"Let me get to the point," the Chief said as he stuck a piece of ham in his mouth. The world is watching us."

Flores's palms began to sweat as the Chief warned him of the consequences of not solving Kijamba's murder. He told Flores he wanted daily updates and that he wanted to be kept apprised of every step of the investigation. The Chief drilled him. Why was the investigation moving so slowly? Why didn't they have any suspects? The Chief complained that his own phone rang all day with inquiries from top officials including Kijamba's business manager, who threatened to sue the department. The case drained department resources each day it wasn't resolved. That meant budget cuts and layoffs, the Chief forewarned. By the time lunch had ended, Flores felt even more stressed.

Back in his office, Flores took off his tie and jacket and went to his desk. He sat for a moment to calm himself; then he turned on his computer. He reviewed his notes and went over the interviews they'd taken. The information they'd learned from the coroner meant that the perpetrator had to be someone who could have gotten close enough to Kijamba to inject Botox in the singer's ear. Standard police procedure dictated that they consider the spouse as a primary suspect. She checked all the boxes. Shada would have had close proximity to the singer, especially when they went to bed and if he'd fallen asleep first. Flores decided to search her background to see if she had a criminal history.

He checked the police records, which yielded no information. So, he decided to do a computer search. The fact that they were a famous couple meant information was readily available. Shada Smith, nee Nassir, was born in Tanger, Morocco to poor parents. The family had immigrated to America when she was young for a better life. Stories suggested Shada faced abuse as a child and left home at the age of seventeen. She'd met and married Terrence Smith, aka Kijamba, whom she met while on a modeling gig. Shada's life changed. She became wealthy and famous. The couple lived in Vivirrambla for a number of years but now they split their time between Spain and New York. Flores perused numerous tabloids and magazine articles about the couple. By all accounts, they had a happy enough marriage by celebrity standards. Flores didn't find any big scandals reported. They were a celebrated couple, revered by the music industry. In fact, less reputable tabloids speculated that the couple seemed too perfect and wondered if there were any skeletons in the closet. They featured sensational headlines like, '*What is Kijamba really up to?*' One tabloid reported a rumor that Kijamba had had a brief affair several years ago. Some of the most outrageous articles discussed Kijamba's secret life as an alien and his other family on another planet, but nothing concrete or plausible was written about the pair.

Vivirrambla Today magazine had snapshots of Kijamba and Shada mingling with the wealthy at one of Vivirrambla's elitist nightclubs, Olivia Valere, where celebrities liked to be seen. Shada looked adoringly at her husband in the photos. Flores, a skeptic by nature, especially regarding famous people, wasn't convinced the couple lived the perfect life portrayed in the magazines. Experience had taught him that what appeared on the surface could be a manufactured illusion. Flores stumbled on one story from several years back that he found interesting. The article stated that Shada had been arrested several years ago as a teen for passing bad checks. The case had been dropped, but it was enough for Flores to delve deeper.

He telephoned Marco. "We need to investigate the widow. I've been doing some research. I just read an article about her passing bad checks several years ago," Flores said.

"I don't think she had anything to do with her husband's death. According to Belen, they were a genuinely happy couple. When I saw her at the bullring, she seemed excited for him. She looked devastated when we went to see her," Marco said.

"That doesn't prove anything, you know that. We've seen it before, the supposed grieving widow. She had the proximity to slip poison into his ear when they were home alone. Everything points to her and no one else right now. We've got no other lead. She's all we've got, and the Chief wants some answers," Flores said.

"What would be her motive? She lived a lavish life with her husband. That bad check case was when she was a teen, hardly a notorious criminal," Marco said.

"We need to dig below the surface. Who knows what else may have been going on. Maybe she was having an affair, maybe she wanted more money, or maybe she was tired of her husband. I'm going to focus the investigation on her. If there's a motive, we'll find it. She'll talk to you. I need you to gain her trust. Speak to her in Arabic and find out all you can about that relationship." Flores said.

Chapter Nine

Marco slipped on a gray sweater and black pants. Belen had gotten tickets to the Teatro de Malaga. In truth, Marco felt too tired to go, but he'd promised her, and he admitted he could use a nice evening out.

He splashed on a bit of Hugo Boss from the bottle Belen had given him. Despite his reluctance to wear *"perfuma,"* as he called it, he liked it.

Belen sniffed the air as she came out of the bathroom. "You smell sexy," she said.

He watched her slip into a mid-length teal dress and put earrings into the two small holes in her ear lobes. It amazed him she could put on the earrings without looking. She took another moment to put her hair up and clip it in place. She wore only the slightest makeup on her olive skin. Marco admired her creamy smooth skin and silky dark hair, her petite figure. She dabbed a slight bit of Hugo Boss for women behind her ears.

"It's going to be a great night," she said.

"I love you," Marco said, kissing her.

She smiled. "Don't mess up my makeup.

They took a taxi to Malaga, so they could enjoy a beer and a bottle or two of wine later with dinner and after the theater. The streets of the city were crowded with the Semana Santa revelers still celebrating from the procession that had taken place earlier in the afternoon. The weeks before Easter were always busy; parades of floats bearing the Virgin Mary and other saints, as well as young boys carrying incense, marched through the streets. Marco and Belen wound their way through the crowds to the theater.

Belen had gotten good seats near the stage through her theater connections. Marco enjoyed the play. He looked forward to a good meal as now he was hungry. They'd made reservations at one of their favorite restaurants in Malaga city, Las Goldondrinas. A smiling waiter showed them to their table in front of a decorative armoire painted with colorful butterflies. The restaurant was cozy, like a large fancy dining room. Marco ordered a beer, while Belen requested a glass of Rioja. For dinner, Marco had Rabo de Toro, bull tail stew, which they simmered for hours, and roasted potatoes. Belen ordered mariscos, a seafood medley with rice.

I spoke to Shada the other day," she said as they were eating.

Marco shoveled food on his fork and looked at her. "You did? I didn't know you kept in touch with her."

"She called me. I was surprised to hear from her. She said you'd been to see her and had mentioned I was your girlfriend. She wanted to know if I knew anything about what was happening with Kijamba. She said the family and his fans back in the states were hounding her about giving him a proper funeral, and his parents wanted him to come home. I told her you didn't tell me that type of information about your investigations."

"That was the right thing to say," Marco said.

Belen took a sip of her wine. "The funny thing is, though, she started to confide in me like an old friend. I'm sure she gets lonely sometimes being the wife of a pop star. She doesn't know whom she can trust. Anyway, she told me that she and Kijamba had been trying to have a baby, but that they hadn't been successful. They were thinking of going for fertility treatments after the tour for the new album. She said they'd been trying for three years."

"Wow, that's a long time. Had they been arguing about it? Was she upset about not having children?" Marco asked.

He remembered Flores's orders to find out what he could about her.

Belen twirled her glass. "She said Kijamba was supportive and was willing to do whatever it took. They were even thinking of adopting. Now he's gone, and they'll never get that chance. It makes me think about us, Marco. You never know how much time we're going to have together."

Marco grabbed her hand across the table. The glow of the candlelight made her seem luminous. "I love you, Belen, and I love our time together. I cherish every day."

"I love spending time with you, but I worry about our future though," Belen said.

As Belen spoke, Marco wondered if trying to have a baby had caused a rift in Kijamba's relationship. Even so, it didn't seem reason enough for Shada to kill her husband if they were thinking of adoption.

"Don't worry, we'll have kids soon enough, when the time is right," Marco said.

Belen rolled her eyes. "Yes, we've been through this before; Shada's husband died before they could have children. We don't know what's going to happen in the future. I didn't really mean to talk about this tonight. We're having such a good time," Belen said.

He gripped her hand tighter. "Yes, let's not talk about it now," Marco said.

She squeezed his hand. "Okay, but I'm serious. We are going to have to really figure this out. I told you before, I'm not going to wait forever, Marco. I don't want to waste all my years."

"I know, I know. It won't be forever, I promise," he said.

They switched the conversation as they ordered *postre,* a dessert of molten chocolate cake, which they shared, and a scoop of ice cream, followed by a *café con leche.*

Marco rubbed his stomach. "I'm stuffed. It's been a wonderful evening, Belen. Thanks for dragging me out," Marco said.

Belen smiled. "I knew you'd enjoy it once we got here."

They both looked up when they heard a voice at their table.

"Hi, Marco, is that you?"

A woman with a mass of curly hair approached their table. She had large, dark eyes. She wore a form-fitting black dress, which accentuated a tiny waist and full hips, and high-heeled sandals. A silk multi-colored scarf draped her shoulders. She sported gold earrings and several gold bracelets. Her oval-shaped face was the color of maple syrup.

Marco looked up, startled. He pushed his chair back and stood up. "A… Amira," he stammered. "How are you?"

She kissed him on each cheek. "Good, how are you? What are you doing here? I haven't seen you for such a long time. How's your mom?"

Marco stammered. "She's good. She always asks about you."

Amira pointed to a group of women walking in the door, talking with each other. "I'm here with some friends. We're going to another friend's wedding this weekend. Good news. I may be moving to Spain permanently," she said.

"Oh really," Marco said.

Marco glanced over at the table. Belen sat stoic, staring at the young woman who'd interrupted their evening.

"I'm sorry, Amira. This is my girlfriend, Belen," he said.

Amira looked over and nodded. "Encantada," she said.

"Mucho gusta," Belen said.

"Listen, I've gotta catch up with my friends. Marco, give me a call sometime. I'm still at the same number. We need to catch up. I saw your grandmother not too long ago. She is doing well. She still calls me her little daughter." She glanced over at Belen. "Nice to meet you, Beatrice," she said, batting her long lashes.

"Belen."

"Oh, sorry, Belen. I'm terrible with names."

The woman went over to join her friends. Belen played with the rest of the dessert on her plate, pushing it around with her fork. Marco suggested they call it a night.

Chapter Ten

Flores and Marco met up early to go and see Shada to tell her the news that her husband had been murdered. Flores insisted that he drive. Marco had wanted to take his car as Flores' car was old and always looked like it was about to break down. Marco felt it was his way of asserting control and showing he was in charge. Flores parked in front of the villa. They were invited into the house and shown into the drawing room, where Kijamba's business manager, Thomas House, greeted them.

House shook their hands with a firm grip. "Detectives, good to see you again," he said. "I understand you have some news for us."

"We have some news for Mrs. Shada Smith," Marco said.

House nodded and bobbed his head up and down. "Yes, yes of course, Shada's upstairs she'll be here in a minute."

"I see," Flores said.

"Won't you sit down?" House asked.

Flores and Marco looked at each other and took a seat on the silk floral couch in front of them."

"Do you live here, Senor?" Flores asked.

"Why do you ask?"

"You seem very comfortable here," Marco said.

House hmphed. "Oh no, I live in the mountains of BenaHavis. I like the quiet country life. Vivirrambla is too lively for me. Although, my little town is getting too many tourists these days. We're thinking of moving to Fuengirola; that's as far as I'll stray into city life."

"You're American, right? How long have you been living in Spain?" Marco asked.

"Hmmmm, I've lived here for about twenty years as long as I've been with Kijamba. I used to live in the States, but my wife and I like Spain, better quality of life. So, we decided to settle here permanently," House said.

"You're married then?" Flores asked.

House nodded. "Oh yes, a Spaniard, twenty-five years, three children. They're grown now. They're still hanging around the house, though. I can't seem to get rid of them," he chuckled.

Flores laughed.

The door to the room opened. The three men turned as if watching Cinderella enter the ballroom. Shada wore a navy tunic top with a split on the side and navy wide-legged pants. Her hair, pulled back, revealed fine, delicate features and full lips. She wore a copper-colored lipstick, which set off her dark skin.

She gestured with her hands as they started to rise. "Don't get up," she said.

"We won't take up much of your time, Mrs. Smith," Flores said.

Shada turned to House, who gave a reassuring smile. "What can I do for you?"

"We have some information about your husband's death," Flores said.

Marco turned to look at House, who stared expressionless, like a mannequin in a dress shop.

"News, what news? I thought they said it was a brain aneurysm," House said.

"That's what we thought at first, but the coroner ran more tests. A more extensive autopsy revealed that Kijamba's death was due to other unnatural causes," Flores said.

Shada frowned. "More extensive autopsy, what other causes?" she asked.

"Senora, did Kijamba complain about any problems with his ears?" Flores asked.

"His ears? You mean his hearing? That's a strange question." Shada said.

"Did he complain at all about any ear pain, hearing loss, ringing in the ears, or headache?" Flores asked.

Shada sat back in her chair. "No, he…why do you want to know about his hearing?"

"The autopsy showed your husband was murdered," Flores said.

Her voice quivered. She let out an audible gasp. "Murdered? Thomas, what are they talking about?"

House shrugged his shoulders. "I don't know."

"Who could have murdered him? What does that have to do with his ears?" Shada asked.

"I'm sorry to upset you, Mrs. Smith, but Kijamba's death has now been ruled a homicide; looks like he may have been injected with poison," Flores said.

"Poison, but how? Why would anyone kill Kijamba?" Shada asked.

"That's all I can say for now, Senora," Flores said.

Thomas patted Shada's hand like a small child who needed comforting after a scary dream.

"Were you and your husband getting along well?" Flores asked.

Shada looked up at Flores. "Of course, we were. I loved my husband. I don't know what all this is about. It's a nightmare, Thomas."

House patted her hand again.

"Had you had any recent arguments or disagreements?" Flores asked.

"No more than any married couple," Shada said. "Why are you asking me these questions? What are you implying?"

"Just routine. We have to ask, Senora," Flores said.

Marco echoed him in Arabic. "I know it's uncomfortable, especially after you've just had a shock, but they have to ask you these questions."

House put his arm around her and rubbed her shoulder as she dabbed her eyes with a nearby tissue.

"Did Kijamba have any enemies? Were there any threatening letters or known stalkers?" Flores asked.

"Nothing other than the occasional hate letter that all celebrities get. Thomas made sure we didn't see most of those, but nothing out of the ordinary."

"Kijamba got his share of hate mail from the public. It's not unusual for a huge star to get some negative feedback. I personally monitored the mail and email messages for anything unusual," Thomas said.

"Were there any new threats?" Marco asked.

House pursed his thin lips. "Nothing we couldn't handle. Most of the negative mail Kijamba got related to his changing his style from traditional R&B. That was Cipi's influence. Some of his fans didn't like it but I doubt if anyone would kill him for it," House said.

"You'd be surprised by the reasons people kill. We'll need to go through his mail," Flores said.

"But of course, Detective," House said.

"Who's Cipi?" Marco asked.

"Cipi's one of Kijamba's band members. He's a blues singer and music composer. He encouraged Kijamba to change his musical style to more fusion. A lot of Kijamba's fans missed the old sound. Cipi had too much influence if you ask me," House said.

"From what I read, Kijamba's R&B pop fusion was popular and sold millions of records," Marco said.

House shrugged. "I guess."

"Cipi's is one of Kijamba's best friends. They've known each other for years. Kijamba trusted him with everything," Shada said.

"Does Cipi live here in Spain?" Marco asked.

Shada nodded. "Yes, he lives in Vivirrambla."

"Can you get us his information, his full name, address, and cell?" Flores asked.

"Sure."

Shada pulled out her phone, retrieved Cipi's information, and gave it to Flores.

"You told us that you and your husband went to bed early that night, is that right?" Flores asked.

"Yes, like I told you, he had to get up early the next day to meet with his lawyers and get some things done. I think some of it had to do with Cipi," Shada said.

"Like what?" Flores asked.

"I think he was signing some kind of contract with him," Shada said.

Flores jotted a note in the small black notepad he'd brought with him. "Are you a light sleeper?"

Shada balled up the Kleenex she held in her hand. "Not really. I can sleep through anything, especially if I've had a glass of wine. Kijamba used to laugh at me about that; we had had wine with dinner," she said, sniffing.

"Who cooked the dinner that night?" Marco asked.

"Our cook made a special dinner. I asked her to. I wanted to celebrate wrapping up the video shoot," Shada said.

"What did you have for dinner?" Flores asked.

"Let's see," Shada paused. "Sauteed beef tips with roasted potatoes and a vegetable medley."

"You said you each had a glass of wine. Did you have dessert?" Flores asked.

"We had sorbet," Shada said.

"What time did the servants leave?" Marco asked.

"They left around nine, right after dinner."

"I don't see what that has to do with anything," House said.

Marco shot a look at House who squirmed in his chair, as people often did when Marco fixed his gaze on them.

"This is all too much. I need to lie down," Shada said.

"Can't you see you're upsetting her? First, you tell her that her husband was murdered, then you ask her all these questions." House said.

"Of course, of course, we'll leave you alone for now, Mrs. Smith. We know this is hard, but we may have to ask you more questions as the investigation proceeds," Flores said.

"You don't know when my husband's body will be released then?" she asked.

"I'm afraid not," Flores said.

Marco and Flores rose from their places and walked toward the front door. Shada followed them. House lurked behind.

"Thank you for your time. Give me a call if you remember anything else, even the smallest detail," Flores said, handing Shada his business card.

"We'll give you a call if we remember anything," House said, taking the card from Flores.

"You will find out who did this to Kijamba, won't you?" Shada asked.

"We are going to do all we can, Senora," Flores said.

The housekeeper walked Flores and Marco to the door. Once they reached the car, Flores turned to Marco.

"She certainly is good at playing the weeping widow," he said.

Chapter Eleven

Flores and Marco climbed the stairs to the third floor of an apartment near the beach and knocked on the door of the address Shada had given them for the man they called Cipi. A well-built, dark-skinned man in his late forties, with neck-length Rastafarian salt and pepper-colored braids and a gold earring in his left ear, opened the door.

"Mr. Jacobs," Flores said. "Police."

The man unlatched the door and let them in. "What can I do for you?" he asked. He spoke with a Jamaican accent.

"We're here to talk to you about Kijamba," Flores said.

He gestured to them to sit. "Yes, of course, call me Cipi," he said.

Singer-songwriter Cipriano Jacobs lived in a two-bedroom condo on the edge of Vivirrambla. The white carpet they stood on looked new. Marco wondered how a man could keep a white rug so clean. He'd have stained it with beer and pizza in no time. Belen constantly nagged him about keeping food off their tan sofa. The furniture was a colorful array of different fabrics and styles, like upscale IKEA. A large armoire cabinet stood between the living room and another part of the house. The room seemed almost feminine, except that numerous guitars were scattered around, including atop the cabinet. Pictures of Cipi standing with famous people, including Kijamba, filled the walls.

"What can I do for you?" Cipi asked.

He was not very tall, but he couldn't be described as short. His rugged face looked lived in. Scattered black and gray hairs sprouted from his chin.

Flores introduced himself. "Buenes tardes, I'm Detective Alberto Flores.

Marco shook his hand. "Soy, Marco."

"We need to speak to you, Senor, about Kijamba," Flores said.

"Please make yourselves comfortable. Can I get you anything?" Cipi asked.

"No thanks," Flores said. "We won't take much of your time, Senor Jacobs."

Marco surveyed his surroundings. An ochre-colored kitchen was visible from where he sat. Copper pots hung from the ceiling. Marco thought the decorations were very eclectic. He sensed it matched the owner's personality.

"I'll get right to the point. We believe Kijamba was murdered," Flores said.

Cipi fell back into his chair. "Murdered? By whom? Who would murder Kijamba?" he asked.

"That's what we intend to find out. How long had you known, Mr. Smith?" Flores asked.

"I can't believe it. I've known Kijamba for almost thirty years. Since we were teenagers," Cipi said. "I'm a musician, too. That's how we met, auditioning for a band. I can't tell you how upset I've been ever since he died. I write the blues, but I haven't been able to write anything since he died. It's ironic. I can't think of anything sad that I want to sing about."

"You two were still close, then?" Flores asked.

Cipi nodded. "He was like a brother to me. We'd been through a lot together. Geez, with my lifestyle, I thought I'd pass on before him. It doesn't seem fair," Cipi said, shaking his head.

Cipi said that he'd moved to America from Spain to follow Kijamba. He was Haitian but his parents had moved to Baltimore when he was young. Cipi played in various bands and wrote music. He'd been married once a long time ago, but he'd been divorced for years. Drugs, traveling and some other things had ruined his marriage. He'd had a drug habit a few years back, but he'd been clean for a long time. Now he lived alone and had an occasional girlfriend. He'd been seeing one woman on and off for a couple of years.

"Kijamba and I met long before he was well-known. Obviously, I haven't made it as big as he did, but Kijamba was nice to me from the beginning. He always took care of me, made sure I played good gigs. I've lived well thanks to him. I gave Kijamba a couple of my original songs for this new album. We were going to sign a deal in a couple of days."

"What kind of deal?" Marco asked.

"A contract for music royalties. I was going to sell him the copyright to a couple of songs I wrote in exchange for future royalties. I've sold more than one hundred thousand copies of my music in Spain, so I have a track record. We were going to sign the deal right after the video shoot. When Shada called to tell me, he was gone I couldn't believe it."

"Do you ever resent Kijamba's success?" Flores asked.

"Of course not. I told you—he always made sure I was taken care of; Kijamba was generous to all his friends," Cipi said.

"Did you know any of his other friends in the music business?" Marco asked.

"Yeah, I know most of them. I can give you a list if it'll help."

"Sure, that'll be great," Marco said.

"Where were you the day the video was shot in the bullring?" Flores asked.

Cipi hesitated. "Me? I was, let me think, I was here at home. I'd been home all day."

"You didn't go to the video shoot then? I don't remember seeing you?" Marco asked.

Cipi turned to Marco. "Oh, that's right, your girlfriend's one of the dancers. No, I didn't go to the shoot. I had an appointment that afternoon."

"What kind of appointment?" Flores asked.

"I had a meeting with my agent, to talk about the deal. Then, I had a doctor's appointment in the afternoon," Cipi said.

"What about that evening? Can anyone vouch for your whereabouts?" Flores asked.

"I was here alone all night."

"You said you were dating someone; did you see her that night?" Marco asked.

Cipi shook his head causing his braids to move. "No, she lives out of town. We only meet up when she's in Vivirrambla," Cipi said.

"When was that the last time you saw, Kijamba?" Flores asked.

"About a week before he died. He had a party at his house with the crew and a few friends to celebrate the video."

"Had you two had any arguments?" Flores asked.

"Of course not. I told you; he was about to sign a major deal with me."

"What about other enemies? Did Kijamba have any enemies that you know about?"

Cipi twisted his lip. "Everyone loved, Kijamba," he said.

"Can you possibly get us that list of his other friends as soon as possible?" Flores asked.

"Sure. His album is going to be big now that he's gone. I hate that he won't be here to see it."

"He'll be missed by a lot of people," Marco said.

Cipi nodded in agreement.

"Okay, Senor Jacobs, that's all for now. Thank you for your time," Flores said.

Flores and Marco rose from the couch. Cipi lifted himself up from his chair.

"Hey, have you spoken to Thomas House, Kijamba's business manager?" Cipi asked.

Flores knitted his brow. "Yes, we've spoken to him. Why do you ask?"

Cipi shrugged. "I just wondered. Kijamba offered to have him manage me too once we signed the new deal. My manager's retiring, but I said no thanks. There's something about House I don't trust."

"Is there something you want to tell us?" Marco asked.

Cipi shook his head. "Nah, I just wondered if you talked to him."

"We're talking to everyone. Thank you for being so cooperative, Senor Jacobs. If you think of anything please don't hesitate to contact me," Flores said.

"Gracias, Senor Jacobs," Marco said.

"I'm not the only one that gets a bad vibe from House," Marco said to Flores as they exited Cipi's condo.

Chapter Twelve

We're always at the mercy of time, but time has no mercy on us. Marco looked at his watch in disbelief. He tapped his pen on his desk to the sound of a tuneless drumbeat. The day dragged on. When Marco was working, time most often passed without notice. Before he knew it, it'd be time to wrap up and go home. Today, for some reason, that was not the case. He couldn't concentrate. He and Belen had gotten into an argument the night before, Marco had wanted to go and watch Barcelona futbol with his best friend, Oscar at the bar. Belen wanted him to accompany her and some friends to a Berlioz concert, music he couldn't much stomach. It wasn't that Marco hated classical music. His father, un pescadore, had gotten pleasure out of angling to the sound of Mozart while he caught the day's fish for the local restaurants. Marco had come to enjoy the music of Mozart and Beethoven, but he couldn't abide listening to Berlioz for two hours when there was a Barcelona match. He'd gone to the concert, but he pouted the whole time. Belen said she was appalled and embarrassed at his childish behavior. He told her he didn't appreciate being treated like a child, and on it went. The next morning, they were still angry at one another. He moved to give her a quick kiss goodbye before he left for work. She'd ignored him and turned over on the pillow.

Marco loved Belen's warm and caring nature, how she always wanted the best for him. He hated it, though, when caring turned to mothering. The argument had escalated. She told him she felt frustrated by his seeming lack of seriousness, including his lack of commitment to their relationship. Every argument they had came down to that, Marco's unwillingness to commit.

He wasn't Peter Pan; she'd told him more than once. At forty, on his next birthday, he was getting too old to care about only futbol and beer. He knew what was said wasn't untrue, but he didn't like being told so.

He buried his head in his work and pledged not to look at the time. When the workday was finally over, Marco thought about his options for the evening. He didn't want to go home. He felt they could use some time apart. He texted Oscar and invited him to grab a few beers at the Townhome Bar.

He'd just finalized his plans when Eva rushed in flushed and panting.

"Marco!" she said.

"What is it? What's wrong, Eva?"

"You're needed in the harbor in Puerto Bella. Detective Flores said it's urgent."

"Why, what happened?"

"A woman's been murdered at the Barre Azule. Flores said it's a horrible scene, and the second line of the port is chaos," Eva said, still struggling to catch her breath.

Marco knew what the second line meant, as did everyone who lived in Vivirrambla. Puerto Bella, five minutes from Vivirrambla, was the play spot of the rich and famous, who parked their yachts on the Mediterranean Sea for weekends of golf and partying. Celebrities could often be seen strolling along the port and shopping at its high-end stores such as Versace and Chanel. The pier in front of the docks, known as the front line, was comprised of expensive bars and restaurants. One of the most popular being the Ellington Bar situated next to the water, where tourists with deep tans sipped mojitos and sangria while people-watching.

Behind the wholesome, shiny glamour of the front line of Puerto Bella, the second line had a different atmosphere. At night, immigrants who worked as dancers/strippers enticed the male patrons who swigged Moet champagne and high-class bourbon and Hennessy.

Marco had gone to Barre Azule only once with some friends. He recalled being awed at the women. Women who looked different than the dark-haired, olive-skinned ones he'd known all his life. Beautiful blonds with light eyes from faraway places approached him.

"Are you like a real-life Gypsy?" they'd ask.

He'd gotten plenty of offers, but for Marco, it was nothing more than an adventure he wasn't eager to repeat. He much preferred the local Spanish bars where he felt comfortable.

Marco shut down his computer and rushed to his car. Eva hadn't gotten many details, only that a woman had been shot. When he arrived, the scene was still high energy. Marco squeezed his way through the crowd of local reporters and onlookers lining the streets. Once he reached the Azule bar, he pushed open the heavy grayish-blue padded doors. He was met by police talking on their phones and camera bulbs flicking. Flores and another group of police stood at one spot, looking down at the floor.

Flores gestured for Marco to approach. "Over here, I'm trying to make sure we preserve this crime scene, so walk carefully," he said.

Marco tipped toed through the area and over the metal anti-contamination stepping plates to the scene. The sight of a dead body didn't often faze him, as it was expected in his career. This time, though, his stomach churned.

A young woman lay, her body contorted on the shiny dance floor. She had blond hair cut to the nape of her neck. Her head was twisted sideways, her eyes shut in the macabre look of death. She had long legs that stretched beneath a short gray skirt. Her white cotton top was stained with blood. She rested in a puddle of liquids.

"Wow, she's so young. Do we have any information on her?" Marco asked.

Flores pulled out a box of Altoids from his jacket pocket and offered one to Marco. Marco shook his head no. He noticed it was a habit Flores had when he got nervous.

"Couldn't have been here too long as the blood's still fresh. She had ID on her. Her name's Elaina Petrov, a Russian or Eastern European national. She lists an address near here. We don't have any information about her immigration status as of yet, but we should have it by this afternoon," one of the other officers on the scene said.

Flores knelt, lifted one of her arms, and turned over her head, examining it with his gloved hands. "I see defensive wounds on her body," he said.

Marco bent over closer. "The way her body is laid out, it looks like she tried to put up a fight."

Flores dropped the lifeless arm. "Yeah, there are wounds near her hands. Bortello can tell us for sure."

"Why did you call me, anyway? Shouldn't this be handled by the Port police and immigration?" Marco asked.

"The mayor called the Chief and demanded we put all efforts out on this one. A death in Puerto Bella isn't good for the city. When we questioned the manager and a couple employees, they were all Moroccan, so we called you," Flores said.

"Oh, I see," Marco said.

"I need you to talk to the manager and see what you can find out," Flores said.

Marco questioned witnesses in Arabic, those who didn't speak much English, while forensics took several more hours to examine the scene and remove the body of the dead young woman. The police roped off the whole Port, including the front-line boardwalk area, leaving many tourists confused. Business owners, upset at losing money as their customers couldn't reach them, voiced their concerns to the police.

The entire port was in chaos. Marco didn't return home until late in the evening. Belen was still at work. He went straight to bed and fell asleep right away. The next day, he was up early and over to Alvarez's for a coffee. He sat on his usual stool in front of the bar and picked up one of the newspapers. The headline in *El Pais* read, "*Young woman shot in swanky exclusive Port strip joint. Bad for Puerto Bella Tourism.*"

The round-faced proprietor stood in front of Marco. "Cafe? That's some business in the Port," he said, shaking his head. "I never let my children go there," Alvarez said.

"It is," Marco said. "I can't really talk too much about it.

Alvarez shook his head and wiped the table in front of Marco. "Entiendo," he said.

Marco gulped down the café con leche. After bidding Alvarez good day, he drove back to the Port to speak to more club employees. The entire Port was still roped off, so parking was easy, and he pulled up right to the front entrance. The pier seemed eerie without the usual tourists mingling around. When he entered the Club Azule, the manager, a middle-aged Moroccan man named Ahmed, introduced himself. He was darker skinned, olive-completed, with a balding spot in the middle of his head surrounded by sleek, dark hair. His once handsome face looked worn, and there were deep creases under his brown eyes. He spoke in Arabic. Ahmed said he'd been in the kitchen with the staff at the time of the murder. One of the cleaners, a man named Idan, had run in screaming that Elena was lying on the floor bleeding.

"I called the police right away," Ahmed said.

"Elaina was one of your employees, right? Can you tell me about her?" Marco asked.

"Yes, she is one of our dancers," Ahmed said.

Ahmed said Elaina had been a dancer at the club for a little under a year. She came from Russia.

"All the dancers seem to be from Eastern Europe," Marco said.

Ahmed shrugged his shoulders. "A fair number. The owner, Hassan, does the hiring. He gets the girls. I just manage the club."

"Had Elaina been threatened by anyone, clients, or anyone that you know about?" Marco asked.

"No, not that I'm aware of; we try to watch out for our girls, but we can't control everything."

Ahmed said he'd been the manager since the club opened. The owner, Hassan, spends most of his time in Morocco. Ahmed had day-to-day contact with the girls, but Hassan had the final word on anything that went on in the club.

"She was one of our best dancers," Ahmed said.

"How do I get in touch with this Hassan?" Marco asked.

"He spends most of the time in Tanger. He doesn't come to the club often."

"Can you give me his phone number?" Marco asked.

Ahmed looked sideways at Marco. Then he pulled out his phone and gave Marco the number. "Look, I shouldn't really be talking to you. If Hassan finds out, he's going to be upset," Ahmed said.

Marco furrowed his brow. "Why is that? These are routine questions about a murder."

"Hassan doesn't like me to talk about his business," Ahmed said.

"I see. Who else was here that day? Can you get me their names?"

Marco spoke to the kitchen staff and the other employees of the club, who verified Ahmed's story. Idan had come running into the room, upset and screaming. Ahmed went to the dressing room, where he found Elaina bleeding on the floor. Marco noticed the staff seemed nervous and shaken. One of the employees started to visibly sweat whenever they mentioned Ahmed's name. They seemed to have rehearsed what to say to the police.

Marco relayed this information to Flores, who agreed they needed to look deeper into the Club Azule and its operations under Ahmed.

Chapter Thirteen

Marco and Belen took seats near the back of the packed church. Shada, dressed in an all-black chiffon dress, her hair up in a chignon, entered Iglesia Incarnacion, leaning on the arm of Thomas House. Large dark Chanel shades shielded her eyes, but her slow gait betrayed her despondency. Thomas House looked as if he was auditioning for the lead in a Mafia film in his sleek black suit. Once they were seated, the long service began with tributes to Kijamba from around the world. Marco did all he could to comfort Belen when she snuggled nestled into his shoulder and cried.

"It means a lot to me that you came with me. I know you don't like funerals," Belen whispered.

What she'd said was true. Marco had an aversion to funerals. As a child, he'd been dragged to the funeral of a great aunt, his father's grandmother's sister. The aunt had been cruel to him. She resented Marco's father for marrying a Moroccan woman. She made sure Marco knew he wasn't wanted in her family. He'd overheard her telling his father that Marco was a *Gitano,* a gypsy mongrel child. Though he really didn't know what the term *Gitano* meant, there was no mistaking the implication that he was different and he didn't belong. When Marco was forced to attend her funeral and watch relatives cry over her body, he developed an aversion to them. It all seemed surreal and fake. Be nice while you're still alive, then I'll care what happens to you when you're dead.

Following the service, Bentleys, Ferraris, and Maseratis parked along the streets of the Golden Mile. Residents of the neighborhood barely had access to their own homes as mourners piled in to pay their respects at an invitation-only repast. Belen had been invited to the luncheon. Flores insisted that Marco attend.

Inside the same room Marco and Flores had interviewed Shada, Belen mingled with famous music legends and other celebrities with ease. Marco stood aside, and people watched. He'd never been impressed by stars. He was more interested in House, whom he watched bark orders to the servers who offered nibbles on silver trays to the guests.

Marco turned to Belen, who'd been talking to another famous singer. "Did you see how he's talking to staff?" he asked.

Shada, who stood nearby, walked over to them. "Belen, I'm so glad you came. Don't worry about Thomas, he's sometimes short with people. The servants are used to it. I admit he's been more short-tempered than usual. We're all on edge," she said.

"I suppose," Marco said.

"Please help yourself to anything you want," Shada said.

Marco grabbed a beer from the server, who passed. As he started to drink, House sidled over.

"Your girlfriend's quite charming," he said, grinning.

"Yes, she is," Marco said.

Marco's cell vibrated. He took it out of his pocket, happy not to have to talk to House any longer.

"Excuse me," he said, walking away.

Flores was on the line. "How's it going at the memorial service?"

"It's interesting, makes me glad I'm not a celebrity. Thanks for calling. You just saved me from having to talk to Thomas House," Marco said.

"He's not so bad. Let me know if you learn anything new. I've got some news. Our Puerto Bella case just got more complicated. That club manager you talked to at the Club Azule, Ahmed, is in the hospital in a coma. He's been attacked, and he's not expected to make it."

Chapter Fourteen

Someone didn't like the fact that Ahmed had spoken to him. Maybe the owner of the club, who lived in Morocco, had learned of their conversation and felt threatened. Something was going on in that club. Marco face-timed his cousin, Karim, who lived in Morocco and worked part-time for the police.

"What's up?" Karim asked. He was unshaven, and black hair stubble stood out on his chin, and his dark hair sat matted to his head.

"I didn't mean to wake you," Marco said. It hadn't occurred to him that it was early in the morning.

Marco explained the details of Elaina's murder and the information he'd obtained from the Club Azule manager, Ahmed, who was now in the hospital fighting for his life. He asked Karim if he could find any information about the club's owner, a Moroccan man named Hassan Alami.

"We need to find everything we can about him. The manager said Alami lives in Tanger," Marco said.

"I'll see what I can find out," Karim said. "Jaddah asked about you the other day."

"Tell her I'll call her soon," Marco said, feeling his usual guilt for not calling his grandmother.

Karim never missed the opportunity to remind Marco that he didn't contact his grandmother as often as he should.

"I need anything you can find as soon as possible," Marco said.

"I'll see what I can do. I've got to get ready for work now," Karim said, disconnecting the call.

Marco performed his own research while waiting for Karim, who phoned a few days later with his findings. Hassan Alami was a majority owner of Club Azule registered in Spain. Alami owned several nightclubs in both Spain and Morocco. Alami had been arrested in Morocco a few years earlier for human trafficking at one of his clubs. The police had dropped the investigation. Alami knew powerful people in the government, Karim told Marco.

"He has a silent partner who owns part of the Club Azule. I couldn't find any information about the partner," Karim said.

"Do you think you could arrange a meeting for me with Alami?" Marco asked.

"I might be able to let me ask my contacts. It may be dangerous, though; you'll need to be careful. Hassan's very shrewd," Karim said.

"I get it. I'll be careful," Marco said.

Marco was on his way home from La Cañada, where he'd gone to pick up a few groceries when Karim called him back several days later. He'd arranged a meeting in Morocco for Marco with Hassan.

Flores sounded skeptical when he heard the plan. "It sounds too dangerous. I'm not sure it'll work. It sounds like you'll use a lot of resources going undercover."

Flores had to be convinced. He didn't have the same instincts that Marco had. He did things only by the book. He had no flair.

"My sense is Elaina's death is tied to what's going on at that club with only Eastern European dancers. This is the only way we'll get any real information. The club's owner, Hassan Alami, is protected by the Moroccan police," Marco said.

"Okay, I'll let you go undercover to see what you find out. At least it'll keep the Chief off my ass for a while," Flores said.

Undercover work always came with a risk, though it could be the most exciting part of investigations. Marco had gone undercover in Morocco before; one case resulted in the arrest of a large money-laundering cartel. So, he had an idea of what to do, but he still felt his heart flutter. He booked a ferry to Tanger. Eva helped Marco create an alias, Abdul Elani, a Spanish businessman of Moroccan descent who wanted to invest in a nightclub in Morocco to avoid paying Spanish taxes. He'd say he'd been referred to Hassan by mutual friends. He stepped on the ferry, ready for the adventure.

Chapter Fifteen

"Since kif trafficking wasn't enough for him, every two weeks he filled some old boats with poor bastards who gave him everything they had to get to Spain."

Leaving Tangier, Tahar Ben Jelloun

Flores shifted the papers around on his messy desk to get to his computer. He couldn't think straight; he felt exhausted. Working two high-profile murders, with now a third attack, was taking its toll on him. He hadn't been sleeping well, and he'd caught a cold, which kept him up coughing all night. He'd drugged himself with cold medicine, which made him feel sluggish, and his reddened nose constantly ran. His normally red jutting ears were even redder. He wanted to crawl under the covers for a few days. He had to keep going, though; the Chief had been clear. He wanted results.

Flores grabbed a tissue from the box on his desk for an expected sneeze. As the sneeze never materialized, he put the tissue down and typed in Club Azule in the search engine. He perused pictures of the club, which advertised itself as a European getaway. Marco had been right; the dancers all seemed to be Eastern European women. Flores wondered how they got into Spain. The police, including his department, had been reluctant to investigate trafficking. On occasion, some religious group would complain to the mayor, and the department would be called upon to look into individual cases, but since the popular nightspots brought in millions in tourist dollars from the wealthy British, Arabs, Russians, and Germans, any investigation into trafficking was short-lived.

Flores couldn't find anything in his computer search that would give clues as to the murder of Elaina. He decided he'd visit the club again. He grabbed the box of tissues on his desk and headed to his car. It was a hot afternoon. The sun's rays reflected on the water. Contented-looking tourists strolled along the paseo, eating ice cream. Some sat at outside bars drinking cocktails. Flores walked over to the second line of Puerto Bella. Club Azule had a different atmosphere during the day. At night, it was a shiny discotheque. In the daylight, the club looked dingy and smelled musty. The furniture looked worn, and the bar seemed outdated as if it'd been used in the 80s in a Miami Vice set. A brown-skinned man greeted Flores when he entered the bar. He had jet-black hair that glowed in the fluorescent light. His dark eyes were large and searching. Flores showed him his badge and asked to speak to someone in charge.

"No one's here," the young man said.

"Who are you? Do you work here?" Flores asked.

"Yes, I am, Idan. I do the cleaning," he said.

Flores furrowed his brow. "How long have you been working here?"

Idan eyes grew wide. "Only a few weeks. I've only been here a few weeks," he said, sticking his hands in his pockets and looking down at the floor.

Idan spoke broken Spanish with an accent that Flores didn't recognize.

"I'm not here from immigration. I'm investigating the murder of the young woman a few weeks ago."

Idan looked up. "Oh yes, Elaina. I can't believe she's dead."

"Did you know her? Flores asked.

Idan nodded his head.

"How well did you know her?" Flores asked.

"She was a friend."

"Did she get along well with everyone?" Flores asked.

"Oh yes, everyone liked her. She was nice to me. Some of the people around here snub their nose at me." Idan's voice softened. "Elaina was always kind and polite. She took the time to say hello and to talk to me."

"So, you knew her for some time?"

Idan stammered when he spoke. "Only for a few weeks."

Idan picked up the broom standing near to him and started sweeping.

"You seemed to really care about Elaina," Flores said.

"Like I said, she was nice to me."

"Were you here the afternoon Elaina was killed?"

Idan swept the floor in front of him. "Si, I was here cleaning. I found her lying on the floor like that."

"Like what?"

"Lying on the floor in all that blood."

"Where were you when you found her?"

"On my way to clean the dressing room. I can still see her with her clothes all wrinkled. She was changing for work. She didn't deserve that; she was beautiful."

"Did you normally clean the dressing rooms while the dancers were changing?" Flores asked.

Idan blushed. "Oh, no, no, they're usually changed by the time I get there late in the afternoon. I make sure all the costumes are hung up, and the room is clean."

"Did you see any of the other dancers that day?"

Idan shook his head. "I didn't see anyone. A lot of times, I'm here by myself in the afternoons with the kitchen staff and or a couple of dancers."

"Could anyone else have gone in the dressing room without you seeing them?"

"They could've come in the back door."

"Can you show me?" Flores asked.

Idan put down the broom. "This way."

Flores followed Idan into a large room that had costumes and hangers on a pole. The costumes seemed skimpy and gaudy. The rest of the room had tables with lighted mirrors and make-up on them. It looked like an old, abandoned Hollywood dressing room. Idan pointed to the floor where he'd found Elaina.

"The manager, Ahmed, said he was here that day," Flores said.

"He'd just come in when I found Elaina. He called the police."

"Do you know anyone who'd want to attack Ahmed or Elaina?"

Idan shook his head vigorously. "No, I keep mostly to myself."

After a few more routine questions, Flores felt he'd learned all he could from Idan. He circled his phone number on his card and handed it to him. "Don't leave Spain. Let me know if you remember anything else," he said.

Flores felt glad to escape the musty club. The smell exacerbated his stuffy nose. He walked along the pier and stopped to get an ice cream. He'd begun to sweat from walking in the sun. Although he'd been born in Vivirrambla, he never adjusted to the heat. He sometimes wondered if he'd be better off in a colder climate. As his ice cream dripped onto his shirt, he decided to take a seat on one of the blue and white colored benches decorated with Spanish tile. As soon as he sat down, a woman with light brown hair and pale white skin approached him.

"Perdone, Senor," she said.

She spoke with a Russian-sounding accent. "You're the police officer who was just in the bar asking about Elaina, aren't you?"

Flores studied the woman. She was slim with peach-colored skin and dimples, the kind of woman he would have liked if he weren't married. She wore blue pants and a peasant top. Flores retrieved his badge from his coat jacket, which he now carried over his arms, and showed it to the woman.

"Si, Senora, I'm detective, Alberto Flores. I didn't see you in the club a few minutes ago."

"Buenas tardes. I'm Ginka Kovalenko. I came in while you were talking to Idan," she said.

Flores gestured to the empty spot next to him. "Please, have a seat. Did you know Elaina?"

"Si, Elaina was my best friend."

"Really, do you work at the club?" Flores asked.

"I'm a dancer like Elaina."

"How long had you known, Elaina?"

"I've known her for a couple of years. I helped Elaina when she started dancing at the club. We were both in school at the University. We only worked at the club to pay for school. Now I don't know what I'm going to do here alone," she said.

"I'm sorry to hear that," Flores said.

"I saw you talking to Idan. He's a creep. He'd been stalking Elaina for months. She told me she wanted to get away from him, but she didn't want to hurt his feelings," Ginka said.

"Idan said he and Elaina were friends and that she'd been nice to him," Flores said.

"Elaina felt sorry for him. She was a kind person. I told her he was obsessed and that she shouldn't encourage him. She said she sympathized with him because she knew how hard it was for us immigrants here in Spain. She had a big heart."

"Do you think he could have harmed Elaina?" Flores asked.

Ginka was silent for some time. "I don't know. He was really into her. I've seen him get angry and protective of her. He grabbed my arm one time when I told him to stop drooling over Elaina. I thought he was going to hit me."

"Did you ever see him touch Elaina?"

"No, I didn't see him touch her. I think he was getting desperate, though, following her around. That's why I tried to warn Elaina. Now she's dead. I hope you're going to arrest Idan."

"We're going to do a thorough investigation. Thanks for coming over to talk to me. You've been very helpful." Flores said. "If you think of anything else, please give me a call."

"I have to do what I can for Elaina," she said.

Ginka rose from the bench. Flores watched as she walked towards the Club Azule. He sat for a few more moments before heading to his car.

When he returned to his office, Flores commenced a search of the police and immigration records. He found no record of Idan having entered the country.

Desperate souls willing to take great risks to migrate to a safer, more prosperous nation than the one that had been their lot are like dangling bate to the unscrupulous. Idan had entered Spain like so many thousands who crossed the border and snuck in under cover. Flores had seen many such immigrants roving the sandy beaches selling sunglasses. The police didn't have the manpower to crack down on all illegal entry. Many came in unnoticed. Unless something happened to drive them from underground.

Flores requested a search warrant for Idan's apartment which was granted by the prosecutor. He rose before dawn and led a team of men and women wearing bright green neon jackets into a small two-bedroom dwelling on the edge of town. The place looked like several people shared it. Mattresses with people asleep on them were scattered around the living room and clothes were strewn on chairs and a sofa. Flores heard the cry of a baby coming from another room. The sleeping residents jumped up when the police entered. Flores could see the fear in their eyes. They stood yelling *"tengo papeles,"* indicating they had legal immigration papers, as police searched the home. They located Idan in one of the bedrooms where he'd been asleep on a mattress. An officer gestured for Flores to come over to a closet.

"Sir, you need to see this," he said.

In the back of the closet, Flores spotted a picture of the dead woman, Elaina, smiling and waving at the camera.

"Take him in," he said.

One of the officers grabbed Idan and jerked him up from the mattress. Idan walked with his head down as they dragged him out of the apartment.

Chapter Sixteen

Marco had taken the first morning ferry to Tanger. Despite two cups of coffee, he yawned. He still hadn't fully awakened by the time he arrived in Morocco. He tugged his suitcase over the entrance to his hotel room and flopped onto the hard bed. He fell asleep within seconds. He awakened a few hours later, ravenous. He ordered room service and ate the cold, tasteless food served under a metal cover as if it were a gourmet feast. His phone said it was still early in the evening. He couldn't go into town for fear of seeing one of his old childhood friends or his relatives and blowing his cover. He felt restless. He clicked on the television and surfed the channels. He reached for his pants and took out his wallet, where he found the business card Amira had given him that night he saw her at the restaurant. He hesitated, then punched the numbers on the card into his cell. She answered right away.

"Hello," she said.

"Amira, it's me. How are you?"

"Marco, I can't believe you called."

"It was great to see you the other night. Are you back in Tanger? I'm in town for a few days and I wondered if you'd like to go on a day trip?" Marco asked.

Amira didn't answer for some time.

"Just to catch up," he said.

Amira said she was in Tanger to see her family. Marco explained that he was in Morocco for business but that no one could know he was there and that he couldn't go into town. They'd have to drive and meet somewhere else.

"That sounds very suspicious. You don't want your girlfriend to find out?" she asked.

"It's not that," he said.

Marco assured her his anonymity was for legitimate business reasons. She agreed to meet him the next afternoon.

He felt guilty after he hung up the phone with Amira. He wasn't sure what he was doing was right. So, he picked up the remote and searched for a futbol match to take his mind off things. He landed on a match in Saudi Arabia. He made a pot of complimentary Maghrebi tea that came with the room and settled back. Soon, he found himself drifting off.

He awoke early the next morning. After picking over a tasteless breakfast, he showered and dressed in a white shirt and navy pants. He got into the rented car the department had gotten him and drove to the edge of town where Amira had agreed to meet him.

She wore a tan dress and gold jewelry. Her red ruby earrings flashed red like fire. She looked like a goddess or princess from ancient Carthage. Her massive hair was pinned up. She was taller than Belen, but not too tall, and she had larger hips and more curves.

She slipped into the car's leather seats. "Kind of flashy," she said.

Marco laughed. "I know, not my usual style."

Marco explained to her that he was there on police business and that he'd rented the car to make him look like a rich businessman.

She laughed, "I see. That's why you wanted to get out of town, so no one would recognize you."

Marco nodded his head. "Yep, that's right. I shouldn't be telling you this, but I've always trusted you, and I wanted you to understand. You can't tell anyone, not even my grandmother, that you saw me."

She narrowed her brown eyes. "You can trust me."

Marco owed Amira the truth. He knew she'd never betray him. They'd dated for a long time and knew almost everything about one another. Marco's whole family was devastated when they broke up. Everyone assumed they'd get married. She'd been a regular at his grandmother's dinners and all family gatherings. They considered Amira to be part of the family. They'd been together since they were teens, but over time, Marco and Amira grew apart. Marco broke off the relationship. Amira was everything his mother wanted for him, but he began to feel unsure that a traditional Moroccan woman was what he wanted. Marco's mother had that permanent disappointed look on her face, like only a mother can, for some time afterward. A year later, he met Belen at his friend Laila's bar. He was intrigued by the dark-haired flamenco dancer, a modern Spanish woman with her own mind, not tied to tradition, not dependent on him. After a few months of dating, they'd moved in together.

Amira had stayed in touch with his family, but Marco himself hadn't seen her for some time. He'd been startled to see her in Spain that day when he was at dinner with Belen. He noticed that she seemed different somehow.

They drove to the town of Asilah, Paradise Beach, nineteen miles outside Tanger, a seaside resort on the Atlantic coast saturated with white-painted buildings with blue doors.

Marco parked on one of the streets along the coastline. They took their shoes off, and the two strolled towards the beach. As they walked side by side, Marco remembered what he'd loved about Amira: her gentleness, her captivating smile, and her kind spirit. They decided to stop for lunch at a local restaurant. They ordered freshly made bread and a salad, followed by pescado, the catch of the day. Over *a-tay-bnah-nch*, sweet tea. Amira revealed that she had a boyfriend in Vivirrambla and that she lived there with him most of the time. They had been dating for a while, though their relationship had become rocky of late, but she still loved him and hoped to spend her life with him. He sold high-end jewelry, she said, and he was generous with her.

"He really loves me for who I am. He doesn't try to change me," Amira said.

Marco leaned over the table. "I'm happy for you, Amira."

She told him she worked for a clothing company as a buyer and stylist. The job allowed her to travel between Spain and Morocco. When Marco saw her at the restaurant, she'd gone to the wedding of one of her colleagues.

After lunch, they resumed their seaside saunter. The breeze wafting from the cool waters didn't shield them from the beating sun, and they grew hot. They sipped cool tea in a colorful glass stuffed with fresh mint at a local cafe. Things seemed different between them now. Marco looked at Amira. His face grew serious.

"Amira, I just wanted to tell you that I'm sorry how it all ended with us."

"It doesn't matter now. It was a long time ago, Marco. We've both grown up since then. We're in different relationships now," she said.

Marco admired how she'd gained confidence. When they were together, she'd always seemed to depend on him, now she seemed self-reliant.

As dusk approached, they got back in the car to head back to Tanger. On the way, they shared funny stories and reminisced. When they arrived at the drop-off spot near town, Marco stopped the car to let her out and kissed her on the cheek.

"It was good to see you again, Marco. It felt like closure," she said as she shut the car door.

"It was good to see you too, Amira."

Marco watched her ample hips swing back and forth as she walked to her car. He sat for a moment, *hmmm...closure,* he thought. He headed back to his hotel.

Chapter Seventeen

Marco zoomed down the motorway in his rented car. He had an appointment at eleven o'clock at a club called *Recorda*. He parked in front of the club and stepped out in character. He wore a white shirt and black pants. His hair had recently been cut, so it cooperated and fell into place. When he opened the door to the club, he shielded his eyes as the inside of the club was dark in contrast to the gleaming sun. Marco sensed right away that it wasn't his type of atmosphere. A pink disco light, like something from the 1970s or 1980s, trying to be Studio 54 back in the day, hung from the ceiling providing the little light there was in the room. The dark gray leather furniture scattered around looked cheap and worn. Gold trim surrounded the glass bar, which reflected the light from the silver disco ball.

A middle-aged, tan-skinned man with a head full of salt and pepper hair and gray eyebrows greeted Marco.

"As-Salaam-Alaikum," he said, flashing yellowing white teeth. "Welcome to our little club."

"As-Salaam-Alaikum," Marco said.

"Marco nodded a greeting to another man seated on one of the bar stools. The man stared at him through small, squinty eyes. His hairline receded. A small moustache dressed his chin. Marco handed the first man one of Eva's homemade business cards. The man on the bar stool grabbed the card from Marco with his large hands. He nodded to the first man as if to signal the business card looked legitimate.

The first man gestured for Marco to follow him.

"I'm Hassan Alami, and this is my associate, Omar Yousef. I hope you like our little club. Can I get you a drink?"

Marco looked around the room. "Nice, it's just the kind of club I'm looking to invest in," he said. He'd started to say it was too early for him to drink, but then he thought of the image he wanted to portray. He eschewed his usual beer in favor of scotch and soda.

Hassan snapped his finger, and the bartender, a young Moroccan woman smiled and handed Marco a drink.

"What makes you want to get into this business?" Hassan asked.

Marco pulled a stool from under the bar and sat on it. He took a sip of his drink. "I'm looking for a new kind of investment, something that will bring me pleasure as well as money. I've made a lot of money, but now I want to get more out of it. Something fun, just for me," he said.

"We checked you out, of course. You have several real estate investments. You've done well," Hassan said.

"I'm impressed you did your homework. I want to expand from real estate," Marco said.

"Why did you choose me for your next investment?" Hassan asked.

"A nightclub was recommended to me by a friend as a good investment. I was told you own several popular spots and are the best in the business as far as running clubs. I heard you surround yourself with beautiful women," Marco said."

Marco winked at the woman bartender who'd served him. "I see that's no exaggeration," he said.

The bartender smiled and wiped off the bar with the rag in front of her.

"You seem to have a lot of confidence," Hassan said.

"That's how I've made so much money. I believe in myself. Once I've decided to invest, I need to believe in what I'm doing."

"You believe in nightclubs?" Hassan asked.

"I believe I can do well investing in them. I have access to some classy-looking women. They'd make great dancers for your club," Marco said.

Omar lit a cigarette and smoke drifted to Marco's face. "We've already got good dancers," he said.

"Ah yes, but I can get you women who're used to only the finest things," Marco said.

Hassan raised his right eyebrow. "Then why do you need my help?"

"I have the women; now I need the club. I want to invest either here or in Spain, and you have a great reputation. It's a win for us both," Marco said.

Hassan shifted on his bar stool. "Tell me more about these dancers of yours."

"I've got connections in Russia, Ukraine, and Estonia, all over Eastern Europe. I have access to the best that want to come to Spain," Marco said.

"How do you have access to all these women?" Hassan asked.

"I have friends I met in Spain. I've done some favors for them over the years. They've encouraged me to make use of their assets," Marco said.

Omar frowned. "We haven't had any trouble finding our own women."

"Yeah, but I can take it up a notch. I think your clients will really like the women I bring in," Marco said.

"We already have a partner from Spain," Omar said.

Hassan shot him a stern look.

"Oh, my contacts told me you were the sole owner of all your clubs, Hassan. It doesn't matter. I prefer to be a silent investor. I don't want it to interfere with my real estate business. I won't have much to do with the day-to-day operation," Marco said.

"Our other partner is also silent," Omar said.

Hassan glared at him. "Omar means we have some other friends from time to time. When could we get these new dancers if we agree to work with you?"

"My friend owns a model management agency in Spain. He has access to women, migrants from Eastern Europe, with dreams of becoming top models. He glamorizes them and tells them they'd be sent out on modeling jobs. He sends them to me. I send them to the club to become dancers. By this time, they owe my friend thousands of Euros for bringing them over to Spain and for modeling fees. So, they have no choice but to work at the club and do whatever we ask them to do," Marco said.

Hassan twisted his lips. "How do I know what you are saying is true?"

Marco handed Hassan one of his manufactured business cards, this one bearing the name of the model management agent. Flores had been reluctant and balked about spending police resources, but he'd agreed to provide an undercover to pose as a model agent. They'd set up a small office space and secured women to pose as models. "I'll tell you what, here's my friend's modeling agency; check it out. Let me know what you think. We can work out the rest of the details," Marco said.

Omar snubbed out his cigarette and grabbed the card from Marco's hand.

"I still don't know why you need me to open a club since you're so well-connected yourself," Hassan said.

"Ah, but only in Spain. You have the contacts in Morocco and can cut through the red tape. As a Spanish citizen, it'd take me years to open a club here. I don't want to wait years. It's a great opportunity for us both. It'll be the hottest club in Morocco," Marco said.

Hassan rose from his bar stool. "I'll let you know what we decide."

Hassan and Omar said they'd get back to him after they'd looked everything over. They invited him to come back that evening to the club for free drinks. Marco declined. He told them he had important business he had to get back to in Spain and needed to take the next ferry back.

Marco messaged Flores when he got back to his hotel and let him know that Hassan and Omar would be contacting the model agent.

"I hope you know what you're doing. I had to take my undercover from another assignment," Flores said.

Marco finished packing and closed out his hotel bill. He turned in the rented car and headed home on the ferry. This time, the ride was smooth. Belen greeted him at the door with a warm kiss. He inhaled her perfume scent. He was glad to be home.

The house smelled of herbs and spices. He walked into the kitchen, which looked as if it'd been hit by a whirlwind. He peeked into the pots on the stove. Belen was making mariscos, clams and shrimp in saffron, and rice, the smell was as intoxicating as her perfume.

"I'm so glad you're back safely. I was so worried. I'll finish cooking while you unpack," she said.

Marco put his clothes away and joined her. The table had been set, and candles scattered around the room. A bottle of Rioja sat open on the table. She'd gone to a lot of trouble to make a special meal.

During dinner, Marco told Belen what had happened in Morocco.

Her eyes narrowed. "This seems dangerous. Those nightclub types can be real sleazes. You read about it all the time."

"They're definitely low lives. Don't worry, Flores will pull the plug if it looks like there's any danger."

Belen looked into his eyes. "I'm sure you won them over. You can charm anyone. You charmed me when I first met you."

Marco blushed. He thought about mentioning his outing with Amira, but he didn't want to spoil the mood.

Chapter Eighteen

Belen planned a five-day getaway trip to Barcelona. She wanted to go to the annual party of one of the dancers whom she met during Kijamba's video shoot. Marco didn't like the idea of a party at the home of someone he didn't know, but Belen convinced him they needed the time away. Eva, who always spoke on behalf of Belen, assured him she could keep things going while he was away.

"I'm glad you two can get some time alone. I've got to leave early today. I probably won't be here when you get back. Have a great trip," Eva said.

"Okay, thanks," Marco said.

Eva took a keen interest in Marco and Belen's relationship. At times, it was endearing; at other times, she seemed like an annoying little sister.

Marco walked over to Alvarez's to tell him he'd be out of town for a few days. The café was empty after the lunch rush. Few customers gave Alvarez the opportunity to philosophize while he made Marco a café. Alvarez had many opinions, the most recent involved America. He theorized that American democracy was on the decline, which he somehow connected to Kijamba's death, and that Spain would take America's place as the world leader. Marco found it best not to argue. Alvarez's passion amused him. Alvarez finished his rant, handed Marco his coffee, and went back into the kitchen. Marco took a sip of the foamy drink in front of him. He picked up the newspaper, *El Pais,* on the counter and folded it for easy reading. The paper had a feature story about Elaina's death at the Club Azule. The article talked about the effect of the murder on tourism in a town that depended in large part on its wealthy visitors. The writer implied that the Vivirrambla police were inept and unable to solve such a high-profile crime. Marco felt guilty now that he was going on vacation in the middle of the investigation.

Marco's phone vibrated in his pocket. Flores was calling. He shouted on the phone.

"Have you seen today's paper? We're getting pummeled. We're under pressure to solve Elaina's case," he said.

"I saw it," Marco said.

"This is not a good time for you to be going on vacation," Flores said.

"It's only for a few days. I'll leave my phone on so you can reach me anytime," Marco said.

"Stay by your phone at all times," Flores said.

Marco put the paper down and ended the call. He walked over and said goodbye to Alvarez. Belen texted him as he was leaving.

"What time will you be home?"

"I'll be there in just a bit. I just need to clean up a few things at the office before we leave."

He walked back to work. He needed to organize his files and clean his desk. Since Eva was gone, he wouldn't be distracted.

Marco sensed something was wrong as soon as he reached the door, one of those inexplicable premonitions of disaster. He put the key in the door. He gasped. Someone had broken in. His office had been ransacked. Eva's desk had been overturned, and papers were scattered all over the floor. He went into his own office. The scene was the same. The intruder had thrown the furniture about, and his computer lay on the floor. He picked it up and examined it for evidence of tampering. Marco only had a few papers in his office, but they'd been rifled through and tossed aside like someone was searching for something. The entire place was in disarray, as if a tornado had stormed through. He went back to the front and checked Eva's computer. It didn't appear to have been turned on. He let Belen know what had happened and that he'd be late coming home. He wanted to cancel the trip to Barcelona, but they had tickets, and everything had been arranged.

He phoned Eva. "Broken in? How could this have happened? Was anything taken? I'm sure I locked up everything before I left," she said.

She apologized for leaving early. Marco assured her it wasn't her fault, and the computers did not appear to have been touched. She encouraged him not to change his plans and told him she'd take care of everything while he was gone. He opened his computer and changed all the passwords, then he filled Flores in that he'd be calling the police to report a break-in.

"Any idea who this could have been," Flores asked.

"Not a clue," Marco said.

"Maybe it's good that you are getting away for a few days. Someone could be after you," Flores said.

Chapter Nineteen

Belen had finished packing by the time Marco got home. He scurried around, throwing things in travel bags. As he gathered his shaving kit, Belen yelled to him that the taxi was waiting out front. They made it to Malaga airport an hour before the flight. Marco panted as he checked in. He felt relieved to get to his seat. As the plane cruised to its highest altitude, Marco settled back with a beer. Belen rested her head on his shoulder and closed her eyes. He felt comforted that he'd be taking her away from potential danger.

They'd booked a room at a hotel in the center of Barcelona, recommended to him by a friend. The room was spacious, with a view of the city. After a restful sleep and breakfast in the hotel, Marco and Belen decided to walk along Las Ramblas, the street of entertainment, with live animals, animated mimes with faces painted white, and tall people on stilts all sharing the sidewalks of the paseo, enticing passersby. The street bore tapas bars and Catalonian restaurants. The sky was crystal blue, and the day was warm but not uncomfortably hot.

They strolled along the avenue, a mosaic of colors, sights, and sounds. They marveled at the pantomime figures, wearing colorful garbs, human statues seemingly unreal until they switched positions and came to life and the huge, exotic birds in cages for sale. Everywhere they turned brought new sights and magic tricks. They made their way, arms linked, through the crowded streets. At lunchtime, hungry and exhausted, they stopped for a Vino Tinto and tapas at an outdoor café, where they met a group of American tourists who seemed besotted to talk to real Spanish people. That evening they had dinner at a well-known, Michelin-starred restaurant that required booking a year in advance. Belen's friend, who was hosting the party, had gotten them a table. She used to date the owner.

They ordered cava from a stuffy-faced waiter.

"I can't believe Catherine got us in here; wait till I tell everyone. I can't believe this place," Belen said.

Marco had to admit the ambience was nice, though the food was overrated, small portions, and tasteless. He couldn't see why the restaurant was so famous. He tried not to look shocked when he got the bill, but his face softened when he saw how happy Belen was; he closed his eyes and paid the bill.

The next day, after a long afternoon of touring Sagrada Familia and other famous sites of the architect Antoni Gaudi, they stopped at a small local bar/restaurant that Belen had discovered near the Plaza Real. The bar advertised authentic Flamenco. Belen watched the show with interest. She told him the dancing was good but not up to her standards. As the dancers swirled around them, Marco fought distraction as thoughts of Amira and their afternoon together had invaded his mind without warning. He tried to push his thoughts aside. He drew Belen closer, and she smiled.

The impetus for their trip, the annual party held at the home of Catherine Taylor, was set for the end of the week. Catherine, a close friend of Shada and Kijamba, used to be a dancer. She'd retired a few years ago. She and Belen had become friendly during the video shoot, and she'd invited Belen to her annual party.

When the day of the party arrived. Marco wanted to skip it and just let Belen go, but he knew she'd be upset. He ran a comb through his thick hair and shook off the dampness. He slipped on a pair of black slacks and a silk shirt, clicked on the hotel television, and waited for Belen. When she finally emerged, she looked elegant in her diamond stud earrings and a navy cocktail dress she'd purchased for the trip, which hugged her figure, and silver heels. She'd pinned her hair up, which showed off her features.

The party was in full swing when they arrived at the large apartment in the center of Barcelona. The lights of the city shined through the open curtains hung on large bay windows. Guests mingled, holding drinks in their hands, which were served on trays by women and men dressed in black and white penguin attire. The servers passed around a variety of tapas; sturdier dishes of food sat on an antique wooden buffet in warming trays in the dining room. The room smelled of a mixture of expensive perfumes and savory dishes. Marco smiled and nodded at several women who spoke to him. He filled his plate with food, which he had to admit tasted good. He grabbed a beer from one of the trays that went by. Marco never felt comfortable at parties. He wished he was back home yelling at the TV with Oscar. Belen thrived in this environment with her charm and ability to talk to anyone. It was one of the things he most admired about her.

The host, Catherine Taylor, walked towards them. She greeted Belen with a smile through pursed lips and kissed her on the cheek. The two of them engaged in conversation while Marco continued to eat something on a cracker and sip his beer. Once Catherine had gone, Belen whispered to Marco.

"I swear if she uses any more Botox, her face is going to crack. When I get old, don't let me do that; just let me age gracefully."

Marco put his arms around her waist. "You won't need that stuff. You'll always be beautiful to me."

Belen smiled and gave him a kiss. She spotted other dancers she knew, so she flitted over to greet them. Marco made his way across the crowded space to a sitting room/library where he could drink his beer in peace and not have to smile at people he didn't know. As he entered, he was surprised to see Kijamba's business manager, Thomas House, leaning on a bookshelf, talking on his cell phone. House wore a crisp white shirt and highly pressed black trousers with creases. He didn't notice Marco enter the room as he seemed distracted. He sounded curt.

"Look, Danny, we do this my way, or I find someone else," House said.

House had dropped his smooth facade. His voice sounded harsh. "I told you I can't talk now. We'll talk about it later," he said.

House ended the call and stuck the phone in his pocket. *"Red-haired idiot,"* he said under his breath as he grabbed a glass of champagne from the waiter who'd come into the library with a tray of drinks. He downed it in one gulp, then reached for another. He noticed Marco as he went to grab the second drink.

He grinned his toothy grin as if nothing had happened. "Hey, aren't you that detective?"

He walked over and shook Marco's hand like he greeted an old friend. "How's it going? What a coincidence; what are you doing here?"

"Senor House, what a surprise to see you," Marco said. "I'm here with my girlfriend. What are you doing here?"

House slurred his words. "Ca…Ca…Catherine's an old friend of mine. I come to her party every year. Great party, isn't it? Catherine's a hoot."

"Yes, it's a very nice party. That seemed like an intense conversation you were having on the phone," Marco said.

House reached for another glass from another floating waitress. "Oh, that, no big deal. That was one of my former employees. Can you believe he called me during a party to argue with me about his last paycheck?" House asked.

"You seemed pretty upset," Marco said.

House waved his hand as if swatting away an annoying fly. "It was nothing really. He's angry that I fired him, and he claims I owe him money for some work he did. I told him I'm not paying him until he finishes the job."

"I see," Marco said. "How's Shada? Did she come with you to the party?"

House shrugged his shoulders. "She's okay. I invited her to come with me. I told her a party would be good for her. She could take her mind off things, but she said she didn't feel like being around a lot of people. She never leaves the house these days. She's afraid she'll be attacked by cameramen and paparazzi."

Marco furrowed his brow. "I don't think she's ready to go out in public. I'm sure it's going to take quite some time for her to recover from her husband's death."

House took a swig of yet another drink. "I suppose. I think the best way for her to get over it is to get out there and have some fun," he said, shaking his hips in a mock dance.

Marco noticed House's shoes were top-of-the-line, and perfectly polished, as was the rest of his clothing. Marco sensed it was all an act, like the pantomimes in Las Ramblas, that his immaculate look disguised something sinister. "Everyone grieves in their own way, Senor House. It's hard for some people just to 'move on,' as you say."

"I guess," House said.

House waved at Catherine, whom he spied across the room. "I'm sure, you're right. Good to see you again, detective. Excuse me, I haven't had the chance to properly talk to Catherine. Catherine," he shouted.

He grabbed a drink, sprinted to the other side of the room, and kissed Catherine on each cheek, "You look fantastic," he said, putting his hand around her waist.

Marco grabbed a beer. The server smiled at him and walked away. Marco watched House, who was in an intense conversation with Catherine. He never trusted men like that. He'd seen that type before, charismatic and ingratiating. The type that would make a good cult leader. They used charisma to hide their controlling nature. Catherine stood close to House. She seemed mesmerized by what he was saying.

Marco went to find Belen. She glowed, hobnobbing with celebrities. He didn't want to rush her, yet he hoped she'd soon be ready to leave. As he turned to go to her, Catherine Taylor sidled up to him. She wore a ruby necklace and a ruby bracelet surrounded by filigree. Marco noticed it as her jewelry reminded him of Amira and her fire-red earrings.

Catherine could be described as glamorous. She wore a black flapper-style dress with sequins. Like House, she looked like the type of woman Jay Gatsby would have at one of his flamboyant parties. Standing close to her, Marco could see the effects of the Botox use Belen had spoken about. Her eyebrows looked as if they couldn't move.

"My, my, Belen's got herself quite a handsome boyfriend, lucky girl. Those eyes would make me do anything you wanted," she said, smiling.

Marco felt his cheeks heat up. "Thank you," he said.

"I see you know, Thomas," Catherine said.

"Yes, Senor House and I have met. He said he comes to your party every year," Marco said.

She flicked her wrist, and her bracelet shone red in the moonlight coming through the window. "I've known Thomas forever. He used to manage my dancing career," she said.

"Really, he was your manager. When was that?" Marco asked.

She leaned in closer, exposing a view of her cleavage. Marco drank in her scent, which was stronger than Belen's subtle perfume.

"I haven't always been old. I used to be quite a versatile dancer, quite limber," she said, winking at Marco.

She spoke in a whisper. "I don't think Belen even knows about my past. I've got nothing to be ashamed of; I needed the money, and I had a good figure. Shedding a few clothes seemed a small price to pay."

She gestured her arm around the room in a fluid motion. "All this. My dance career paid for all of this, I don't know why I'm telling you these things; for some reason I feel comfortable talking to you, like I can tell you anything."

"You never married?" Marco asked.

"I was married for a few years once. I think I loved him more than he loved me." She sighed. "Now I'm a free spirit."

"I see," Marco said.

She grabbed a drink, moved closer to Marco, and spoke directly into his ear. "I can give you a private showing of some of my old routines sometime if you want. I still have some of my costumes."

Marco spotted Belen coming towards them. He grabbed her by the arm. "Belen, where've you been? Are you ready to go, darling," he asked.

Belen nodded. "Yes, let's call it a night."

She turned to Catherine and kissed her on the cheek. "Great party. It's been wonderful to see you again."

"You too, querida. I'm so glad you came to my little party," Catherine said. She put her hand on Marco's shoulder. "Take care of this gorgeous man."

Belen put her hand in Marco's. "I will."

Belen and Marco weaved their way through the party crowd and headed out the door.

"I never did trust that woman," Belen said as they walked arm and arm out into the still lively streets of Las Ramblas.

82

Chapter Twenty

"When he closes his eyes, death begins to dance around the table where he sits almost every day to watch the sunset and the first lights scintillating across the way, on the coast of Spain."

Leaving Tangier, Tahar Ben Jelloun

Belen sniffed. Something reeked of stale water, and it hit them both as soon as they stepped into the kitchen. They looked down and saw a pool of water on the floor. Marco stepped through the water and opened the cabinet under the sink. He had little talent for plumbing or fixing things, but it appeared to him to be just a small leak in the sink. The leak had just started since their entire kitchen wasn't flooded. He needed to get to work. So, he called the plumber and left Belen to deal with it. Thank goodness the plumber had agreed to come right away and had not given him the amorphous *mañana*, which meant whenever they got around to it.

Marco was happy to escape the water crisis. When he arrived at the office, Eva had a stack of messages for him. He thumbed through them while he waited for his computer to power up. The trip to Barcelona had proved interesting, with his unexpected interaction with House. He resolved to see what else he could learn about the business manager. He input the names of Thomas House and Kijamba into the search engine. Predictably, the top articles were about Kijamba's death. Several magazines had pictures of House at the funeral with Shada. They appeared on the cover of the local and national papers, including *El Pais*. Marco scrolled through more web pages. He stopped at an article in a US magazine about House as a young entrepreneur in Spain. The story touted him as an American lawyer who'd made his way to Spain and had become a business success. House stood smiling before the cameras at some awards ceremony where the Mayor of Vivirrambla gave him the key to the city. His hair was blond and not partly white as it is now. His face was unlined, and his nose, sharp and angular, a Matinee idol. The article said he managed the business affairs of the famous singer Kijamba. Marco paused at the next section. The column described House's other interests and mentioned that he'd had a stake in a nightclub that had been closed due to a drug scandal. Marco recalled an incident that occurred while he was with the police force. They'd shut down a night spot popular with the young party set. The club featured Moroccan décor, round orange velvet couches, and Hookah pipes. They'd arrested the owner, who'd been receiving heroine in boxes of wine and selling it at the club. The then-mayor of Vivirrambla had been implicated in the scheme. The article portrayed House as a victim whose establishment had been used for nefarious purposes without his knowledge. Marco now doubted the verisimilitude of that theory.

Marco was deep in concentration when Flores pinged him. He'd sent a message to say that they'd named a suspect in Elaina's murder, a young illegal immigrant who worked at the club. The man had come to Spain from Tunisia a few weeks earlier and worked as a cleaner in the Club Azule. A witness said he'd been stalking Elaina for weeks before her death. They were about to bring him down for questioning. Flores wanted Marco to sit in on the interrogation and translate it into Arabic.

Marco knew the story of these migrants. They risked their lives to get across the sea. The rides Marco took on the ferry from Tanger North Africa, to Vivirrambla, Spain, were uneventful. As a Spanish citizen, he could rest assured that he would be made to feel as comfortable as possible. On the ferry, he was free to roam around, to get a drink, or to watch the sea. He knew that these immigrants had no such luxuries. The lure of the siren's call from the horizon of Spain often led hopeful migrants to a life of despair. They'd entered the country on unstable rocky boats or hidden away in the bowels of larger vessels. Many had used their life savings or borrowed from family to pay unscrupulous *passeurs* thousands of Euros to cross the Mediterranean. They came eager for a better life. Most ended up in debt and at the mercy of the smuggler. Some died on crossings on smaller unstable boats. If they made it safely across, they had a great chance of being deported and sent right back to the circumstances they tried to escape. Many who stayed ended up poor, yet their debt to the ferryman remained, and everything they earned went to pay off the smuggler.

Marco let Eva know he'd be leaving for a meeting with Flores. Ever since the break-in, he'd been leery about leaving her alone in the office, but she assured him she was fine.

"I'll lock everything up, don't worry," she said.

It was the middle of the afternoon as he drove the coastal highway to Malaga. The ride was pleasant. The weather had been atypical, mild, and not humid. Marco rolled down his window and took in the fresh smell of the salty sea. He turned up the music of U2 and sang along to the words to "Beautiful Day," belting out words in English, most of which he didn't understand.

Flores invited Marco into his office, which was a disaster as usual. His desk was full of papers and a half-full coffee cup that sat perilously close to the computer keyboard. Marco, who wouldn't consider himself fastidious, wondered how Flores got anything done. Flores shifted some papers on his desk and offered Marco a seat in front of him. He briefed Marco on the suspect they'd arrested. His name was Idan. He'd worked as a cleaner at the bar for the past several months. Flores had interviewed him at the club. After the interview, he'd spoken to a witness who said Idan seemed fixated on Elaina. The witness said she'd warned Elaina that Idan was dangerous. After Marco had been briefed, they headed through the police station to the interrogation room, where they waited for Idan. Flores sat at the head of the table. Armed guards ushered in a young man with dark hair, shaking, with his head bowed.

"Have a seat," Flores said, gesturing to the empty metal chair opposite Marco.

Marco thought about how, because of his darker skin tone, he could have easily been in the same situation, at the mercy of Spanish police, had he not had the protection of his Spanish father.

Flores raised his voice, as if talking louder would make the immigrant understand him better. "What are you doing in Spain?" he asked.

Idan spoke in Arabic, which Marco translated. Idan confessed that he'd come to Spain hidden on a boat with several other people. He'd been given a job at Club Azule as soon as he arrived. He worked to pay off his debt, several thousand Euros to the boatmen who brought him over. He'd been desperate to get to Spain to escape political persecution in his own country. He believed the smugglers when they told him they would get him a good job and he could start a new life. Idan said he'd heard of others who didn't pay. They'd been beaten or, worse, killed.

"What do you do at the club?" Flores asked.

"I'm the cleaner," Idan said.

"How do you get paid?" Flores asked.

"I earn one hundred Euros every two weeks. My boss gives me forty euros in an envelope," Idan said.

Marco and Flores looked at one another.

"What happens to the rest of the money?" Flores asked.

Idan shrugged. "I never see it. My boss keeps all the money."

"How do you live? Who gets the rest of your money, do you know?" Marco asked.

"I don't know. A man comes to the club and collects it. I don't know his name. He's from Morocco. That's all I know about him."

"Have you ever seen this man?" Marco asked.

Idan nodded his head. "I've seen him a couple of times. He goes in and talks to my boss."

"Do you see everything that goes on in the club?" Marco asked.

"I see most things that go on. Most of the time, people don't notice I'm around."

"Were you watching, Elaina?" Flores asked.

Idan looked at Flores. His large brown eyes were moist. "I saw her sometimes. She was my friend."

"You wanted her to be more than friends, didn't you?" Flores asked.

"She was beautiful and smart. I knew she'd never like someone like me," Idan said.

"So, you followed her around, didn't you?"

Idan stared at Flores through pleading eyes. "I never followed her. She's the only one who'd talk to me at the club. She was a nice person. The other women at the club won't even look at me. They're immigrants too, but they think they're better than me."

"Did you ever ask Elaina out on a date?" Flores asked.

Idan shook his head. "No, no, I'd never have enough courage to do that."

Flores's voice rose to a high pitch. His face turned the color of Spanish clay. "You're lying. She turned down your advances. So, you decided to get even and kill her. Isn't that what really happened?"

Idan squirmed and rose from his seat. Immediately, the guard at the door sprang towards him. He looked at Marco as if pleading for help. They spoke in Arabic to each other. Then Idan calmed down. "Kill her? I would never kill her. She was my only friend here. I would never hurt her. I told her she should stop dancing at that club, that she was too good for that."

"You were jealous of her and other men, weren't you? Our witness says you stalked, Elaina," Flores said.

"I just didn't like her dancing in that club," Idan said.

"We found pictures of her in your apartment," Flores said.

Idan hung his head. "Yes, she was beautiful, and she let me take her picture. She was thinking of sending it to a modeling agency. One day before work, we went to the beach to take pictures. I kept copies. I liked to look at them."

"You were obsessed with her, and you knew you couldn't have her, isn't that right, Senor?" Flores asked.

Idan turned to Marco. "I don't understand. What does it mean to obsess?"

"It means you thought about her all the time. That you followed her around. That you wanted her for yourself. Our witness says you threatened her," Flores said.

Marco translated what Flores had said to Idan in Arabic.

"No, no, no. I know you spoke to that friend of hers, Ginka. She hated me. She looked down her nose at me and told me I wasn't good enough to talk to Elaina. She threatened me to leave her alone," Idan said.

Flores slammed the pictures of Elaina his officers had found in Idan's house on the table. "Senora Kovalenko tried to protect her friend from you. When Elaina rejected you, you killed her. Isn't that what happened?"

When Idan reached for the pictures, both Flores and Marco noticed that Idan's arm was bruised and black and blue. Flores and Marco looked at one another.

"Where'd you get that bruise on your arm? Was that from Elaina when she tried to fight you off?" Flores asked.

Idan looked down at his arm. Squirming in his chair, he answered. "I had an accident at work. I slipped on the wet floor?"

Flores raised his eyebrows. "When did that happen?"

"The other day."

Marco watched the beads of water trickle down Idan's face and converge with the tears that dropped on his cheek. He felt the fear and pain Idan experienced.

Idan seemed to sense that Marco was sympathetic to him. He turned his attention to him. "It's true. I kept her picture, but I would never do anything to harm her."

Flores leaned over the metal table. "Bruises on Elaina showed she put up a struggle. If we find your DNA on her, I have enough to charge you with murder."

Marco explained the significance of what Flores had said to Idan.

Idan's eyes widened. "I didn't kill her."

"Can you get an attorney?" Marco asked.

Idan shook his head. "I'm not a legal resident. Senor Marco, please help me."

Marco told him he would find out what he could do and let him know.

Marco was skeptical of Flores's hypothesis that Idan had killed Elaina because he couldn't have her. He'd seen the murder scene. It didn't look like a passion killing, more like a hit. From Marco's experience, a passion killing out of jealousy would be more personal; more care would have been taken with the victim. Elaina was shot with her clothes left in disarray and her hair disheveled. The assassin directed the shot like he or she knew what they were doing. Idan didn't seem like a trained killer.

"I'll see what I can do to find out about a lawyer for you," Marco said as Idan was led back to his cell.

Marco turned to Flores, whose normal color had not yet returned. "I think you've got the wrong person. He's not a killer. He's too timid, and this doesn't seem like a crime of passion."

"The evidence says otherwise. Our witness says he drooled over Elaina like a sad puppy. The other dancers thought he was creepy and tried to avoid him. Everyone noticed his obsession. He was in the club at the time of the murder, and he kept pictures of her in his house. That's enough to charge him."

"I know all that, but my instinct says he's not a killer. I think he genuinely admired Elaina and she was the only one who was nice to him. He might have been in love with her, but I think he knew nothing would happen. The other dancers looked down on him because he was from Tunisia. They blamed him right away for the murder," Marco said.

"I've told you before, we follow the evidence, not your instinct. I think we've got our man," Flores said.

Chapter Twenty-One

When politics guides the decisions of the rulers, humanity is forsaken. Marco had read that somewhere, and it was proving to be true. Flores informed Marco that the department would no longer pay expenses for his undercover investigation of the Club Azule since the murder of Elaina had been solved. Flores's decision had been driven by politics. The police wanted the case solved. The department was anxious to preserve the reputation of Puerto Bella, to keep the tourists' dollars flowing. Flores refused to listen to Marco's pleas to continue the sting operation. Elaina's murder was more complex than a jealous lover. He argued to no avail. When, finally, Flores refused to budge, Marco vowed to keep digging. Politics wasn't a sufficient reason to blame murder on an immigrant who couldn't defend himself.

Marco was too upset to go back to work after his meeting with Flores. He went straight home. When he walked in the door, Belen reclined on the couch wearing a pink tracksuit. Her hair was in a ponytail. She sat with her legs folded, looking at her iPad. He told Belen of the interrogation and his intent to keep searching for Elaina's killer. She frowned and turned up her small nose.

"There's nothing for you to investigate. The case is over. The police said she was being stalked by the guy who worked there. I don't think you should put yourself in any more danger," Belen said.

"You must understand how frightening it is for an undocumented immigrant to be interrogated by the police. I need to do what I can to help him. I think the police have the wrong man."

"This isn't about his being an immigrant. This is about a man who stalked a stripper and killed her out of jealousy. It's not the first time that's happened," Belen said.

"I spoke to Idan. He's a gentle person. He was genuinely upset about Elaina's death," Marco said.

"I understand your point, but that doesn't mean all immigrants are innocent either," she said. "The police have plenty of evidence to charge this man. He was obsessed with the dancer. As a woman dancer, I understand this fear."

Marco put his arm around her. "Has anyone ever stalked you," he asked.

She put the iPad down and pulled her knees up close to her chest. "I've had my share of gawkers, and some men have made me feel uncomfortable," she said.

Marco hadn't really thought of Belen being in any danger when she danced. Now that she performed solely in the theater in Malaga, she was no longer vulnerable to drunken tourists like she'd been while dancing at local clubs and restaurants in Vivirrambla.

"You need to let me know if anyone approaches you," he said.

She smiled. "I'm fine. My point is that stalking happens. Crime of this kind is common. It's got nothing to do with him being an immigrant."

Marco chuckled. "You sound like a police expert. I used to be on the force, remember?" he asked. "I've seen how they operate. The police are quick to close the case when it's an immigrant, especially one from Africa. They spend less time investigating. I think that's what happened here, besides the fact that Flores is under a lot of pressure to solve this case."

Belen stood up from the couch. "I see your point, but stalking is real, and many women have died because of men's obsession. We can agree to disagree on this one. Do you want a beer?"

Marco nodded.

Belen walked into the kitchen and returned with two beers. She handed one to Marco. "It's not your job to finish La Guardia's work. It's enough you're helping them solve high-profile murders."

Marco took the beer from her and popped open the top. Some of the beer drizzled from the can. "I know but don't you see I have to help, Idan."

"I get it. I just don't want you to be in danger," Belen said.

Marco put his arms around her. "I love you. I'll be okay."

"I love you too," she said.

Belen finished her beer, rose from the couch, and walked into their bedroom. Marco grabbed another beer and flicked on the television. His mind was still on Idan. He thought of his Moroccan relatives, like his cousin Karim. If they emigrated to Spain, they could be in the same situation dealing with the police.

Marco soon fell asleep on the couch in front of the television, which blared some program when he woke up the next morning. He decided to go for a swim to clear his head. Belen was still sleeping, so he crept into the bedroom and grabbed his swimming gear. He walked to the beach and dove into the water. His anxiety eased. His thoughts turned to Amira. He tried to dismiss her and concentrate on the feel of the water against his skin. Amira would have understood the feeling of being a vulnerable immigrant. He wasn't being fair. Belen had supported him when he lost his job on the police force. She'd understood how he'd been treated. She'd adopted his Moroccan family. His grandmother, Jaddah, loved her like one of her own grandchildren. Amira though, would have had a deeper understanding as to why he needed to help Idan.

Marco's muscles glistened in the yellow sun when he stepped out of the water. He smoothed the wet hair off his face and dried himself off. The gesture reminded him he needed a haircut as the shaggy strands fell into his eyes. He gathered his flip-flops and headed back to the apartment.

Belen had gone to an appointment when he returned home. Marco headed to the shower and dressed for work. As soon as he got into the office, he contacted a criminal defense lawyer he knew from working on the force who spoke Arabic. The lawyer promised to go to the prison to talk to Idan. Marco felt better after the call. There was nothing else he could do for Idan.

After making a notation in his phone's calendar to check up on Idan in a couple of days, Marco turned his attention to Kijamba's murder. He asked himself who would have a motive or who had something against the popular singer. He needed to look into those who'd worked with or surrounded the pop star. He created an Excel spreadsheet of Kijamba's friends, band members, stagehands, and employees and checked off those on the list that had already been questioned by the police. Others who had not, he placed on an open list. He narrowed that list to those closest to Kijamba and those who had the most access to him.

Once the list was complete, Marco went for lunch. He couldn't think on an empty stomach. The restaurant was crowded with regulars and tourists who chatted amongst themselves in various languages or on their cell phones.

Alvarez ushered Marco to his regular table. "Buenes tardes, Marco. *Pollo con patatas fritas* on special today."

It was Marco's favorite daily special. Alvarez placed a basket of bread and olive oil in front of him. The smell of olive oil augmented his hunger. He poured some of the smooth light green liquid from the olive trees that grew from the soil in Spain onto a plate, took a piece of bread, and dipped it like a religious rite. He poured a glass of wine from the carafe that came with the meal and settled down for lunch. When he finished eating, he felt stuffed. He turned down the *postre,* and settled for coffee, which Alvarez delivered along with a sermon about the latest world events. Then he asked Marco about Kijamba.

"Any progress on finding the killer of the singer? The papers are saying our police aren't capable of handling such a high-profile case," Alvarez said.

"It's a complicated case. We're doing all we can, but it may take a while to solve," Marco said.

"I see. I hope they find the killer soon. It makes the whole town look bad. We can't afford negative publicity. If tourists think it's not safe, they'll stop coming," he said.

Marco thanked Alvarez for his opinion and headed back to the office, walking in the hot afternoon sun. Eva, who sat typing at her computer when he arrived, told him there'd been no new messages. So, he went straight back to his Excel sheet. Alvarez wasn't totally wrong. The police did seem inept. They'd spoken to the film crew, the video crew who worked the set, the sound crew, costumes, and props, but they'd obtained little useful information.

He scrolled through his list. A couple of names piqued his interest. One was a Spanish guitarist who played background in the video named Juan Lopez. His website advertised him as a local flamenco guitarist who played with several musical troupes. Marco had access to police files. He searched for Lopez's name. The musical accompanist had been arrested five times for drug offenses.

Marco phoned Belen to ask her if she remembered Lopez from the video shoot.

"Ah, Si, Juan, I've known him for some time. He plays at some of my gigs. He's a bit odd, but a great guitarist," she said.

"What do you mean odd?" Marco asked.

"Too much drug usage has aged him. He reminds me of a wanna-be rockstar who never quite made it," she said.

"Did he get along with the other performers and musicians? How did he get along with Kijamba?" Marco asked.

"We all got along with him. The dancers knew he was a burnout, in and out of jail. I'm not sure Kijamba knew him that well. We were all hired by an agency," Belen said.

"Has he ever been violent when you were around?" Marco asked.

"Not that I can think of. I saw him lose his temper a couple of times during rehearsals when we couldn't get it right, but nothing violent," she said.

"Did he ever lose his temper with you?"

"Oh no, we got along fine. He taught me a lot about music. He's a musical encyclopedia, that's why I like to dance when he's playing guitar, he knows the history and background of every song. You can sense it in the feeling he puts into it."

Marco worried again about the people Belen worked with; he looked up

Juan Lopez's address. Lopez lived nearby in San Pedro Alćantara a small town, 10 km West of Vivirrambla. Marco phoned Lopez and told him he needed to speak to him regarding a police investigation. When he hung up with Lopez, his own cell rang. He didn't recognize the number but decided to answer it anyway.

"*Dime*," he said.

The caller's voice sounded muffled, but he spoke broken Spanish with an accent. "I'm giving you one warning. Keep away from Amira. The next time, you won't know what hit you," the voice said.

"Who is this?" Marco asked.

The line disconnected.

Chapter Twenty-Two

Marco weaved his way through the crowded streets of the Plaza Mayor in the pueblo de San Pedro Alćantara. He blended in with the joyous revelers who languished along the streets enjoying St. Ana's feast. The entire town, it seemed, had come out for the procession and the colorful pageant of religious statues and floats constructed in honor of the mother of Mary and grandmother of Jesus. Concession stands offering a variety of foods and Sangria, as well as other drinks, surrounded the town center. *Las calles*, the streets, smelled of incense, fresh *jamon*, and oranges from the blooming naranja trees. Women in elaborate patterned flamenco dresses and black Mary Jane's danced and twirled, seemingly oblivious to the heat. Olive-skinned men with raven hair, wearing black vests trimmed in yellow, rode astride Andalucian horses as they galloped alongside the parade floats.

The citizens of San Pedro went all out for this yearly feast celebration. *Confradias,* fraternities, or brotherhoods vied for the opportunity to carry the large, heavy floats and to wear their signature uniforms. Marco had attended many such feasts and Semana Santa celebrations the week before Easter. His Catholic father was a proud member for many years of a fraternity that carried a parade float. Churches spent months preparing figurines to ride atop the structures through town, one more grand than the other. Giant figures of St. Ana and the Virgin Mary, their skin dark, as if they'd been warmed by the Andalucian sun, road on the floats surrounded by live flowers. Cherub-cheeked altar boys swung incense thuribles right and left like a pendulum as they strode through the town; others held giant candles that inspired emotions of tears from devout onlookers.

In the town center, bells pealed from la Iglesia Santa Ana, the white church decorated with candles. It was at this spot where the procession would end in the wee hours of the morning. Marco stopped in front of the church to check the address he'd entered on his phone. The locator showed he was around the corner from Juan Lopez's apartment.

Marco walked up to the front door of the three-story building and pressed the entrance button. The sounds of the parade dissipated, though the church bells still rang. The door opened automatically to an old-fashioned style lobby with big velvet furniture, which looked like a holdover from the Victorian period. No security guard manned the entrance, so Marco was unsure as to who'd let him into the building. He ventured straight to Lopez's door and knocked. He knocked louder a second time.

"I'm coming. Calm down!" Marco heard a craggy-sounding voice yell from behind the door.

After the click of several chains being unlocked, the door opened. A middle-aged man of medium height with long dark thinning hair and lined skin, like a Spanish Keith Richards, answered the door. He wore baggy jeans and a faded black t-shirt bearing the name of some forgotten rock band. His feet were bare, but his arms were dressed with various tattoos.

"Sr. Juan Lopez?" Marco asked.

The man squinted his dark almond eyes and stared at Marco. "Si, who are you? What do you want?"

"Soy Marco. I called earlier. I need to talk to you about Kijamba. I'm a private detective working on the case.

The bells from the church pealed again as Marco spoke.

Lopez looked up. "Darn that noise. I hate those damn bells. Come in."

He ushered Marco into a small living room with an enormous red sofa and a couple of chairs, which looked much like the furniture in the lobby.

Lopez shuffled across the red-tiled floor over to the sofa. He gestured to Marco to sit.

"Make yourself comfortable, hombre. What do you want to know about Kijamba? It's too bad what happened to him. He was a great singer. I felt honored to be in his video," Lopez said.

"Full disclosure: my girlfriend was one of the dancers," Marco said.

Lopez stared at Marco. "Your girlfriend? Who's your girlfriend?"

"Belen Romero," Marco said.

Lopez raised his dark brows and smiled. "Ah, Belen. Good looking. Nice legs. I've played at a lot of her gigs."

Marco ignored the comment about Belen's legs. He looked around the apartment. The dining area contained a table full of papers and sheets of music. Pictures in frames of a younger Lopez, without the cragged old skin, rested on the cupboard.

"As I told you, I'm a private investigator assisting the police in finding out what happened to Kijamba. You were hired by an agency like Belen to play in the video, right?

Lopez nodded his head. "Yep, someone told me Kijamba was making a video in town and that he needed guitarists. I jumped at the chance."

"So, you'd never met Kijamba before the video shoot?"

"Nope, my first time meeting him. I didn't really get to talk to him much, though. We were hired for a few days, came in for rehearsals, then for the final cut."

"There was a big party a week before the shoot at Kijamba's home. Did you go?" Marco asked.

Belen had also been invited. It was to meet the crew and everyone involved in the video, but Belen didn't attend as she was in Madrid visiting her parents.

"Yeah, I went for a while. I brought one of my guitars and played some music for them. I didn't stay long as that crowd isn't really my scene."

Lopez picked up one of his guitars and started to strum a couple of notes. Marco recognized the melody.

"Did anything unusual happen at the party?" Marco asked.

"Like I said, I wasn't there long, too many beautiful people. Some woman kept coming on to me, flashing her ruby bracelet like she wanted to prove to me she had money. Not my type, too much Botox. I hate those tight faces." Lopez said.

"What about after the video shoot? Did you go out with the rest of the crew to celebrate that afternoon?" Marco asked.

"No, I was wiped out from standing in that sun all day. A few beers and a smoke, and I crashed."

"Can anyone vouch for your whereabouts?" Marco asked.

Lopez shook his head no. "I live alone. I've been divorced from my husband for some time. He lives in America. We were married for five years. I'm alone now, just me and my music."

Marco raised his eyebrows. "Do you remember anything unusual happening that day? Even the slightest thing may be important. I know there was a lot going on during filming, but did you see anything out of the ordinary on the set, any fights or disagreements?"

Lopez paused for a second and scratched his head. "I remember one incident. While we were on break, I think I was the only one still standing on the set, me and Kijamba, that is. Anyway, someone looked like one of those delivery people, as he was on a bike, handed Kijamba a note. Kijamba looked mad after he read it. His face turned red. He balled it up and threw it on the ground. Then we went back to rehearsal, so I didn't think any more about it."

"That's interesting. Do you have any idea what happened to the note?" Marco asked.

Lopez shook his head. "No idea. They came and swept the set before we went back to rehearsal. I thought it was the lunch order since lunch was late and they had some problems with delivery. I figured Kijamba was mad they'd screwed up the order."

"Can you describe the person who handed Kijamba the note?"

"Delivery guy…youngish, medium height if I remember right."

"Do you know who let the person on to the set? I would think the set was closed," Marco said.

"One of the stagehands let him in. Probably thought it had to do with the lunch order like I did," Lopez said.

Marco rose from the low-seat sofa. He felt a pain in his back. He was getting old. "Muchas gracias, Senor Lopez, you've been really helpful."

Lopez rose from his seat and escorted Marco to the door. "Not sure what

I did, but glad to help. Do you know when Kijamba's album is going to be released? It's going to be even bigger now that he's dead."

"I'm sorry, I don't know," Marco said.

Marco handed Lopez his card. "Let me know if you think of anything else," he said.

"I will. Come back anytime and bring Belen," he said.

"I'll tell her you said hello," Marco said.

Chapter Twenty-Three

"They look at the sea, at the clouds that blend into the mountains, as they wait for the twinkling lights of Spain to appear."
                              Leaving Tangier, Tahar Ben Jelloun

Flores turned over, groaned, and shut down the piercing noise coming from his landline phone.

His wife raised her head from the pillow. "What's going on?" she asked.

Flores answered the phone. "I'll be right there," he said.

He turned over and got up from the bed. "Go back to sleep, honey," he said to his wife.

"It's five o'clock in the morning. What are you doing up? Are you going fishing?" his wife asked.

Flores kissed her on the head. "I've got to go. I'll call you later."

He went into the bathroom and showered, no time to shave. He slipped on a pair of jeans and a shirt. He grabbed his bluish-gray police jacket in case it was cold by the sea this time of the morning. He made a cup of instant *Nescafe* and hopped in his Citroën. The drive took fifteen minutes. By the time he arrived at the sea, he felt awake. The sun had also begun to rub the sleep from her eyes.

Flores parked right next to the boat; a blue unstable contraption now covered in police tape. Several of his officers had already boarded the vessel. As soon as Flores stepped onto the unsteady boat, he felt disgusted at the thought that with its cracked floorboards, chipped paint, and rusted handles, it had been used to transport humans. He thought of the perilous voyage of men, women, and children, all squashed together like crabs captured in a net.

His colleagues and SASEMAR milled around searching for evidence of smuggling, Operation Contrabando they called it. They dusted for prints and bagged evidence. The ship had come to the attention of the police after they received complaints about its coming and going at odd hours and strange-looking people going on and off the boat and about the noise. They'd received an anonymous tip that the boat intended to leave the dock in a few days, a recognized sign of smuggling. They'd obtained a search warrant before the boat could leave Spain.

Before the police arrived, the boat crew had been warned that the police were coming. Most of the smugglers had scattered like rats exposed to daylight. They detained those who remained. Costal officers rummaged through the boat, shining flashlights in corners, nooks, and crannies. They found over 100,000 Euros and firearms, as well as ropes, torn clothing, hair, and other evidence that humans had been restrained on the boat's deck. To their surprise, they also found bags of shiny red gems hidden in a cushion under the floorboards. Flores and SASEMAR gathered dozens of bags of red jewels, which appeared to be rubies, and tagged them as evidence. The search took several hours. Preliminary evidence indicated that the boat had originated in Scotland.

Chapter Twenty-Four

Eva sat at her desk, staring at the internet. Her shoulder-length blond hair hung loose, and a pair of large gold earrings dangled from her ears. She was one of those people who exuded happiness, her infectious smile, contagious.

"Anything new?" Marco asked, invading her thoughts.

She jumped, startled. "Nope, *jeffe*, everything seems calm right now."

"I'll be in my office the rest of the day if you need me," Marco said.

The visit to Lopez had proven fruitful. He'd confirmed that Kijamba had received a note, delivered on set by a courier, which had made him visibly angry. Marco looked up courier and messenger delivery services. He found ten in the Vivirrambla area.

He picked up the phone on his desk to call each of the services. He'd almost finished entering the number of the first when Flores appeared at his door panting and out of breath. His large ears were bright red. His shirt was not fully tucked in and hung on his pants.

"Detective, what are you doing here? Marco asked.

Eva appeared at the door after him. "Sorry," she said. "I was on the phone when he came in."

"Don't worry, Eva," Marco said. "Make yourself comfortable, Detective. It's pretty hot out there, huh," he said.

Flores flopped onto the available chair in front of Marco's desk. Marco thought it would be a good idea if Flores took up exercise or swimming to get in better shape.

"Darn right, it's hot," Flores said, wiping his forehead with a handkerchief.

"Can I get you anything? "Eva, can we get him some water?" What are you doing here?" Marco asked.

Eva came in a few seconds later and handed Flores a glass of water. Flores grabbed it and slurped it down in one gulp.

"Ah, thanks," he said, setting the glass on Marco's desk. "I need to speak to you right away. We've had an incident. You may have been right about that Tunisian. He didn't have anything to do with Elaina's death. He's been stabbed in jail."

Marco gasped. "Idan? Stabbed, by whom, where is he now?"

"He's in Malaga hospital clinging to life. It doesn't look good. The doctors say the next forty-eight hours should tell us whether he'll make it through," Flores said. "If he survives, we're going to need you to speak to him."

Marco nodded his head, "Yes, of course. What changed your mind?"

"Idan has an airtight alibi for the time of Elaina's death. He was being held on a smuggling boat. I just came from a raid. We arrested some of the smugglers. We found out they'd been holding Idan on the boat the entire night until right before he'd come to work. We have some of the crew in custody. When we interrogated one of them, he used Idan as an alibi. Can you believe that?"

"Why were they holding, Idan?" Marco asked.

"The smuggler told us that he was "questioning" him about some money he owed the company, more like a brutal interrogation, I'd guess," Flores said.

Flores chuckled. "I've never heard of such an alibi. The smuggler identified the man that he'd been questioning as a cleaner at the Club Azule. We figured out it was the Tunisian. So, we had to let him go. A few hours later, someone attacked him with a knife."

"No wonder Idan looked so frightened when we spoke to him. He was afraid the smugglers were after him," Marco said.

Flores nodded his head. "You were right. I jumped the gun. We're going to have to start the investigation into Elaina's death from scratch. The Chief's not going to be happy."

Flores, who'd cooled off and was no longer sweating, rose to leave and then turned to say something. "The odd thing is we found some gems that appear to be rubies stashed all over the boat. They're at the lab for analysis."

"Rubies? That's interesting, smuggling rubies along with people. I'm sure there's more to that story," Marco said.

Chapter Twenty-Five

Marco visited Idan in the hospital. Tubes ran throughout his body, and he was unconscious. He lay still, not moving, his eyes closed. The doctors said they weren't sure he'd pull through.

The police had no information on Idan's family. Only Marco and Flores had been to see him at the hospital. If Idan died, no one would know.

Marco's cell beeped as he was leaving the hospital. He looked down at the phone and was surprised to see Amira's name. "*Dime*," he said, still thinking about Idan.

"Hi Marco, I hope I'm not disturbing you," Amira said.

He felt nervous at hearing her voice, though he couldn't explain why. "No, it's okay. What can I do for you?"

"I need to speak to you," she said.

He leaned back in his chair. "Uh, okay."

He thought of his grandmother in Morocco, and he hoped Amira hadn't heard any bad news about her.

"In person…" she said.

"Okay, where are you?" he asked.

"I'm here in Vivirrambla. Is there a possibility we can meet somewhere this evening?"

"Uhm, I'm not sure this evening will work," he said.

"It's important," she said.

Marco thought for a moment. He'd planned an intimate dinner with Belen, a date night. Belen had been working a lot. Since word had gotten out that she'd been one of Kijamba's principal dancers on the video he was making before his death, she'd been in high demand. She'd become the star flamenco dancer in her troupe in Malaga. Her new fame meant she worked every night, many times during the day, and on weekends, so she was rarely home. Ironically, she'd been upset with Marco about his work schedule. Now, she was the one who was never home. He knew she'd be disappointed if he canceled. "Can we make it tomorrow? It's just that I had plans with Belen."

"I'm sorry to ask, but it's really important," Amira said.

Marco paused. "Okay, let's meet in Malaga for dinner at eight."

"Thanks, Marco. I wouldn't bother you, but you're the only one that can help me."

"I know, I'll be there," he said.

Marco did worry. How could he tell Belen that instead of their romantic evening together, he was going to spend the evening with his ex-girlfriend?

Eva had left hours ago. He'd let her go early since the air conditioning was only partially working. He began to sweat even though the sun had gone down, yet he delayed leaving. Belen had texted to ask him when he intended to come home.

"I'll be there in a little while."

"See you soon. I'm excited about tonight."

After procrastinating for another hour, Marco decided he'd better go home and face Belen. He stopped at the florist on his way and brought a large bouquet of flowers. The aroma was sweet and intoxicating, with the mixture of roses, baby's breath, and orchids. He took the long way home through the Old Town, Casca Antiqua, past the white stucco homes and orange trees. He stalled, giving himself time to think of what he'd say to her. He thought about how nice it would have been to have dinner in *Casco Antigua* with Belen.

"Belen," he called out once he reached the door.

"In here," she said from the bedroom. "Hurry up and get dressed."

He entered the bedroom and saw that she wore a sleeveless peach dress. She looked beautiful.

He hesitated. "I'm going to have to postpone the evening," he said.

"What? When did you find that out? You didn't say anything earlier. You know I only get a few nights off."

"I know, I know. I'm sorry. It's work. I thought it would be better to tell you in person."

He explained that he'd received a call about one of his cases and that it sounded urgent. A witness needed to meet with him.

She stared at him through the mirror. Her long, thick, dark hair came past her shoulders. Her large oval eyes stood out with black liner and long lashes. She smelled of jasmine and lilac from the bottle on her bureau. Marco thought about canceling his meeting with Amira.

He handed her the flowers. She sniffed them, then placed them on the bureau without looking up. "I'm sorry, sweetie. You know I wouldn't go except she said it was urgent. I'm a detective, I have to go."

Belen frowned. "She? Your client is a woman?"

Marco grabbed her face. "It's just business."

She pulled back from him. "Okay, I get it. We can reschedule for my next day off," she said.

He couldn't tell her it was Amira he was going to meet. He showered and changed into a blue shirt and jeans. He reached for his aftershave, but then he thought the better of it.

"I won't be too late," he said to Belen, who had changed into a more comfortable outfit and settled in front of the television. She held the remote in her hand, surfing the channels.

Marco slipped on his black shoes and walked to the door. His dark, wavy hair was slightly wet, and a couple of drops hit his shirt.

"I'll see you when you get back," she said.

He shut the door and left before he could change his mind.

Marco picked Amira up, and they drove to *restaurante* Paco Jiminez, a well-known eatery in Malaga. They were seated at a table by the open patio door. The evening breeze that had now developed felt good in contrast to the heat of the day. The intimate surroundings of the restaurant, with white tablecloths, made it feel romantic. A young waiter dressed in a black tux and white shirt handed Marco the wine list. He chose a white wine, Amira's favorite. They perused the menu. Amira ordered *Cocktail de Langostinos* for an appetizer, and Marco ordered Jamon Iberico. For the entrée they both chose *Parillada de Pescado y Mariscos*—grilled seafood and fish.

They exchanged small talk over the appetizer. Amira said she'd been busy at her work. But her visa was about to expire. She hoped that it would be renewed by her employer so she could stay in Spain.

The waiter returned to the table. "Can I get you anything else?" he asked.

"No thanks," Marco said.

Then he turned his attention to Amira. He felt a sharp stabbing pain to his heart, which caught him off guard. He grimaced. "What is it you wanted to talk to me about?" he asked.

She stared at him for a moment. Her brown eyes danced in the candlelight, and her bronze skin glowed. "I've been having some problems with my boyfriend."

She took a sip of wine. "I think it's serious. He's been acting weird lately, and I wanted to get your opinion as a detective. I'm worried he may be involved in something illegal. I heard him talking on his cell the other day."

"I see. Talking about what?" Marco asked.

"It sounded dodgy, like he was doing some kind of deal. I couldn't hear all of it, but he was saying someone owed him a lot of money for something he'd done for them. He's changed. He doesn't come home sometimes, and he's become withdrawn. When I ask him about it, he clams up and tells me not to worry."

"Sorry to hear that; you deserve to be happy, Amira," Marco said.

"Daniel used to be so sweet. He brought this shady-looking guy over to the apartment the other day. They made me leave the room," she said.

Daniel, it was the first time Amira had said his name.

"I don't want to seem like I don't trust him. I don't want to chase him away like I did you, but things aren't like they used to be." Her eyes glistened. "I'm scared," she said.

"Amira, you didn't chase me away. We grew apart, it happens. Whatever has made Daniel change is of his own making and has nothing to do with you, I'm sure. You said you tried talking to him?"

"Do you and Belen have rocky periods?" she asked.

Marco shifted in his seat, "Uh."

"Never mind. I shouldn't have asked that. He says everything's fine. He's been hiding money in the house. He thinks I don't know."

"Money, where does he get this money? What does he do for a living?"

"He's a jewelry dealer. He keeps meticulous records. He used to make deposits every day, but recently, he's been stashing large sums of cash. I found it when I was cleaning one day. I know I shouldn't have called you, but I don't want to get him in trouble." She took a sip of wine and looked at Marco. "Ever since I saw you again at that restaurant, I've been thinking about you."

Marco looked down at the table. "I've been thinking about you too," he said.

They didn't speak for some time.

"What should I do?" she asked.

"I don't know what we should do right now, Amira."

"About Daniel," she said.

"Oh, you need to try to talk to him again. See if you can find out what he's up to but be careful. Don't let him suspect you've been talking to anyone about it."

"Daniel's been good to me. I just want things to go back to the way they used to be," she said.

Marco noticed she wore a ruby ring on her right hand.

"Where did you meet Daniel?"

"I met him at a party at one of my colleague's houses here in Spain. We hit it off right away."

"How long have you been dating?"

"It's been two years. At first, it was great. He was nice to me. He gave me gifts. He said I was his princess. He gave me this ring last year," she said, pointing to the ruby on her engagement finger.

"Are you engaged," Marco asked.

Amira shook her head, no. "We talked about marriage, but neither of us was ready. You were always straight with me, Marco. That was one thing I loved about you. You'd tell me if anything's wrong, wouldn't you?"

"I'll see what I can find out. Don't let him know you spoke to me," Marco said.

"I won't. I don't want to be involved in anything criminal," she said.

Once dinner was over, Marco drove Amira to her car, and they said good night. When he arrived home, Belen was asleep, or at least she pretended to be. He thought he saw her eyelids flicker. He slipped into his pajamas and climbed into the bed next to her.

Chapter Twenty-Six

Flores lit a cigar, something he rarely did, and poured himself another scotch from the bottle hidden at the back of his desk drawer. He deserved a drink after the morning he'd had. The Chief had virtually threatened him with a demotion if he didn't stop these murders from running amuck in their city. The Chief had exaggerated, of course, when he'd referred to murderers running amuck in Vivirrambla. Flores had been doing all he could with the manpower he had. The boat raid of the smugglers had been a drain on the department, which had been required to absorb most of the cost. Once they'd seized the boat, the larger smuggling inquiry also diverted resources away from the Kijamba and Elaina investigations. Morale was low, and the budget was even lower.

In some respects, he agreed with the Chief. The death of the young woman gnawed at Flores. He saw his own young daughter in the dead Elaina. What if he and his wife didn't do a good job, and their daughter started selling herself in the port for money from rich men who didn't care if she lived or died? What if she'd run into the wrong crowd and ended up like Elaina? He recognized that his own children were lucky not to be immigrants desperate to find better lives in another country. Still, he worried.

Flores gulped the last bit of scotch and stamped out his cigar. He'd trusted the word of Ginka Kovalenko, but she'd turned out to be unreliable. Idan had been cleared. Flores spent an hour flipping through documents without gaining any new insight. If he were to learn anything more, he needed to re-interview the dancers and employees of the Club Azule.

Flores grabbed his brown jacket from its permanent place behind the door in his office. He popped an Altoid into his mouth and headed out. He ambled down the *paseo,* walking past the half-drunken tourists enjoying the sea. He nearly ran into an inebriated Brit who stumbled in front of him onto the street. He could've arrested him for disorderly conduct, but that would take away time from his intended purpose. He stepped over the man, who grunted at him and proceeded down to the port.

The Club Azule looked even shabbier than it did during his last visit. The once glitzy club had been losing money since the murder occurred, and one of its employees was arrested. Flores wondered how long it could stay in business. He wouldn't be sad to see it close. He'd long been an advocate of cleaning up a lot of those back-end bars on the Port. Too much questionable money flowed into Vivirrambla from those establishments. He hated that the mayor and the Chief ignored the corruption in favor of the money it brought into the town.

Flores spoke to the bar manager and requested a complete list of the addresses, phone, and email information of everyone who worked at the club at the time of Elaina's death. The manager protested that he'd already given the police that information. Flores threatened to obtain a warrant and inspect the financial books of the club.

"I'm going to need you to give it to me again," Flores said.

The manager disappeared for a time, then returned with a list in the form of a printout. Flores thanked him and handed him his card.

He returned to the office to review the printout. The six dancers from the club shared flats in the same building, so he could speak to them all in one day. He checked his watch. If they danced at night, they would not be at work yet, he surmised. He decided to meet with them before they could learn of his coming. He drove to the building where the dancers lived. Three of them shared one flat, and two shared another flat. He knocked on the door of the first three on his list. They were attractive blonds in their early twenties. They shared the same story; they were in Spain on temporary visas and were enrolled in school at the University of Malaga. They worked at the club to help pay for school.

Flores then went to the two-bedroom, sparsely decorated flat of Ginka

Kovalenko. The witness from Ukraine who'd accused Idan of stalking Elaina. Ginka shared the apartment, a small space with tile floors, with a new roommate, another woman from Eastern Europe who, like the others, had come to Spain to go to school. Ginka told Flores that she worked at the club to pay off her trip to Spain. She informed him, as she had the first time they met, that she was in school. She said that she was enrolled at the University of Malaga with the others. Elaina had also been enrolled in the university, and they studied and went to school together during the daytime. It didn't seem to Flores to be a coincidence that they all went to the University of Malaga and worked at the same club.

"Who sponsored your trip to Spain?" Flores asked.

Ginka looked away. "I'm not sure what his name is, but they paid for my trip when I was back in Ukraine. It was all done through my parents. I was told I'd be working in exchange for my tuition and living expenses. I want to be a nurse."

It was the classic story of dreamy-eyed immigrants being lured across the seas with the promise of a good life. Instead, they'd been forced into virtual prostitution to pay off their debt.

"Who found you your job at the club?"

"When I first arrived, I was approached by someone who said he was a lawyer. He said he represented the owner of Club Azule. He told me that they'd found me a job. I was sent to talk to Ahmed, the manager of the club."

"So, you never actually met the owner?" Flores asked.

"No, I've never met him. We get all our instructions now from Ahmed. Well, we used to until he got attacked. Now we have a new manager," Ginka said.

"Why did you tell me Idan was stalking Elaina?" Flores asked. "You almost caused an innocent man to go to jail. He's been stabbed and is in the hospital, you know."

Her eyes widened. "I didn't know that. I'm sorry. I was so upset at Elaina's death. I thought he killed her. He followed her around all the time like a puppy. Will he be okay?" she asked.

"The doctors aren't sure. Did anyone tell you to blame Idan for Elaina's murder?" Flores asked.

She shifted in her seat. "No. Of course not. I told you. I thought he was obsessed with Elaina."

Flores looked around the flat. "Who pays for this apartment?" he asked.

"The owner pays our rent as part of working in the club."

"I must be blunt and ask you an uncomfortable question, Senorita. Do you do any special favors for men who come to the club?"

Ginka shifted in her chair. "I don't think that's any of your business, Detective."

"This is a murder investigation. Everything's my business," Flores said.

"Sometimes. Ahmed would threaten us. If I didn't do what he wanted, I'd have to pay back thousands of euros for my trip, and they'd stop paying for school," she said.

"I see. Did you see any of the men paying special attention to Elaina?"

"Elaina was beautiful. She was popular with our customers. A lot of men paid attention to her. She had a great personality. She was always smiling. She'd tell me not to worry, that soon we'd graduate from school, and we wouldn't have to work at the club. She said things would get better. I don't know what I'm going to do without her."

"Did you see anyone in particular, any of your customers, giving her extra attention or harassing her?"

Elaina shook her head. "No, none of the regulars."

"Did Elaina have a boyfriend?"

"I think she might have been dating someone."

"Really. Do you know who?" Flores asked.

Ginka furrowed her brow. "I don't know. She didn't talk that much about it."

"Why do you think she didn't tell you about her boyfriend?"

Ginka hunched her shoulders. "I guess she didn't want Ahmed to find out about it. Ahmed would have made her give him up."

"Is there anything else you want to tell me about Elaina's boyfriend or anything else that would help me find her killer?" Flores asked.

Ginka looked at her feet. Then she answered. "No, nothing else."

Flores didn't pursue it any further. He told Ginka to let him know if she remembered anything else and cautioned her that lying to the police could lead to deportation. Ginka assured him that she'd cooperate in the future. Flores sensed Ginka was hiding something. She could have been covering up for the manager or her pimp. He phoned Marco. "I need you to begin a full surveillance on Ginka Kovalenko. I got the feeling she's not telling me everything."

Chapter Twenty-Seven

Marco parked behind a tree outside of the small apartment complex Flores had visited and pulled out his iPad and camera. He had a clear view of who entered and left the building. The sky was blue with no hint of rain, as is usual in Vivirrambla, so there was no obstruction. He wasn't sure what Flores wanted him to find, but he'd see if the young Ukrainian woman Flores had described was up to anything.

Surveillance often took hours, so Marco had come prepared with a bocadillo de jamon, a thermos of coffee, and olives. He propped the telephoto camera lens on the car window and pushed the driver's seat back so that he could read. Marco had been an avid reader since his teenage years. The latest novel he was reading was a spy thriller about a woman who played tennis. It sounded like a strange concept, but it was surprisingly good and kept his attention.

He'd only read a few pages when he saw the target exit the building. She headed towards the beach on foot, but Marco was able to follow her along the highway in his car. She stopped and entered one of the bars on the paseo near the edge of the sea. Marco parked his car and walked into the crowded bar, a trendy place with metal tables. The woman met up with a Moroccan-looking woman with a mass of dark hair. Marco could only see the back of her from his vantage point. The women exchanged the traditional Spanish kiss on each cheek. When the Moroccan woman turned her head, Marco almost dropped his phone. Amira, his ex-girlfriend, greeted Ginka like an old friend.

Marco wanted to ask her what she was doing, but he knew he couldn't compromise the surveillance. Instead, he left and went over to a nearby bar so Amira wouldn't see him. It was early afternoon, so the bars were empty. He had a clear view of the two of them. He watched as they found a table and ordered *vino tintos*. Ginka looked around the bar; then she handed Amira a small envelope. In return, Amira handed her a larger manila package. Amira stuck the envelope in her purse, and they continued to sip their drinks for a time. Then, they exchanged another Spanish kiss and departed.

Marco slouched down in his seat and planted his head in the restaurant menu as the two women headed out into the street. He sat for a while. He knew he should inform Flores of what he'd seen but he couldn't let him know about Amira. He didn't know if she was involved in anything illegal. He left her name out of his report.

Conflicted as to what to do next, Marco decided he needed to follow Amira to find out what was going on. He pinged Eva to tell her that he would not be back for the rest of the afternoon. He parked in front of Amira's building and adjusted his camera to where it was easiest to get a good picture through one of her windows with a wide-angle lens. An hour into his surveillance, a pale-skinned man with thick red hair and freckles entered Amira's apartment. He was medium height, and he wore jeans. Marco snapped photos of the man from every angle he could get.

Chapter Twenty-Eight

Flores wiped up yet another coffee spill and vowed to clean his desk. He'd had to replace several keyboards because he'd dropped his coffee or his drink from lunch inside the board, making the keys sticky. He'd gotten a nasty note from the property department the last time he requested a new keyboard. Once his desk had some semblance of order, he began to examine the surveillance video Marco had sent via scan to his phone. Ginka Kovalenko handed an envelope to an unidentified woman. The rest of the video was too grainy and not discernible. Marco claimed he couldn't get a better shot of the woman because the bar was crowded.

The video was enough for Flores to put in the paperwork to get a subpoena of Ginka's bank accounts and phone logs. Finding her income wouldn't be easy. Most strippers and dancers were paid under the table in cash, difficult to trace. He thought about the student angle; he may be able to find a record of tuition payments paid to her in a bank account. University was a good place to start.

The University of Velaquez (sometimes called the University of Malaga), situated near the Alcazaba, across from the Port of Malaga, was constructed of red brick Spanish architecture. Its majestic collection of buildings stood out in the city. As he parked in the newly built university lot, Flores thought about his time there as a student where he'd studied criminology.

Flores hesitated to leave the air-conditioned car. Outside felt brutal. He could barely stand to put on his jacket. He walked down the path to the front and pushed open the grand wooden doors. Inside was an atrium surrounded by glass and light. Past the atrium was the administration building where the offices were located. Flores entered the main office, identified himself as a police detective to the woman behind the desk, and showed her his badge. He asked to speak to the school administrator. The woman got up from her desk and disappeared. A lanky, tall, distinguished-looking man with graying temples emerged a few minutes later. He extended his hand, neatly cut nails out to Flores. He escorted Flores to his impressive office with large dark furniture surrounded by bookshelves full of important books Flores was sure he never read.

"Buenes tardes, Senor, soy Doctor Rubio, head of the school. How may I assist you, Detective?"

"Mucho gusto, Senor," Flores said, shaking his hand. 'I'm investigating the death of a young woman, a student at your university. You heard about her death?"

The administrator twisted his thin lips. "Oh, my no, I don't think so. We have a lot of students; some are part-time. The University can't keep up with them like we'd like to. I'm not sure I can help you," Rubio said.

"The school is not in any kind of trouble, Senor. I just have a few questions about the student's tuition payments."

Rubio raised his brows. "I see. Which student and what is it you want to know? We have over twenty-thousand students in the university, so we don't know them all."

"Senorita Elaina Petrov, she would be an international student," Flores said.

"Let me see. I'll check our enrollment to see if we have a student by that name."

Rubio phoned his administrative assistant over the intercom and asked her to pull up on her computer the students currently enrolled and whether any student deaths had been reported. She responded a few minutes later.

"Yes, we do have a student by that name, one of our international students. We don't have any information about any of our students being recently deceased," the assistant said.

"As I said, Senor Doctor. She was killed. Can you print out all the information you have on that student?" Flores asked.

"Certainly," Rubio said.

"Let me ask you about another student."

"Oh, who?" Rubio asked.

"A student from Ukraine by the name of Ginka Kovalenko. She may be studying nursing in the same international school."

Rubio paused. "Just a moment. She's a current student, you say?"

"Yes," Flores said.

Rubio buzzed the assistant again. "What was her name again?" he asked, turning to Flores.

"Kovalenko, Ginka," Flores said.

Flores looked around the office. It was tidier than his, even though it was much bigger. Everything seemed to be in place. Flores made a mental note to keep his office cleaner. His mind jerked back to reality when the assistant buzzed Rubio.

"Yes, we have a student by that name. She is in her second year here at the University. She seems to have dropped out for a couple of semesters, but when she was enrolled in our school, her academic record was good," the assistant said.

Rubio thanked the assistant.

He looked over at Flores. "Is that what you need or is there anything else I can do for you?"

"Yes, one more thing. Who paid her tuition, and how was the tuition paid for Elaina Petrov, the deceased student?" Flores asked.

"You really should have a warrant if you are going to ask for any confidential information, Detective. I can't just go around giving out students' personal information," Rubio said.

"I appreciate your cooperation; this is a murder investigation, and anything you can tell me would be helpful."

Rubio sat up in his desk chair and turned to the computer. He put on a pair of glasses, which sat on the desk and studied the screen. "Her tuition is paid in full."

"Can you tell me how her tuition was paid?" Flores asked.

"We received a check from a foreign account."

"Can you tell me whose name is on the check and where the check originates?" Flores asked.

Rubio leaned back. "To give you more information, Detective, I really will need a warrant. We don't release any personal information, even to the police."

"I see. That's all for now, then. Thank you for your cooperation," Flores said.

"Why certainly, anything I can do to help," Rubio said.

Flores shook Rubio's hand and handed him his crumpled card with the bent sides. He'd meant to get new cards, but he'd been busy, and he never remembered until he went to hand someone one of his cards. He rose to leave. He was starting to cool off, so he hesitated to go back outside in the heat.

He'd have to go back and ask the prosecutor for permission to search Rubio's computers. Flores had wanted to avoid that. Besides the fact it was more paperwork, a request for a search warrant always drew the attention of the Chief, who would then query Flores as to the status of the murder cases.

He drove straight to the prosecutor's office. The prosecutor seemed uncertain but agreed to allow a limited search of the University records. It was enough to find out the information he needed. Flores headed straight back to the school.

"What is it you want now?" Rubio asked when Flores was ushered into his office for the second time that day.

Flores handed him the warrant for records and account information. Rubio frowned and took the paper from Flores. Rubio wore a white shirt, which was not a good idea, as visible sweat stains appeared under his arms. He scrutinized the warrant, then went back to his computer.

"Have a seat. My assistant is out. I will look for the information you require," he said, gesturing for Flores to sit in the chair in front of his desk.

Rubio turned his attention to his computer. After a few clicks, he looked up at Flores. Here's the information you desire, Detective. Ms. Kovalenko's and Ms. Petrov's tuition was paid by an anonymous person."

"You don't know the name of the payer?"

Rubio folded his hands. "No. We don't ask questions like that about tuition, Detective. It's not really any of our business as long as the tuition is paid."

"Do you have an address or any information on the person who paid the tuition?" Flores asked.

"No, we just have an address for the student. The tuition money was sent via wire transfer from a bank in Scotland," he said.

Flores's eyes widened. "Scotland?"

Rubio nodded. "Yes, the check was drawn on the National Bank of Scotland. The payer wired the tuition for the entire year. We're not in the habit of asking people where they get their money. Now, if you will excuse me, Detective, I must get back to work. That's really all of the information I have," Rubio said.

"Gracias, Senor. I'll let you know if we need anything else," Flores said.

"I trust there's nothing else you'll need from me," Rubio said.

Flores rose from the chair and extended his hand to Rubio, who huffed and went back to typing on his computer.

As he walked back to his car, Flores pondered his next step. Rubio's attitude had raised his suspicion. It was his experience that hostility during an interview meant there was something to hide.

Chapter Twenty-Nine

Marco waited until Belen left for work before he pulled the number up on his cell. He hesitated for a minute, then punched in the numbers.

"Hello," the voice on the other end was soft.

"Amira, I need to see you," he said.

There was a long silence.

"Why?" she asked.

"I want to talk to you about Daniel. I was concerned after I spoke to you last time," he said.

"Oh, no need to worry about that. I was just venting. Everything's fine," she said.

"I'm sure, but still, I'd like to talk to you. Tomorrow night let's have dinner in Malaga," he said.

He knew Belen would be out until late as she was dancing at the later show, so she wouldn't be home until the early hours of the morning.

"Alright, I'll see you then," she said.

Marco debated telling Belen. It was business, part of a murder investigation, no different than meeting any other suspect or potential witness, he reasoned. If she even found out, Belen would understand once the dust settled and the murders had been solved.

Marco splashed on Armani cologne, Amira's favorite when they were together. He wore his white button-down and black slacks.

He met Amira at a popular restaurant in *Malaga Centro* that looked more like a home than a restaurant. Comfortable sofas rested against the wall, and China cabinets containing knickknacks and a buffet with a large mirror graced the entrance. The restaurant was not yet crowded. Amira arrived a few minutes after Marco. He handed her a bouquet of flowers he'd picked up on the way from one of the roaming sellers on the streets. He wasn't sure why he bought the flowers. It was on impulse. Amira sniffed the array and smiled. She looked stunning in a knee length green dress, her mass of dark hair tamed, up in a clip, Marco always liked it when she wore her hair up.

Marco pulled out a chair for her to sit. "You look wonderful."

Amira smiled. "You smell good. I remember that smell."

Marco laughed. He felt his cheeks flush.

They were seated under a marble statue of some ancient Spanish figure. Marco ordered a bottle of Muga Rioja, delivered to the table by a young, cheery-looking fellow. He poured some of the wine into a glass and stood before Marco with one arm behind his back. Marco twirled the glass, then smelled and tasted the wine and nodded his approval. The waiter then filled each of their glasses.

The same young man returned after a polite interval to take their order. To start, pate to share and green salad. For an entrée, Marco ordered grilled steak smothered in sauce *con patatas,* boiled potatoes. Amira ordered a dinner salad with couscous and raisins.

"What did you want to talk to me about?" Amira asked after they'd eaten several bites of the entrée."

"How are things with Daniel?" Marco asked.

Amira shrugged. "Things with Daniel are okay. I know I said it was fine when you phoned. I'm thinking of going back to Morocco."

She pushed around the food on her plate. "I'm not sure this relationship is going anywhere."

"What about your job here in Spain? I thought you liked it," Marco asked.

"I do. It's a good job. I make more here than I would make in Morocco. I've become a buyer for a good clothing chain. I've had a call from Zara in Spain to become an assistant buyer. I'm not sure it's enough, though, to keep me here. Daniel's becoming more and more distant. He used to pay attention to me. Now it's like I don't exist unless he wants something. He can be very charming when he wants to be. Did I tell you he's Scottish?" Amira frowned. "Life is strange. I'd never envisioned myself with a Scottish man."

"How did Daniel end up in Spain?" Marco asked.

"He moved here after visiting a few times to expand the market of his company's jewelry. He has a lot of Spanish customers. He's been in Spain for three years. He'd been married for a few years in Scotland. He told me it was a good opportunity to escape the scene with his ex-wife. He makes good money, so we have a nice apartment, but…"

She leaned across the table. Her neck displayed a necklace with a shining ruby at the center.

"That's a beautiful necklace. Did Daniel give it to you?" Marco asked.

She clutched the necklace and nodded her head yes. "It's a job perk. He gets jewelry at good prices. He's given me some nice pieces."

She picked up her fork and scooped up some of her food. "When we first got together, he doted on me, showering me with gifts and flowers. I thought he loved me and wanted to take care of me forever. Then things started to change."

"When did things start to change?" Marco asked.

"In the last six months, he's been different. We barely even talk now. He usually comes home, grabs a beer, and sits in front of the TV. I asked him if it was another woman. He assured me there was no one else. I don't know what to do."

"Maybe he's going through something with the ex. Does he talk to you about his marriage? Did they have any kids?" Marco asked.

She took a bite of the flan they'd shared for dessert. "He talks about it sometimes. He has one child, aged ten. He says he misses his son," Amira said.

"Maybe that's it. How often does he travel to Scotland?" Marco asked.

Amira smiled. "This is beginning to sound like an interrogation, Detective."

"Oh, sorry, forgive me, habit. I've been thinking a lot about you lately. You've changed so much. I like the way you've become your own woman."

She batted her eyelashes. "You've changed too. You've grown. You don't seem so arrogant. That girlfriend must be good for you." She pulled her napkin from her lap and wiped her mouth." I'm probably just paranoid. Daniel's been good to me."

"Never underestimate your instincts, Amira. A lot of times, your instincts are warning signs."

"Good advice," she said. "I'll think about it. Let's get some coffee."

During coffee, they talked about their time together, when things were good between them.

"You were my first love," Amira said, gazing at Marco.

Once they'd finished dinner, Marco walked Amira to her car. "Let me know if you need me. You can tell me anything, Amira. No matter how bad it is, you can trust me. I'm always here for you," Marco said.

"I know. I should never have let you go. You've stirred up old emotions in me," she said.

Marco shut her car door and walked through the cool night breeze to his own car. He wondered when Belen would be home.

Chapter Thirty

Oscar staggered off to the kitchen to get more beer. He'd come over for the first time in months to watch futbol. Belen was out with friends, so Marco and Oscar drank beer and ate pizza while they cheered for Barcelona and Messi. Marco hadn't felt this relaxed in some time. It was a big win for the team's standing in the Europacupa. The two men were giddy and cheered one another as if they'd played in the match. Marco's phone vibrated just as he opened another cerveca. He thought about ignoring it but looked down and saw that it was his cousin Karim. He sat up on the couch. Since Jaddah's heart attack a while back, his heart raced every time Karim called.

"Karim, *dime,* what's up? Is Jaddah okay?" he asked.

"Yeah, she's fine. I'm calling about your undercover mission. The man you met with has been in touch about your interest in buying a nightclub," Karim said.

Marco had given Karim a throwaway cell phone with a Moroccan phone number to use if Hassan called. Karim was to be his assistant.

"Really? What did he say?" Marco asked.

"He wants to meet with you again. I did a little more digging into Hassan. He's a bad actor. Rumor has it that he wants to form a consortium of club owners, like some kind of Mafia family coalition. They want to freeze out individual club owners and have control of all the clubs here in Morocco and Puerto Bella under one group, a monopoly on the club scene. My contact says an American businessman is behind the whole scheme and is the real head of the consortium.

"That's great work, Karim. Do we know who this American is?" Marco asked.

"All we know is he's in the music business. He keeps a low profile. Hassan works directly for the American. I told Hassan you were willing to set up a meeting," Karim said.

"Excellent. I'll make the arrangements and come over to Morocco. Call him back and arrange the meeting," Marco said.

"Give me about a week to set it up," Karim said.

Marco broke the news to Belen when she got home.

"I've got to go to Tanger. I'll be gone for a few days," he said.

Belen frowned. "Fine, I'm used to it now," she said.

"I'm sorry. I'll make the weekend up to you."

"Don't worry about it."

She walked over to the bedroom and started to get undressed. Marco went in after her, but she put on her slippers and shuffled off into the bathroom. She emerged with her hair pulled back tightly with a clip, her face freshly washed. She put on moisturizer and got into bed. Marco undressed and slipped into bed beside her.

"I'm just as disappointed as you are, sweetie. I was looking forward to the weekend," he said.

"That's just it. Are you really disappointed? I'm not so sure you are."

"Of course I am."

Belen turned over and switched off the light.

Chapter Thirty-One

"Long pipes of kif pass from table to table while glasses of mint tea grow cold, enticing bees that eventually tumble in, a matter of indifference to customers long since lost to the limbo of hashish and tinseled reverie."
Leaving Tangier, Tahar Ben Jelloun

Marco arranged for the early morning ferry to Tanger. Being July, the air was warm and stale even at sea. He could see the dry air floating like waves across the landscape. He'd left his car in Vivirrambla and didn't take it on the ferry as he usually did so as not to blow his cover. He'd had to take an expensive taxi to the port. He became drenched in sweat in the short time he waited for the taxi to arrive, although it was still early morning. There had been a warning of forest fires, and he hoped none would come to fruition.

Marco nearly fell into the air-conditioned taxi to Algeciras port, where he'd board the ferry. He paid the taxi driver, a round-faced man who spoke rapidly even for a Malagueno, and then walked over to the ferry's entrance. He had to wait outside as the ship was forty minutes late. So, he was soaked again; even his hair was dripping wet. The ferry wasn't crowded, for which Marco was glad. He found a seat, then journeyed to the kitchen area and ordered a drink and pastry. He wandered over to one of the modern-looking tables and found a spot in front of the television, which blasted CNN news. He took out his iPad and began planning for his meeting with Hassan once he arrived in Tanger. Eva had created a fake website for his supposed business.

He chuckled to himself. He had to admit it looked slick. He reviewed the website and made sure he was familiar with all the information it contained. By the time the boat docked, he felt well versed in his highfalutin real estate business.

Noisy peddlers, in colorful djellaba, some in caps that looked like pillbox hats, selling rugs, greeted him when he arrived on the streets of Tanger. Old men sat at tables puffing on hookahs with glasses of mint tea in front of them. The streets smelled of hashish. Marco spotted his cousin Karim who waved to him. Karim looked tan in a light shirt and blue pants. He could have been mistaken for an Ethiopian. He and Marco looked a lot alike; they'd often been mistaken for brothers when they were younger.

The two exchanged greetings—"As-salamu Alakum"—then walked to a nearby parking garage.

Marco nodded his head in approval. Then Karim handed him the keys to the silver Porsche. "Nice job," he said as they approached the car.

"I thought you'd like it. It used to belong to a big drug dealer before it was confiscated," Karim said. "The police loaned it to me for our sting."

"You've got great connections," Marco laughed.

Marco threw his suitcase in the back, and the two set off in the fancy car like young jetsetters. Marco drove to Karim's home in the suburbs of Tanger and dropped him off at the corner. He couldn't risk seeing his grandmother or any of his family.

Then he headed to his hotel, one of the finest in Tanger and checked into his room. He'd booked the room for three days. He'd called Flores and told him about the meeting and convinced Flores not to drop the sting operation.

"We've come this far, and we have a meeting all set up now. We don't have any other leads, so we need to see where this goes."

Flores had been reluctant but in the end, he agreed that what Marco said made sense.

Marco unpacked and settled in. He'd been invited to meet with Hassan the next day, though the so-called invitation seemed more like a command. Marco was to appear at a named hotel at a specified time. He was warned not to be late. It's how thugs did business.

He plopped down on the fluffy queen-sized bed. Before he knew it, the sun in his eyes awakened him. He automatically reached for Belen. When he realized she wasn't there, he rolled over and looked at the hotel clock. It read seven o'clock in the morning. He'd slept through the whole night without waking. The heat and the ferry ride must have worn him out. He showered in the luxury of the warm, soft water, then dressed in a navy-blue blazer, linen pants, and white tee-shirt, his investor look. He'd slicked his hair down with gel. He looked like he could have played Lawrence of Arabia in the film. He splashed on cologne and headed off to the appointed address.

When he arrived, a short man with a scruffy beard and bad skin ushered Marco into the meeting room. The room was a typical conference room with stark white walls, blue carpeting, and plastic chairs. Marco was surprised Hassan hadn't chosen a posher hotel for the meeting. He couldn't imagine the Corleone's meeting with the other families in such a cheap setting. A large table in the middle of the room was occupied by five men.

Hassan and Omar, the other man he'd met at Hassan's nightclub, greeted Marco. Omar introduced him to the other men present, who nodded as their names were called.

Marco sat at the place designated for him. A water pitcher sat in front of him, along with an empty cup.

A hotel server scuttled over with a pot of coffee, mint tea, and small carafes of cream.

Hassan, who sat at the head of the table, spoke. "I want to thank you all for coming. Let me get right to the point. My colleagues and I are interested in forming an organization of businesses. We are the greatest businessmen in Morocco. Instead of competing, we can join forces and earn more money for all of us."

The other men at the table nodded in agreement.

"You want to form a consortium?" Marco asked.

"We want to join forces as club owners here in Tanger. We want to all cooperate to make more money for every man." Hassan said.

The other men looked around the table for each other's reaction. Marco noticed that there wasn't a personality between them.

"Why do you want me here? I don't know any of you gentlemen?" Marco asked.

Hassan looked over at Marco. "I'll be honest, we're interested in your nightclub investment offer. It may be important to us. As a group, we'll be able to purchase all the nightclubs in Morocco. You can get us an interest in Spain. If we accept your investment, you will become part of the consortium, which means you will have a stake in all the nightclubs we purchase."

Hassan made a gesture to all the men around the table. "As you say, you don't know us. We'll have the major share with forty percent of the profits." He pointed to Marco. "You will receive five percent if the Chair decides you're right for us, and the other gentlemen will split the remaining fifty-five percent."

Marco leaned back in his chair. "Who is the Chair?" he asked.

"The chief investor. He will take the largest risk, so naturally, he'll get the biggest share of the profits."

The other men, Moroccans, dressed in expensive suits, whispered amongst themselves. Then one of them spoke.

"We think it's fair. They handle all the risks. We just run the clubs and take in the profits. It's a good deal for all of us."

"I see. Who's the chief investor?" Marco asked.

Hassan grunted and made a face. "Why do you need to know? It's not important to you. You deal only with me directly," he said.

The others stared at Marco. He felt his heart race from fear of this room full of thugs.

"I just wondered if I'd get to meet him. I want to thank him," he said.

Hassan's eyes narrowed. "Don't worry about it. I'll take care of the details. I'll give him your thanks. How many clubs you control in the future will depend on your investment in the business."

"The investment is made through you?" Marco asked.

Hassan nodded his head. "Naturally. You will pay us an initial investment fee as a courtesy."

One of the men squirmed. Everyone turned to look at him. The man cleared his throat. "It sounds like we'll just be nightclub managers," the man said.

"You will be a part owner. It's a fair arrangement," another one of them said.

Hassan glared at the man, who fidgeted in his chair. "Of course, it's your choice to get out of the nightclub business," he said.

The man slinked back and took a sip of water from the glass in front of him.

"Excuse me for one minute," Hassan said.

Hassan called two of the men and Omar over to him and whispered to them. Then he turned his attention to Marco.

"When we met at my club, you said you had access to women from Eastern Europe. Can you still make that happen?"

Marco nodded. "That won't be a problem, but I'm going to need some upfront funding. It won't be cheap getting them over here."

Hassan rubbed the stubble beard on his face. "We can consider it part of your investment. Of course, I'll have to talk it over with the chief investor. How many dancers could you supply?"

"I'll check with my contacts. I'll be here for a couple more days. I'll let you know before I leave," Marco said.

"That will make a difference to the chief investor as to whether he wants you to be a part of our business."

"For the rest of you gentlemen, do we have a deal?"

They all nodded yes in unison.

Omar turned to Marco. "We'll be in touch before you leave," he said.

Hassan rose from his chair. Omar followed like an obedient puppy, and they left the room without saying the meeting had ended. The rest of the attendees quickly scooped up their laptops and phones and exited. Marco followed suit and gathered his belongings.

He decided he needed lunch, but he couldn't eat in that hotel. He drove to the next town to a café and coffee joint that touted itself as being international. He ordered a falafel bowl and couscous. The food was fresh and satisfying. As he settled in for coffee, he called Flores to update him on

CHAPTER THIRTY-ONE

Hassan and his ideas of a club monopoly with Eastern European dancers.

Flores also had news for Marco. Ahmed, the manager of the Club Azule, who'd been attacked, hadn't made it. And he had other news. "We finished our investigation into the break-in of your office. It was the now-deceased Ahmed. A witness saw a man fitting his description circling the building that day, we assume trying to find out how to get inside. We found his fingerprint on a piece of furniture. You'd better be careful; your cover isn't blown. I think we should pull out of the undercover," he said.

Marco felt touched that Flores cared. He was never sure Flores even liked him. A thought popped into his head. Marco wondered if the break-in had anything to do with Amira. Had anyone seen them together? In any case, Ahmed was dead and couldn't reveal his identity. Besides, the operation was in full force. Marco assured Flores he'd take precautions.

"The person, whom they referred to as the chief investor, do we know who that is?" Flores asked.

"Hassan wouldn't say. He said he'd handle the business end of the operation," Marco said.

"We need to find out who that is, good work," Flores said.

Marco felt upbeat when he returned to the hotel. Flores rarely said he'd done a good job, and it meant something to him. Marco pulled the card key out of his pocket and opened the door to his room. He looked up to discover one of the men from the meeting, a balding man with a gray beard and smooth skin, sitting at the desk next to his bed. His feet were propped up on the bed. Marco jumped. He noticed a gun on the table.

"What are you doing here? How did you get in?" Marco asked.

The man grinned, exposing a missing tooth at the bottom. "As-salaam Alaikum. No need to be alarmed. I came here as your friend. Another friend asked me to come and visit you," he said.

Marco felt his pulse quicken. "What is it you want?"

"Our mutual friend, Omar, wanted me to remind you, once we agree to make you a partner, we investors expect you to come up with the full amount in twenty-four hours," the man said.

"Don't worry. I'll have my investment," Marco said.

The stranger stood and slapped Marco on the back. Marco flinched.

"Good. As long as we're clear, *Sadiqi*. I won't take any more of your time. Have a pleasant evening at this fine hotel," the man said.

He rose, grabbed his gun off the table, and left Marco's room.

Chapter Thirty-Two

So I had to... I had to leave my country and my family.
                    Leaving Tangier, Tahar Ben Jelloun

Ginka never thought of herself as the kind of person who would be sleeping with men for money. She had dreams and ambitions, but sometimes you can't control where life takes you. Ginka Kovalenko left her native country wide-eyed, ready to go to nursing school and start a new career that would grant her a better life. She loved medicine even as a little girl. She'd intended to become a nursing aide and then a full-fledged nurse. Eventually, she wanted to go back to Ukraine and work in a hospital. Ginka had applied for scholarships around the world. Her first choice was America, but she could only get a job as a lifeguard on a temporary visa. Spain had accepted her as a student at the University de Velasquez, school of Nursing in Malaga, which accepted international students on a student visa. Ginka spent an entire summer learning Spanish at an immersion school at home in preparation.

Her family couldn't afford her passage to Spain, but as was their fortune, a benefactor, a man her father knew, had come forth and offered to pay for her trip. He promised to subsidize accommodations, an apartment in Spain, and her tuition. Her father didn't question it as he'd known the man for many years, and he'd done construction work for him for minimal costs. The man said he wanted to invest in Ginka as a thank-you. So Ginka's father agreed that she could go. They saw it as a godsend.

Ginka arrived in Spain at Malaga airport after a three-hour flight. She'd been told she'd be living in Vivirrambla in an apartment near the sea. The benefactor had even shown her family a picture of her apartment. When the cab stopped, she looked at the address a second time. In front of her stood a shabby two-story building on the edge of town, nothing like the picture she had in her hands.

"Are you sure this is it?" she asked in broken Spanish.

The driver nodded his head. "Si si, Senora, eso es la direccion," he said.

Ginka paid the cab driver and stepped out of the cab. She walked to the house and stumbled up the flights of stairs with her two large suitcases to the apartment number she'd been given. When she knocked on the door, two women who spoke in Russian greeted her. One of them, an attractive woman with large green eyes, introduced herself as Elaina Petrov and told Ginka that she'd be her roommate. Ginka followed Elaina, who walked with the grace of a dancer, to their shared room. Ginka looked around at the drab, small gray space with twin beds and one chest of drawers. She sniffed at the musty smell. She wanted to cry.

"I've got to go to work now. Make yourself at home," Elaina said, gesturing with her hands.

"Oh, where do you work?" Ginka asked.

Elaina laughed. "Where do I work? The same place you work. Your shift starts tomorrow," she said.

Ginka's head began to spin. She'd checked the schedule for school. Classes were set to start in a few weeks. She'd hoped to tour Spain and become acclimated to her new environment. She hadn't been told anything about working.

"I'm a student at the university. I'm not working right now," Ginka said.

Elaina snickered. "We're all students, but we also work."

Ginka was certain Elaina had her confused with someone else. There must have been a mix-up, and another person was intended to move into the shambled apartment. Ginka's lodgings must be somewhere else.

"I'm not sure what you mean. I'm here in Spain to study medicine at the university."

Elaina tossed her hair. "I know who you are. Daniel told us you were coming and to expect you. He asked me to help you get settled in before you start work tomorrow. I'll be back, but now I've got to get going. The boss doesn't tolerate lateness."

Ginka heard the front door slam a few minutes later. Elaina had gone. Ginka put her suitcase on the small twin bed and looked around. A wave of realization hit her like a sudden tidal wave washed up on the shore. She put her clothes in the single drawer designated to her after wiping it down. Then, she wandered out of her room to look at the rest of the apartment. There was one other bedroom already occupied. She found the bathroom, with its peeling paint and faded tile. At least it seemed clean. Back in her room, she laid her head down to take a nap. She dreamed she was in a beautiful apartment in Puerto Bella on the water, like the ones she'd seen in the pictures she'd been given. She sat on the edge of her small bed and cried.

That had been two years ago. Ginka had since learned that her benefactor was a well-known human trafficker, one of those passeurs who promised to ferry you over to your dream. She owed him thousands of Euros. If she returned to her country, she'd be killed as she couldn't pay him back. Half of her paycheck went to pay the club owner, and the other half went to her benefactor. Over time, she and Elaina became sought-after escorts for wealthy men who visited Spain for golf and recreation. Sometimes, the men gave them jewelry. One day, Elaina confided in Ginka that she'd pawned the jewelry she was given, and that she'd been hiding the money. She also told her that a Spanish man with a high position was in love with her and that he'd asked her to marry him. She'd said yes. They planned to marry in a few months. She'd be able to get away with the money she'd saved. Ginka warned her of the danger of what she was doing, but Elaina was insistent that she could escape their fate. She said her boyfriend was powerful and could protect her. That had proven as untrue as the passeur's promises.

Chapter Thirty-Three

Flores closed the door to his office to shut out the noise from the busy police station hallway and sat down to the drudgery of going through phone records. He'd decided to continue the surveillance of Ginka Kovalenko that Marco had started earlier. He'd use the regular guys as Marco was on an undercover mission. They followed Ginka for several days and produced a video for Flores. Flores met with the computer techs to examine the tape, which showed Ginka receiving a package from a man. Surveillance couldn't identify the man, who wore a baseball cap and jeans. The video was grainy, and they couldn't zoom in close enough to tell much about the package.

Flores then examined Ginka's phone records. She'd been making calls to a burner phone that no longer existed. Since the station had upgraded its technology over the past year, forensics could trace the burner phone and extract all the information from it.

He created a chart showing calls coming in, calls going out, and the duration of the calls for the two weeks prior to Elaina's murder.

He perused the chart for a pattern. He discovered numerous calls to one number, which couldn't be traced. He'd have to have forensics do further work to find out who was associated with the phone number. He hoped he'd found a lead.

Flores then turned to examine Ginka's bank account which she held at a nearby bank. He flipped through the pages showing deposits and withdrawals. Most deposits were in cash from her dancing gig at Club

Azule. Flores knitted his brow. It annoyed him that the town lost a lot of tax revenue from clubs that paid dancers in cash, money that the town could have used for schools and parks. He kept flipping. Halfway through, he stopped and sat up in his chair. A deposit of several thousand Euros had been made to Ginka's account the day after she'd been observed on the surveillance tape handing a package to someone.

Flores looked at his watch, it was still early afternoon, Ginka wouldn't yet be at work. He grabbed his jacket from behind the door. It was 30 degrees Celsius, but the jacket made him look more professional. So he'd sweat it out. He put it on and headed to his car.

Flores took the elevator up to Ginka's apartment and knocked on the door. He heard rustling and scrambling in the background. Yet, no one came to the door. Flores knocked harder.

"Senorita Kovalenko it's Detective Flores. Open the door."

Flores heard more scrambling in the background. Yet, still, no one answered. A neighbor in a pink housecoat peered out of her door. Flores signaled for the woman to go back inside. He banged on the metal structure.

"Senorita, open up, police."

The rustling stopped, and Flores heard the click of door latches being undone. The door flung open. Ginka stood wearing shorts and a t-shirt.

"What do you want, Detective?" she asked.

Flores stepped inside and peeked his head around the room. The room was cool for which Flores was grateful. "Did I hear noises in here? It sounded like I heard other voices."

He noted the patio door was slightly ajar.

"No, just me. I was listening to music. What is it you want? I'm very busy, and I have to go to work soon," Ginka said.

"May I sit down?" Flores asked after he'd already taken a seat on the couch.

Ginka hmphed and sat in a chair next to him.

"Who else was in here?" Flores asked.

She squirmed. "No one. I told you."

"I need to ask you a few questions. We've had surveillance following you. You're on video meeting with a man and handing him some kind of package.

He handed you a smaller envelope in exchange. That seemed like money. Who were you meeting, and what was in the package and envelope?" Flores said.

Ginka scoffed at Flores. "That's my business. It had nothing to do with Elaina."

"I didn't mention Elaina. Who were you meeting?" Flores asked.

Ginka ran her fingers through her hair. "No one, just a friend."

"What was in the package?"

She sighed. "Jewelry. One of my clients wanted a gift for his wife. I needed money, so I was getting nice jewelry for him, if you must know."

Flores twisted his lip. "Where did you get the jewelry?"

She looked around the room nervously, "From a friend who sells jewelry," she said.

"Are you looking for someone?" Flores asked.

"No, I'm just in a hurry. I need to get ready for work."

"I see. I won't hold you up too long. I just need to ask you a couple of questions. What's your friend's name?" Flores asked.

"His name's Paco. He knows where to get jewelry," Ginka said.

"So, you get the jewelry from this Paco and sell it to your client, is that right?" Flores asked.

"Basically," she said.

"What's Paco's last name, and how do I get ahold of him? You realize selling stolen goods is also a crime, right?"

Ginka shifted in her seat. "I didn't steal any jewelry. I got it from Paco. I don't know anything about him. Everyone calls him El Feo. I met him at the club. I only see him when he comes in to see me dance."

"Do you have a phone number for this, Paco?" Flores asked.

"No, I told you, I only see him when he comes in the club. Why does it matter? What does it have to do with Elaina?"

"This is a murder investigation. Everything matters. How much did you get from your client for the jewelry?"

She hesitated. "Three thousand euros."

"I'm going to need your client's name," Flores said.

Three thousand euros was the amount of the deposit he'd seen in her bank account. Her story seemed plausible. One of the rich men from abroad that she slept with, buying an expensive present for his wife to assuage his guilt for sleeping with an escort.

"You'd better be telling me the truth, Senorita Kovalenko."

"Of course, Detective. Is that all?"

Flores got up from his chair, walked over to the patio door, and looked around. "For now, Senorita, you're still under surveillance. I'd be careful if I were you. I could still charge you with giving false information about Idan to the police. You would be deported. If I find you're lying to me again, you'll be charged."

Flores was sure there was more to it than she was letting on. She'd been dealing in stolen jewelry, he felt sure, and she seemed to be protecting someone. He wondered if this Paco was part of a ring. Flores vowed to step up the surveillance.

Chapter Thirty-Four

arco hoped the call coming from Eva's desk wasn't for him as he'd just started to concentrate.

"Call for you, jefe," Eva said, as she transferred the phone call to him.

"Buenes tardes, this is Cipriano Jacobs," the caller said. "I kept your card. I need to talk to you about Kijamba's case."

Marco recalled the Jamaican blues singer with long braids, one of Kijamba's best friends. He and Flores had interviewed him at the beginning of the investigation. "Senor Jacobs, how can I help you?" he asked.

"People call me Cipi. You're one of the detectives working on Kijamba's case, right?"

"I'm a private investigator consulting with the police. What can I do for you?"

"Have you found out who killed Kijamba yet?" I don't think the police are doing anything. Shada is really upset. She wants to know what you all are doing," Cipi said.

"We're doing all we can. It's a complicated investigation, and we're looking at all possible leads," Marco said.

"What about the information I gave you guys?" Cipi asked.

"Information? What information?" Marco asked.

Cipi lowered his bass voice. "Can I come to your office? I don't like talking about this stuff over the phone."

"Si, when do you want to come in? I'll switch you to my assistant to make an appointment."

Marco heard the click of the phone after a minute. Eva popped her head in his door.

"I've set the appointment for tomorrow morning. You look like your mind's turning," she said.

Marco looked up at Eva. "He seems anxious to tell us something."

"Yeah, he sounded pretty determined to talk to you," Eva said.

The next day, Cipi Jacobs arrived at Marco's office a few minutes after Marco himself arrived. Cipi wore jeans and a bright-colored polo shirt, which set off his dark skin. His long, woolly grey and black twists looked neat and fell to his shoulders. The whites of his eyes were bright, and his hazel brown iris sparkled.

"Have a seat, Senor Jacobs," Marco said. "Cipriano is an unusual name."

"My parents named me after Saint Cipriano; very Catholic. That couldn't be further from the truth," he said, laughing.

Marco laughed. "How can I help you, Senor Jacobs?"

Cipi sat in the chair in front of Marco's desk. "Cipi. Please call me Cipi. Senor Jacobs is my father. Like I said on the phone, I wanted to speak to you about Kijamba's investigation. Kijamba was one of my best friends. I want you to find whoever murdered him and put them away for life."

"We're doing everything we can. Investigations take time," Marco said.

"Did the police check into him like I asked?"

"Him? Who is 'him?'" Marco asked.

"House, did you and the police check into House? He's taken over all of Shada's accounts. What is he doing with Kijamba's money? I asked him about it, and he told me in so many words to mind my own business. Something's not right. I mentioned it to that other detective. He said he'd look into it," Cipi said.

"What other detective?" Marco asked.

"Flor…that guy Senor Flores, I think his name is, I told him he needs to really look into House. We never did get along. I didn't trust him, and he knew it. He always seemed a little too smooth for my taste. He's strutting around now like he owns Shada. I tried to warn Kijamba about him." Cipi said.

"Do you have any specific information about Senor House you want to share?"

Cipi shook his head. "House has taken control of all Kijamba's business. Shada says she needs him. I'm afraid he's taking advantage of her while she's vulnerable. I told her it was a bad idea to trust him. She won't listen to anyone but him. It's like he's Rasputin, and she's the Tsarina under his spell."

"House has control of all Kijamba's estate?" Marco asked.

Cipi leaned forward as if to sit closer to Marco. "Yes, and not only his money, but House also dictates everything she does, whom she sees, where she goes, what she buys, everything. Kijamba had been paying me a monthly stipend for doing some work on editing, and for some music, I'd written for him. We'd also worked out an agreement for songs I contributed to his new album. House stopped the payments to me. He said that since Kijamba's dead, he doesn't have to honor the agreement. What kind of way was that to treat me? That was my main source of income. What am I going to do now?"

Marco leaned back in his chair. "When did House stop payments to you?"

"My check was late last month, and I only got half of it. I went over to her place to ask Shada what had happened. She told me I had to go and talk to House. House had fired Kijamba's accountant and hired his own person. The other accountant had been with Kijamba for years, and there was never a problem. Why did House need to fire him? House told me that the new accountant had decided I wasn't entitled to any more payments."

"Senor Jacobs, I appreciate your concern. I can't look into it just because you didn't get a monthly check. It's really Shada's business whom she hires," Marco said.

Cipi sat up straight in his chair. His muscular arms bulged from his shirt. It was evident that he worked out on a regular basis. It reminded Marco that he needed to get back to his regular workouts. "Of course, I need the money, but I'm also worried about Shada. I've known her for years. She's like a sister to me. House is taking advantage of her. I know it."

"Unless you have some evidence he's doing something illegal, there's little the police can do," Marco said.

"Can you look into it as a private investigator? I can pay you," Cipi urged. "Why is he firing everyone? Who is this new accountant, and why did he get rid of Kijamba's old one?"

Marco thought for a moment. "No need to pay me as any work I do will be for the police. I'll see if I can find out anything, Senor Jacobs. I'll let you know if I need any further information."

Cipi stood up from his chair. "Cipi," he said, shaking Marco's hand.

Marco smiled. "Cipi."

"Thanks, I care a lot about Shada. I don't want anything to happen to her," Cipi said.

"Do you think House could have had anything to do with Kijamba's death?" Marco asked.

Cipi shrugged. "I'm not going to say whether he did or didn't, because I don't know for sure. I wouldn't be surprised, though. I think he's a greedy, ruthless bastard."

Marco shared the details of Cipi's visit with Flores.

"It sounds like Senor Jacobs is bitter because he isn't getting paid anymore. Shada can hire whomever she wants. I don't see it as part of our investigation," Flores said.

"Yeah, I told Jacobs the same thing, but I noticed that House seemed more and more in control of things each time we visited Shada. I think there might be something to it," Marco said.

"I thought he seemed protective, like he cared for someone he's known for a long time, whose husband had just died. Besides, he's been good at keeping the media off our backs, which the Chief appreciates. I doubt he'd approve an investigation into him," Flores said.

"Still, it couldn't hurt to do our due diligence. It won't be the first time a business manager stole from his client," Marco said.

"That's true. It might look bad if it turns out he was stealing and we hadn't discovered it. The Chief would really come down on me if we missed an angle. Okay, but don't spend a lot of time on it."

"I'm gonna need your permission to get access to House's business records," Marco said.

"Okay, I'll tell the Chief it's just a routine check. This had better not be for nothing."

"I'll keep you posted," Marco said.

Eva carried stacks of papers into Marco's office a few days later. Flores had obtained the necessary subpoenas. The judge said their evidence was scant, but since it was a high-profile case, he let them dot all their I's and cross all their T's to kill a metaphor.

As a music manager to a star, House was worth millions, and his finances were complex. Marco determined he would need help to decipher all the information he received. He knew of one person who could help him, an old friend named, Roberto Rios, an Argentinian business lawyer. Rios and Marco had attended school together; they still hung out from time to time for drinks and *futbol* at the Townhome with Lars and Laila.

It was a bright day, and the sun's reflection illumined an emerald-green color on the water as Marco cruised down the motorway to the business district of Puerto Bella. Marco had texted Rios, who invited him to come to his office that afternoon. Rios was in the *Cristamar* building, a steel and glass edifice close to trendy bars and restaurants. The lobby stood empty except for a frowning security guard seated next to the entrance. Marco told the guard why he was there, the guard scowled then buzzed him up to Rios's suite.

"*Amigo como estas? Mucho tiempo.* It's been too long," Rios said when Marco entered his office.

He gestured to one of the chairs near a large open window with a view towards the sea.

Rios wore a dark blue suit and a white tie. His hair was cropped short. Gray was beginning to appear at the temples and on the top, a symbol to Marco as to how long they'd been friends. His boyish face was still handsome. Rios went over to a Swedish minimalist-style desk that matched the décor of the office. A sleek black computer sat on the desk. Above his desk was an abstract painting. The rest of the room contained shelves of law books.

Rios spat out questions to Marco in rapid fire, as if to make up for all the time they'd been apart. "What have you been up to? How's Belen? You and Oscar been to any futbol matches? What's new?"

When Rios finally took a breath, Marco responded, then told him the reason for his visit.

"I need your help," Marco said.

Rios's face grew serious. "I see. I got those documents you faxed over. Very intricate financial stuff. What can I do to help?"

"It's about the American singer that was killed, Kijamba."

"Oh yes, I read that you're involved in that investigation," Rios said.

Marco nodded. "Yeah, I'm helping the police. The information I sent you is about Kijamba's business manager, Thomas House. House has been made the executor of his estate, and he's in control of all of his money. His wife gave him all the powers through a notary. Some questions have arisen."

Rios pulled documents out of his printer and flipped through the pages. "I see House Management is listed as a *Sociedad de responsabilidad* limited liability company run by a small Board of Directors. Hmm. The same company owns a subsidiary named Rubio Inc., run by the same Board of Directors that runs House Management."

"What kind of company is Rubio Inc.?" Marco asked.

Rios paused as he perused the information. "Looks like it could be a shell company."

"What's a shell company?" Marco asked.

"Businesses create shell companies to hold funds and manage financial transactions for their other businesses. They sometimes use these companies to hide money, especially profits from real estate transactions. Foreign businesses got away with sheltering money like this for years. Since Mayor Carmen was arrested for fraud and bribery, it's not as easy as it used to be, but they still do it. Strange, I see the company's listed on the US exchange, but there's no record of officers or a general meeting."

Marco thought back to the incident with Mayor Carmen. The mayor, a short, squat, rounded woman, was a popular elected official. She'd brought a lot of money into Vivirrambla from foreign investment. At first, many loved her, Mayor for life they'd called her. Her opponents complained that she'd made the formerly charming small fishing town too commercial. Still, there was no denying the economic boost from foreign investments. Wealthy visitors from Europe now frequented the sun-filled town as a destination tourist spot. Some even bought homes and became extranjeros, permanent residents of Vivirrambla.

The bankruptcy of a major hotel in town led auditors to the discovery that the mayor had been accepting bribes and kickbacks. The mayor herself had made millions. She'd been generous with friends, buying them cars, homes with little to no interest rates, and other gifts. After a sensational trial, Mayor Carmen was sentenced to several years in prison. The town felt embarrassed on the world stage. The newly elected Mayor pledged to crack down on corruption.

"What does all that mean?" Marco asked.

"Usually when you see a company on the exchange, but its stock isn't listed, and you can't find a record of an annual meeting, that means something's afoot," Rios said.

Rios continued to flip through the business records. "I need to do more research and talk to my auditors to know exactly what's going on. Leave the documents with me, and I'll see what else I can find out."

"Gracias, anything you can find out would be helpful," Marco said.

Marco thanked his friend and agreed they should soon get together for a drink. When he got outside, he felt the transition from the air conditioning to the steam heat of an Andalucian summer. When he reached his car, he noticed a note on the windshield. *Oh no, a ticket, he thought.* When he got closer, he saw that it was handwritten. He was becoming weary of these threats. The warning was short and simple. Someone was watching his every move.

Chapter Thirty-Five

Belen had decided to go home for a month to see her parents. She caught the early train to Madrid. Marco didn't discourage her from going as he didn't know who'd been threatening him, and he feared she might be in danger. He hated being alone in the house, but it gave him time to concentrate on his cases. He also wanted to talk to Amira, which seemed too complicated to explain to Belen.

Marco phoned Amira. "What are you doing this evening?" he asked.

"I don't have any plans. Daniel's away on business," Amira said.

"Good, can we meet at Townhome? Laila would love to see you."

"Sure, that sounds good. I'd love to see her, too."

"I'll meet you at the bar at ten," he said.

Marco had a tough time concentrating the rest of the day. He was glad to sign off his computer. He went home, made himself dinner, and clicked on the television to pass the time. When it was time to leave, he changed into jeans and combed his hair. He grabbed his keys and headed out. He stepped out into the warm night air. He always walked to the bar when he knew he'd be drinking. The streets of the Old Town, Casca Antiqua, were full of night owls ready to make merry.

He felt nervous as he entered the Townhome bar, even though he told himself that it wasn't a date. Amira was already there when he arrived. Lars and Laila seemed happy to see her. They sat at the bar catching up.

"So good to see you again, Amira; I see you let your hair grow; it looks good," Laila said.

Marco took a seat on the bar stool next to Amira.

Laila turned to Marco. "What can I get you?" she asked.

"Una cerveza," he said.

"Laila didn't ask Marco about Belen, for which he felt grateful.

Marco and Amira talked small talk for a while. Then Amira told Marco that she was thinking of leaving Daniel. Things were getting worse. He didn't seem committed to the relationship.

"I'm sorry to hear that," Marco said.

Marco ordered more beers while Amira went to the jukebox to choose some music. Townhome still had one of those old-fashioned jukeboxes that played a range of music from modern jazz to American pop and Spanish music. Marco twirled his beer as he watched Amira as she walked away.

Amira returned to her bar stool to the tune of "No Ordinary Love" by Sade.

Marco raised his beer bottle in a toast. "To old friends."

The two clinked bottles.

The music was warm and atmospheric in the dark bar. Couples, some gazing into each other's eyes, retreated to the small dance floor in the back of the bar. Amira grabbed Marco's hand and led him to the dance floor. As they moved together to the smooth rhythm of the music, thoughts raced through his head. He felt confused, conflicted, guilty. He wasn't sure which dominated, the music with the beer or the intoxication of her sweet perfume. He felt giddy.

He moved in closer to her. "Amira, why did we break up?"

She shrugged. "You wanted me to come Spain and I wanted to stay in Morocco with my family. My father didn't want me to leave. You left me in the end. You said we'd outgrown one another. I cried for months."

Marco frowned. "I'm so sorry," he said.

"It's okay," she said. "We were young. It worked out for the best."

"But you don't seem happy with your boyfriend."

Amira looked down. "I'm hoping it's just a phase."

Marco felt her warmth as she rested her head on his shoulder. "That's true. I've gone through many phases myself," he said.

They laughed.

"Daniel's only been this way since he started working for this new company," she said. "He's just getting used to it. His boss is an American, and he's a real jerk. I think he's demanding things of Daniel that he doesn't want to do."

"I thought you said he was in the jewelry business. I got the impression he worked for himself," Marco said.

"He does, sort of, but he has a boss. He works in a high-end jewelry trading business. There's a lot of pressure on Daniel. Once he gets used to it, I think things will go back to the way they were," she said.

Marco knew nothing about selling jewelry, which to him didn't sound like a real job. "What kind of jewelry trade is it? Who does he work for?"

"I don't know that much about it. I just know his boss is an American. I've never met him. Since Daniel's clients are high-end, he sometimes goes to their homes to show them jewelry, some nice houses. Sometimes, he loans expensive pieces as a way of advertising. Some of his jewelry is featured on models in magazines like Vivirrambla Today."

"Wow. He probably meets a lot of famous people that way," Marco said.

She leaned on his shoulders. "Let's not talk about Daniel anymore."

"You're right. Let's just enjoy the music," Marco said.

They finished dancing and ordered more beers. Marco greeted friends who came into the bar. Laila and Lesley's son, Jacob, appeared with shots of Tequila with lime. They stared at the drinks as if to say, *"We'd better not,"* then they each gulped down one shot and then another and another. Marco started to feel lightheaded. They decided to dance again. Without warning, they were close and touching. Her skin felt soft like cotton. Marco felt a stirring. He heard the singer croon, *'I wish this night would last forever.'* At that moment, it felt as if no one except Amira and he were on the dance floor. He pulled Amira tighter to him. Her hair touched his chest. She didn't resist. Before they knew it, their lips were touching, and he could feel her breath.

The music stopped. As if he'd come out of a trance, Marco pulled away from her. "Amira, I'm sorry. I can't. I'd better take you home," he said.

She nodded her head in agreement.

Marco bid goodnight to his friends at Townhome, and he and Amira left. Marco said he'd walk her home. There was an awkward silence on the way. Neither knew what to say. He dropped her off at her front door.

"I'm sorry, this can't happen again," he said.

"I know. Good night," she said.

On his way home, his phone buzzed. "Belen, is everything okay?"

"I know it's late," she said. "I just wanted to check on you and see how you're doing. Not too lonely, I hope."

Guilt washed over him like a wave of seaweed over ancient sedentary rock. Marco's head was spinning from the shots, the beer, and the remorse. He'd gotten swept away in a past remembrance, like a Proust novel. He had a job to do, and that was it: find out what Amira's boyfriend was up to and see how he could protect her from harm.

Chapter Thirty-Six

When he woke up, Marco felt like he'd been in a sword fight. He cringed as he remembered what he and Amira had almost done. He recalled a dream he'd had a while ago about being wicked. He wondered if it was true. At work, he poured himself a strong dark coffee. He rubbed his temples and turned on his computer. As he took a sip of the black nectar, his cell phone lit up. The light hurt his eyes. He sat up when he saw it was the fake business phone he used for undercover work.

"*Dime,*" he said in a hoarser than normal voice.

"What's wrong with you? You sound terrible?" the voice on the other end asked.

"Nothing, I just had a little too much to drink last night."

It was Hassan from Morocco. "Oh, I see," he laughed. "Too many beautiful women, eh, ha, ha, ha," he said.

"Something like that," Marco said.

"You're in," Hassan said.

Marco understood that that meant they'd accepted him as a member of the consortium. "Great, what's the next step? Do I need to meet with the boss?" he asked.

Hassan sounded impatient. "All business is done through Omar and me. I told you that," he said.

"Oh, that's right. I'm not thinking straight," Marco said.

"Hmm. I have some paperwork for you, a contract. This has all got to look legit. I'm coming to Spain in a few days. We can meet then?"

"Sure. Where and when do you want to meet?" Marco asked.

"Are you familiar with Benalmadena? I know of a great bar there. Let's meet for lunch." Hassan said.

Marco knew the town of Benalmadena well. His *futbol,* soccer buddy, best friend, Oscar, lived in the town. On weekends, he and Oscar, and a group of friends, frequented a bar owned by their friend, Juan, to watch Barcelona futbol. There, they enjoyed tapas, fresh seafood, and sizzling brown *albondigas*, meatballs, a specialty of the house. He'd have to make sure none of his friends recognized him in the town.

On the agreed-upon date, Marco prepared to resume the playboy role he'd played when he met Hassan in Tanger. He slicked his black hair back and changed to a white shirt slightly open at the collar and black pants. He looked like a fancy drug dealer. Belen would have said he looked ridiculous. He got into his car and headed down Highway Seven. Twenty minutes later, he entered the roundabout circle, signaling his arrival in Benalmadena. He drove to the marina, where the parking space fairy blessed him with a spot right near the restaurant Hassan had chosen.

The town was full of tourists walking along the *paseo*. Many of those he passed were typical pale, shirtless old men with large bellies, making every effort to brown their sun-starved skin. Hassan had chosen a flashy upscale bar on the Benalmadena Marina. Marco was glad as it was not the type of place his friends would frequent. He walked over to the meeting spot.

The restaurant was the kind of place he hated, the kind that served funny things on little pieces of bread and called it tapas. He looked around. Hassan had not arrived. So, he found an open table, pulled out one of the chairs with a view of the boats bobbing on the water, and ordered a beer. The waiter brought him a small expensive glass of ale.

"Anything else, Senor? The waiter asked.

"Gracias, no," Marco said, thinking he'd go bankrupt if he ordered anything else.

He spotted Hassan approaching, carrying a black briefcase. He wore Ray Ban aviator sunglasses, khaki pants, and a muted pink shirt, which emphasized his brown skin.

"Asalamalakum," Hassan said as he sat down.

A Moroccan man with an arm full of tattoos, yellowing teeth, bad skin, and a smashed-in head emerged from the kitchen and welcomed Hassan. Hassan introduced the chef as El Feo, to Marco. Marco thought the man looked familiar, but he couldn't place him.

"Wa-Alaikum-Salaam," Marco said.

Although Marco considered himself to be Catholic like his father, people assumed he was Muslim. It was simpler not to say anything. In this case, anyway, it was part of his cover.

The chef narrowed his eyes and glared at Marco. Then he disappeared.

An equally strange-looking waiter with greasy hair was sent over to their table. Hassan ordered water. He told Marco he didn't drink. Marco thought how ironic it was that the owner of nightclubs didn't drink.

They ordered lunch, couscous, and ensalada. The meal was horrible, not of the caliber of his friend Juan's food. Marco was glad Hassan was paying for the meal. Flores would have it the roof had he seen the bill on the overpriced meal.

After they'd eaten, they both ordered mint tea. As they sipped their tea, Hassan spoke. "I talked to my boss, and he's interested in giving money to you, a loan to buy one of the bars in Puerto Bella. There's an Irish bar on the port up for sale, and he wants to buy it and turn it into one of our clubs. He'd like to have the club in your name," Hassan said.

Marco squinted. "I thought we were talking about clubs in Morocco?"

Hassan pulled out a set of papers from his portfolio and handed them to Marco. "Yeah, but the boss wants you to run this one. Here are the papers I need you to sign."

Marco felt like he'd been a victim of bait and switch. He perused the documents, a contract, for the purchase of a nightclub with Marco listed as part owner and given an interest in the club. "What are the loan terms?"

"We agree to loan you five million Euros to be paid back over a period of two years at forty-percent interest. We'll remain silent partners with a majority share in the business."

"That's really high interest," Marco said.

El Feo appeared at the table and glared again at Marco. He grumbled, then poured water into their half-empty glasses.

Hassan picked up his glass and downed the water in one gulp. "We've looked into your past. We see you had a couple of businesses that failed. So, we don't know your success rate. You're a risk. Too big a risk for our consortium. We think this is a better deal."

Hassan ordered more mint tea for them both. "This is a private deal. No one else needs to know about it. I hope we have an understanding."

Marco nodded. "Of course.".

"One more thing," Hassan said. "My boss is going to need you to do him a favor."

"Favor? What kind of favor?" Marco asked.

Hassan leaned into the table. "The dancers you talked about from Eastern Europe, how soon can you get them in the new bar?"

"I'll talk to my people. It should take a couple of weeks."

"We need you to arrange transport to get them over here and all the paperwork. We'll take care of them once they arrive," Hassan said.

It took all he could do for Marco to restrain himself. He wanted to call Flores and have Hassan arrested right then for human trafficking. He took a deep breath. "That won't be a problem," he said.

"We're going to refurbish the club, and we'll need dancers in place and ready before we open."

Marco looked into Hassan's soulless eyes. He felt a cold chill run down his spine.

"How many girls do you need?"

"A minimum, five or six to begin with, make sure they're beautiful. The boss is partial to blonds. I'll be in touch with you in a week."

"That might take a little longer to get all blonds," Marco said.

Hassan's eyes narrowed. "This needs to be your priority. One week, we've got clients already lined up."

"Okay, I understand," Marco said.

Hassan put twenty euros on the table and stood up. "I've got another appointment. I've got to go," he said.

The slimy-looking cook appeared from the kitchen and gestured to Hassan to follow him. They both went in, and the kitchen door shut. Marco sensed they were up to something. He wondered if the cook was a part of the smuggling operation. Marco looked around the empty restaurant. It could be a cover for their activities. The food was inedible.

Hassan emerged after some time.

"Is everything alright?" Marco asked.

Hassan grinned a porcelain smile. "We're all set. I'll be in touch."

Chapter Thirty-Seven

lores read over the contract Hassan had given Marco and shook his head. "I don't know much about business, but this contract looks like something written by a consigliere, not a legitimate business contract. I thought the club was supposed to be in Morocco?"

Marco explained that Hassan had changed the venue to Spain to an available club on the Port.

"Great, just what we need: more trafficking in Spain. These people have no heart. Set up the meeting and say you'll accept their contract. I hope we can get to the bottom of Elaine's murder," Flores said.

He informed Marco that plain-clothed Malaga police would be around but out of sight for the rendezvous. They'd arrest Hassan as soon as money was exchanged.

Marco contacted Hassan. They agreed to reunite at the same restaurant in Benalmadena. Marco had signed the contract and had information about the women he could supply, thanks to Flores's help. Marco had to admit that sometimes, Flores could be helpful. He arrived early for the meeting. He stood around one of the tables outside the bar. He couldn't bear the thought of that horrible restaurant with the evil-eyed cook. He felt edgy and nervous for reasons he couldn't explain. Something in Hassan's voice on the phone had seemed different. He ordered a beer and stared at the waves as they trickled over the sand.

Once he'd finished his beer, Marco frowned and looked at his watch. Hassan was forty minutes late. He thought about leaving but decided to wait a little longer. He wondered if Hassan had gotten caught in traffic. As he took a sip of a second beer, he saw Hassan approaching.

At that moment, Marco felt the knife at his side.

"We know you're a cop," a voice said.

Marco jerked his body forward to escape the knife. "You're mistaken. I'm not with the police."

"We know who you are M-A-R-C-O," the voice said, drawing out the letters of his name. The bar was empty. The man with the knife had a clear aim at him.

Marco's mind raced. Somehow, his cover had been blown. He'd been trained as a past police officer to slow down the situation and seek to find an escape or cover. The knife was starting to pinch. He shifted as he felt it getting closer to his ribs.

"I don't know what you're talking about. I'm here to meet Hassan. I think you have the wrong person."

A young couple walked by and looked at them. The man with the knife grinned at the couple, stepped back, and eased the tension from the knife.

"Don't try to fool me." He whispered in Marco's ear. Marco could smell his bad breath. "I'd kill you right now if I could. I hate cops. Start walking, and don't even think about escaping. Now move."

He shoved Marco forward.

"How did you know who I was?" Marco asked.

He stuck the knife in so that Marco could feel the tip of the blade. "I remembered you as soon as I saw you. You kind of stand out. I was arrested a few years ago. Don't you remember? You were with that other Spanish cop that kept hitting me. I had a broken arm from where he twisted my arm behind my back," the man said.

"I remember now. You were arrested for robbery. That was my former partner who hurt you. I tried to stop him. I no longer work with him. He wasn't a good cop. He was the one that hurt you," Marco said.

"You say that now. I didn't see you coming to my aid at the time. He beat me to a pulp."

"I complained about him," Marco said.

The man shoved Marco harder. "I never got an apology from the police. I was in the hospital for weeks."

"You told Hassan who I was when he went back into the kitchen to talk to you, didn't you?"

Shove. "I told you to keep moving."

Marco's heart thumped. He wondered if his assailant could hear it. He could feel the knife moving in, stabbing him. Hassan approached them. The man loosened his grip to greet Hassan.

"I got him for you, boss," the ugly cook said.

Marco bent down and jerked his elbow up into the man's chin. The cook went flying across the ground. He hit one of the tables. His knife slit his own arm as it dropped from his hands. Marco ran. The man clutched his arm and got up and started to limp after Marco. Hassan ran after them.

Marco, now on the paseo amid people walking, pointed at the cook and screamed. "Robbery! He just stole my wallet."

Everyone turned to look. The injured man took off, limping in the other direction. The plainclothes officers Flores had gathered saw what was going on and ran to catch the cook still holding the knife. The cook managed to escape. Hassan spotted them and tried running away, nearly knocking over unsuspecting strollers. Flores messaged Marco that he'd notify the Benalmadena police. After a few minutes, the police swarmed the Marina, which was shut down in all directions. Confused tourists and residents watched the chaotic scene unfold, not sure where they should go as the police ushered them off the beach.

Marco sat inside a police car, too shaken to go home.

Chapter Thirty-Eight

For once, Flores received good news. His team had caught the restaurant cook who'd tried to stab Marco. His name was Paco Gil, but he went by El Feo, the ugly one, because of his pockmarked skin and misshaped head. They found him hiding in a motel near the restaurant. He'd left bloody towels in the bathroom from his wounded arm. When the maid came to clean the room, she was alarmed at the sight and called the hotel manager. The suspicious manager called the police who arrested Paco as he checked out of the motel.

Flores himself interrogated him. He told Paco, who sat nervously fidgeting in his chair, that he intended to charge him with attempted murder of a police officer since Marco had been working for the police at the time of the assault. Paco agreed to confess and to give them information about his accomplice, Hassan, in exchange for a lesser charge. Hassan, he said, was a friend of his from Morocco. He worked for him. Paco had recognized Marco and alerted Hassan as to his identity.

What kind of work do you do for Hassan?" Flores asked.

Paco stuttered; beads of sweat ran down his face. "Wha...t...ever he needs."

Flores and his team had raided the restaurant when they picked up Paco. They'd found little evidence of food preparation. Instead, they identified stacks of stolen goods, including jewelry hidden throughout the kitchen, even in the refrigerator. It looked more like a warehouse for contraband than a restaurant. The jewelry they recovered was the same as Flores's team had discovered in a boat raid a while ago: what appeared to be red rubies.

Paco admitted after pressure from Flores that he used the restaurant mainly as a cover to funnel goods.

"We found jewelry, expensive rubies, hidden in your restaurant. Where did you get it?" Flores asked.

"It's not mine, it's Daniel's," Paco said.

"Daniel, who's Daniel?" Flores asked.

El Feo explained that Daniel was a foreigner he'd met through Hassan, who'd helped him get work at the University of Malaga.

Flores frowned. "What kind of work did you do for the University? I thought you owned a restaurant?"

"My restaurant wasn't making money. I needed to pay off some gambling debts. Daniel hooked me up with the University Administrator to do some jobs for him."

Flores stared at Paco. "You mean Dr. Rubio?" he asked.

Paco nodded his head. "Yeah, that's his name."

That explained Rubio's reluctance to assist him when Flores visited the university.

"What kind of jobs did you do for Dr. Rubio?" Flores asked.

Paco sat slouched in his chair with a smirk on his face. "Mostly helped him arrange for those Russian girls to help out at the clubs."

Flores glowered at Paco. "Sit up," he said.

The guard standing behind him shoved him in the back. Paco sat up in his metal chair.

"You recruited young girls to become strippers at night clubs, and Rubio paid you," Flores said.

"I guess you can say that. I arranged everything and made sure the girls were available."

Flores felt sick at the thought of Dr. Rubio trafficking young girls like Elaina and Ginka. "Do you know Ginka Kovalenko?" he asked.

Paco twisted his lip. Who's that?

"One of the girls you trafficked. That was you on the video swapping jewelry and money with Senorita Kovalenko, wasn't it?"

Paco shrugged.

"We can tie you to her, and we'll tack on other charges for smuggling and trafficking. You won't be getting out for a long time," Flores said.

Flores was starting to see that the whole operation was a complex network, a spider web of bad actors. As much as he didn't like his style, Flores had to admit, Marco's undercover operation had yielded fruit. He hoped he'd pealed enough layers to find Elaina's killer.

Flores turned to the officer standing behind Paco. "That'll be all for now. Take him away," he said, waiving him away with his hand.

The officer nudged Paco to stand up to be returned to his cell. Paco, no longer wearing a smirk on his face, was escorted out of the room.

Flores gathered his papers and walked down the corridor to his office from the interrogation room, where he found Marco waiting, seated in one of the chairs.

"What are you doing here?" Flores asked.

"I was anxious to find out what you did with the man who tried to kill me," he said.

Flores briefed him on what he'd learned in the interrogation of Paco Gil.

"I think Daniel is a jewelry dealer from Scotland," Marco said.

"How do you know that?" Flores asked.

"One of my sources told me about a red-haired man from Scotland who sold high-end jewelry in Spain. I've seen some of his pieces, and they're all rubies," Marco said.

"You never mentioned him before," Flores said.

"I was waiting until I had more concrete information," Marco said.

Chapter Thirty-Nine

lores was skeptical of Marco's explanation, but he didn't question him. He had more urgent business. He needed to speak to Dr. Rubio.

Flores raced to the university. Unlike his prior visits, school was in session. Students carrying bookbags swarmed the campus. Flores scurried between them and entered the main administration building. The receptionist looked at him over her black-rimmed reading glasses.

"You're here again? How can we help you this time, Detective?"

"Buenas tardes, Senora, I need to speak to Senor Dr. Rubio. It's urgent."

"He's on the phone. I'll let him know you're here."

The woman nodded and gestured to two wooden chairs behind where he stood.

"Have a seat. I'll be with you in a moment."

Flores surveyed his surroundings. The high ceilings were freshly painted the same vanilla color as the walls, which were adorned with gray file cabinets lined up behind a high counter.

The stern-faced receptionist returned. "Senor Rubio will see you now. He has another meeting soon. He asks that this be brief," she said.

"Gracias, Senora, this shouldn't take long," Flores said as he followed her into the administrator's office.

The administrator reached out a clammy hand to Flores. Please, sit. I thought I answered all your questions last time, Detective."

"We've gotten some new information. I need to follow up on."

"I don't know how I can help. I'm really very busy."

"Let me be the judge of that, Senor. You said that the tuition for the foreign student, Ginka Kovalenko, had been paid through a foreign money transfer."

Rubio nodded his head. "Yes, that's right."

"Has Senorita Kovalenko enrolled for this semester?" Flores asked.

Rubio shook his head, yes.

"I need to get that transfer information from you, including the bank account numbers."

"I don't know that I have the authority to give that to you," Rubio said.

Flores pulled out a set of papers from inside his coat jacket. "Now you do have that authority."

Rubio put on wire-framed glasses and studied the warrant. He grimaced, turned to the computer on his desk, and pushed a number of buttons. The printer started to make noise, and paper spit from it. He handed Flores a set of papers containing transfer and bank information from the National Bank of Scotland.

Rubio adjusted his glasses. His brow was wet. He spoke in a curt, low voice. "Is that all you need?"

Flores took the information and stuffed it into the portfolio he'd been carrying. "That's it for now. I'll need to speak to you later about a man named Paco," Flores said.

Rubio's eyes widened. Paco? I don't think I know anyone by that name."

"I think you do, but we'll discuss that later. Thank you for the information," Flores said.

He could feel Rubio's eyes boring into him as he walked out of the office.

Flores telephoned the National Bank of Scotland as soon as he returned to the station. Thankfully, the bank was cooperative. A woman with a heavy accent said the payor's name on the transfer of funds to the University of Malaga was Daniel Abercrombie, a citizen of Scotland. He listed his occupation as a jewelry merchant. Daniel, the man Marco had somehow known about.

When he asked for more information about Abercrombie, he was given the number of a Detective with the Scottish police named Shamus Murray. Flores rang Detective Murray. He enjoyed talking to his counterparts in other countries. He liked finding out how other police departments worked.

"It's interesting that you should call. We've been closing in on him," Murray said.

Murray explained that they'd been watching Abercrombie for some time and building a case against him. Once they had enough evidence, they intended to extradite him back to Scotland to stand trial. He gave Flores background information on the case, which went beyond fraudulent bank accounts. Abercrombie had first come to their attention when he started making large deposits of money over a short period of time. After an investigation, they were almost certain that he participated in jewelry fraud. Scotland was flush with natural gems called *"Elie Rubies"* found in the Kingdom of Fife, on Ruby Bay, the Scottish detective explained.

"We call them rubies, because of their color, but they're actually garnets called Pyrope garnets. Authentic rubies are rare and extremely costly. Garnets are semi-precious stones and aren't worth nearly as much. Hang on, let me get my notes," the detective said.

There was a pause. Flores heard papers rustling in the background.

"Okay, I'm back. As I was saying, these rubies are really garnets. A clean garnet with no inclusions can be sold for about 7,000 euros per carat tops on the market. A good natural ruby can start at 15,000 euros per carat. Pigeon blood rubies are the most valuable," Shamus said.

Flores whistled. "Whew. We seized a smuggling boat that originated in Scotland and was filled with rubies not long ago. Those must have been the garnets from Scotland. We sent them for analysis, but now we can trace their origin."

"Indeed, there's a fraud operation that's been using sophisticated machines to repolish Elie rubies to be sold as genuine pigeon blood rubies. They've set up the base operation in Spain, so naturally, they would need to smuggle the gems into the country."

"Oh great, just what we need," Flores said.

The officer laughed. "Only a highly trained jeweler can tell the difference. We've been working with the Scottish Universities Environmental Research Centre of Glasgow to identify these fake jewels."

Besides cheating buyers, the mining of the Elie Rubies has caused an environmental hazard in Scotland, which has led to protests and unrest. They've caught some of the miners, but many of the gems have already been smuggled out of the country in boats like the one you found."

"The boat we seized was also smuggling immigrants," Flores said.

"That makes sense. They wanted to divert attention away from the gems and hoped you would only focus on the immigrants. It's great you found the gems," Shamus said.

"It was some good work by our police force," Flores said.

"We've identified Daniel Abercrombie as a ringleader in the smuggling operation," Murray said.

Flores thanked his counterpart for the information. They agreed that they hoped to meet in person someday. He hung up the phone and leaned back in his chair. *Garnets sold as expensive rubies,*" he thought. *'I've heard it all now.'*

Chapter Forty

Marco sat on his couch sulking with his friend, Oscar, over the Barcelona loss to Villareal they'd just witnessed in a heartbreaking final quarter of penalty kicks. They stared into the abyss slumped in front of the television in silence, nursing beers. Once Oscar left, Marco prepared to clean up the pizza boxes and empty bottles. His cell lit up as he washed dishes.

Flores was calling to update him on what he'd learned from the Scottish police about Elie Rubies and the fake jewelry smuggling ring. As he listened to Flores, Marco thought about the necklace Amira had worn when they met for dinner and her fire-red earrings when they'd walked on the beach in Morocco. He'd noticed their red brilliance. She'd said Daniel had given the jewelry to her as a present.

He forgot about Barca futbol. He had no choice now but to tell Flores about the tape he had from his first surveillance of Amira meeting Ginka Kovalenko in a restaurant and exchanging something. He feared Amira might be implicated in Daniel's scheme. He knew her. She couldn't be involved in anything illegal. Flores wouldn't see it that way; she could even be arrested as an accomplice.

His head banged. He grabbed a couple of aspirinas from the bathroom and shuffled into the kitchen. He swallowed the pills, took a swig from a bottle of Lanjarón water and went to bed. He had dreams of Amira lying dead in a bed of rubies.

He awakened in the middle of the night with an urgency to save her. He turned over, reached for his cell, and woke his cousin Karim, who agreed to help.

Then he called Amira.

She started speaking before Marco could explain why he was calling. "Marco," she said. "You don't need to call me in the middle of the night to apologize. We were both drunk. I totally understand. Daniel and I had a talk, and we're going to try to work things out. He said he's changed. He should be home soon."

"Hold on, Amira. I need to tell you something."

"What? You sound serious," she said.

"You appeared on a police surveillance video a while ago with a woman named Ginka Kovalenko. I never showed that video to the police, so as not to get you involved in our investigation, but they are going to be charging Daniel."

"What are you saying, Marco? You've been doing surveillance on me this whole time? Why? How could you?"

Marco explained that Ginka was a friend of the murdered woman, Elaina. The police had been watching her. He'd filmed Amira at the restaurant that day handing something over to Ginka. The police have discovered that Daniel is involved in jewelry smuggling and that Ginka works for him.

"I can't tell you anymore about it. Trust me,"

Her voice sounded high-pitched. "Smuggling? Daniel a smuggler? That can't be true. He's a jewelry salesman like I told you. I think the police made a mistake."

"There's no mistake. The police in Scotland had an ongoing investigation. They have a lot of evidence against him. He's been passing off garnets made in Scotland as expensive rubies. Did you know anything about his business? Tell me the truth. You could be in danger, Amira."

Her voice quivered. "No, I swear. I don't know anything about it. I believed him when he told me he sold high-end jewelry," she said.

"What were you doing with that stripper, Ginka Kovalenko?" Marco asked.

"You mean a few months ago? Daniel asked me to give that envelope to her. He said she was one of his assistants. I didn't know she was a stripper.

Daniel knew I was going to be in the area, so he asked me to deliver some jewelry to her for a client. I can't believe you've been following me. This whole thing between us has just been a surveillance trick, Marco?"

"No, of course not, Amira. You brought up some real feelings I thought I'd forgotten. I'll always care what happens to you. I've arranged for Karim to protect you. You need to go back to Morocco before the police question you. Karim is expecting you. You need to leave as soon as possible."

"Leave? Why? Can I see Danny before I go? I need to ask him if all this is true. Are all the men in my life just using me? I can't believe this, I really loved Daniel."

Marco felt another stabbing in his ribs, this time it wasn't from a knife. "You can't see him, Amira. You must go now. Get your stuff together and I'll take you to the first ferry over. Karim will pick you up at the port."

Marco took a shower. He hadn't shaved in a couple of days, and his scraggy facial hair itched. He threw on jeans and a T-shirt. He hoped he'd get to Amira's apartment before the police. He drove at top speed. Good. He didn't see any official cars parked in the area. Amira came downstairs carrying a small suitcase. Her eyes were bloodshot when she hopped in the car.

"I only brought a couple of things. Will I be able to come back? What will happen to Daniel?" she asked.

"I don't know if you should come back anytime soon. Daniel will be arrested and go on trial here and be deported to Scotland. Give me your keys, and I'll arrange for the rest of your stuff to be sent to you."

He'd ask his assistant, Eva, to pack up the rest of her things. Eva was good at that sort of thing.

They rode in silence past the small towns with white houses on the way to the Algeciras port. Amira shivered and stared out of the window. Marco took her hand to try to calm her. She snatched it away.

"Don't worry. It's all going to be okay. Karim will take care of you. I'm sorry about Daniel," he said.

"What about you? How could you treat me like this?" she asked

"I'm sorry, Amira."

They reached the large red and white ferryboat moments before the entrance was about to be rolled up. The bright, full moon overlooked the sea like a watchful mother. Marco kissed Amira goodbye under the moon's light. She handed him the keys to her apartment, and then she walked away. He watched her hips sway in the moonlight. She didn't look back. He felt like he was in the final scene from Casablanca.

Chapter Forty-One

"And the Raven, never flitting, still is sitting, still is sitting on the pallid bust of Pallas just above my chamber door."

The Raven, Edgar Allan Poe

Doctor Miguel Rubio pulled back the curtains of the large baroque window in his impressive office and looked out onto the campus, his campus, at the eager students going back and forth across the quad. Rubio had been the Administrator at the University of Malaga for over twenty years. He felt proud of his tenure and the numerous awards he'd won. He looked at them on his shelf. He was set to retire soon, and he looked forward to the next stage of his life: a new wife. His relationship with the Board of Trustees had begun to deteriorate in recent months. They'd questioned the increase of Eastern European students over all other countries in the International School. The Board wondered why there was such a leaning towards those students while rejecting students from other countries who traditionally had done very well in the school. He didn't seem to vet any of the students, one of the board members said. Rubio argued that Eastern European students paid well. Very few of them needed scholarships, so it was profitable for the school. He pointed out that the school had remained financially sound for many years. Another board member said it seemed suspicious. She argued that the school shouldn't risk its reputation for profit.

Rubio had once thought like that naïve, starry-eyed board member. In the past, he'd put integrity above all else. A divorce and bitter custody battle had changed him. He'd become mistrustful, nihilistic. He himself couldn't believe who he'd become. He'd justified his actions with the underworld as his allowing himself much-needed retirement money that he'd been robbed of by his ex-wife. Now, all he'd worked for was being threatened. Still, he didn't blame himself.

He wiped the bead of sweat that had gathered on his forehead the second time he'd experienced a cold sweat that day and closed the curtain. He picked up his cell and pressed the desired numbers. He'd procrastinated long enough. They'd find out by tomorrow. Better it came from him. His heart raced. The loud thumping hurt his ears. He wondered if he should make an appointment with the university doctor. One thing he'd discovered about aging, he could never tell when anything unusual with his body was a serious illness or just a result of getting old. He dismissed it as nerves.

A gruff voice answered his call. "What is it?"

Rubio whispered in a soft voice. "I need to talk to you. That detective came to see me again. He wanted the bank transfer information and deposit numbers for Ginka's tuition."

The voice on the other end sounded frigid. Rubio could sense the coldness through the phone. "Did you give it to him?"

"He had a warrant. I had no choice," Rubio said."

"Then it's only a matter of time before they trace the money to me. This is a bad situation for you," the voice said.

Rubio was old-fashioned, meticulous in his dress and manner. He still wore a pocket square in his suit pocket. He pulled out the neatly folded gray handkerchief to wipe the beads of sweat now falling down his face. "What was I supposed to do? I had no choice, I swear. He said if I didn't give him the information, he'd seize all the school's computers. I couldn't let that happen. You know what's on those computers."

"You always have a choice. You should have let them take the computers. You made the wrong choice. I told him we couldn't trust you."

"He had a warrant. How could I have stopped him? He would have searched through all our records anyway. There was nothing I could do."

"You should have anticipated the police's visit and cleared the computers of *his* information."

There was a long pause.

"How was I supposed to do that?" Rubio asked.

"You're the genius. That's what we paid you for. You were supposed to make sure our names weren't connected to those payments. That was stupid of you. He's not going to be happy. You'd better hope I can fix this mess before it comes back on him," the voice said.

"But. I did what I cou—"

The phone disconnected.

Rubio sat for a while at his desk with his head between his hands. He took deep breaths, trying to slow down his heartbeat, which pounded out of control. When he looked up, he saw a black raven perched outside his window, still piercing eyes, staring at him.

Chapter Forty-Two

Flores needed to apprise the Chief of the latest events. He sat down at his desk to write a memo. The noise in the hallway was abuzz with so much chatter he couldn't hear. He got up to tell the other officers to quiet down.

When he opened his door, he saw several officers and personnel milling around conferring with one another. News had traveled through the station like a bullet train. Dr. Miguel Rubio, school administrator from the University of Velazquez, Malaga, had been found shot, execution-style, in his office on the University campus. His assistant found him barely breathing when she went to work. He'd perished before paramedics could reach him. Flores went back to his office and grabbed his police vest. He'd have to catch the Chief up later.

Flores jumped in his car and drove to the scene. He arrived on campus at the same time as Bortello, the coroner. Rubio's secretary stood outside the building in front of a police car, shaking, as she gave an account of what she'd seen. She'd found him lying on the floor of his office, she said.

Flores walked past her into the school building amidst the hustle and bustle of examiners, forensics, and police, dusting for fingerprints and surveying the room. Bortello lifted the sheet that had been placed over Dr. Rubio's body. Flores kneeled next to the departed.

"The killer meant business. I'd say it was a professional," Bortello said.

Flores nodded his head in agreement. "Do you have a time of death?" he asked.

Bortello shook his head. "Not until I examine the body. It was sometime last night is all I can tell you now. His assistant said he was alive when she left the office around six in the evening. The windows were open, so it was cold in here last night. That might affect the time of rigor."

"We need to make this a priority," Flores said.

Bortello frowned. "They're all priorities."

Flores asked forensics if they'd recovered the weapon. They told him they were still searching, but so far, they hadn't found anything.

"As far as we can see, it was a professional grade silencer, which means anyone in the building may or may not have heard it," one of the officers said.

Rubio's computer had been left on. Flores ordered the computer bagged and sent to data surveillance for analysis. The detective looked around the office he'd just been in a day or so ago. Other than a few papers, everything seemed just as he'd seen it. He looked out of the window. He noticed a black bird fly past. It peered through as if it knew what was going on.

Chapter Forty-Three

Men and women wearing black Ninja outfits gathered two blocks from Daniel's apartment building. Flores wore his bulletproof vest and other protection. The officers drank coffee from thermal mugs and waited until dawn. These raids always raised Flores' adrenaline. It was the thrill of catching the suspect combined with the possible danger of the moment. He took a sip of coffee and shivered from the morning air. As the first light hit, they entered Daniel's home, taking a confused sleeping Daniel, wearing sweats and no shirt, into custody. His flaming red hair and red eyebrows stood on end. His eyes were still filled with sleep.

When they concluded the raid, Flores returned to his office, where he found Marco sitting in one of the chairs.

"What are you doing here? This is getting to be a habit." Flores said, taking off his protective gear.

Marco showed him a DVD.

"What's this?"

"I need to talk to you," Marco said.

"Talk to me about what? Can this wait?" We're about to bring Daniel Abercrombie into the interrogation room," Flores said.

"I know. I need to talk to you before you do."

Flores screwed up his face. "Okay but make it quick."

Marco put the DVD, which showed Amira meeting with Ginka Kovalenko, into the player in the corner of Flores's office.

"I don't remember seeing this surveillance tape. Who's that with Ginka

Kovalenko?" Flores asked.

Marco explained that Amira was his old girlfriend and that he'd filmed her meeting Ginka at a restaurant during the early part of the investigation.

Flores frowned. "Why am I just seeing this?"

Marco explained the sequence of events and told Flores that Amira had left Daniel and was back in Morocco. She knew nothing about his criminal activities.

An angry Flores knitted his brow. "Still, you should have told me. You had no right to keep critical information from me. Did you know about Abercrombie?"

Marco shook his head. "I knew Amira had a boyfriend who sold jewelry. I was starting to realize that he was involved in something illegal."

"You should have come to me with your suspicions."

"I know," Marco said.

An officer knocked on Flores's door to tell him Daniel Abercrombie was ready in interrogation.

Flores grabbed the DVD from the machine. "I'll deal with you later. Right now, I can use this. I've got to go."

"One more thing," Marco said.

"What is it?"

"I think Thomas House is involved in this whole scheme. I had a lawyer friend of mine dig into his finances. He has a lot more than music management going on," Marco said.

"I don't have time to get into that now," Flores said.

Flores left Marco sitting in his office and headed to police interrogation. He felt angry at not seeing the surveillance earlier, but he needed to focus. He entered the room and sat in one of the army green metal chairs next to a woman with long brown hair wearing pants and a police jacket.

Daniel sat, arms folded. His eyes looked glazed.

The click of a tape recorder broke the silence. "This is to advise you this is being recorded. I'm Detective Flores, and next to me is Detective Delores DeLuca. Do you know why you're here?"

Daniel remained silent for a time. Flores watched the freckles on his arm. He observed that the hair on Daniel's arms was as red as the hair on his head, which he found curious. He'd never seen red hair on anyone's arms.

"Does this have something to do with my job?" he asked.

Flores sneered. "Your job? Is that what you call smuggling these days? We'll get to that."

Daniel fidgeted in his chair.

"Where were you yesterday afternoon, Senor Abercrombie?" Flores asked.

"Visiting with a client, why?"

"Senor Rubio of Malaga University was murdered at the school," Flores said.

"Who is Senor Rubio, and what's that got to do with me?" Daniel asked.

"We ask the questions here. Where were you, exactly?" Flores asked.

"With a client, I already told you."

"We'll need the name and address of that client."

"That information is confidential."

Flores looked at Daniel and sneered. "Confidential? Are you a Priest?" he asked.

Daniel sat up in his chair and peacocked his shoulders. "I'm a high-end salesman. My clients are very wealthy. Some are well-known. They don't want everyone to know who they are or what they own for security reasons."

"That's not good enough. This is a murder investigation. You need to give me the name of the client you say you were visiting yesterday," Flores said.

"I can't give you that information," Abercrombie said.

"You can either answer my questions, or we'll charge you with murder right now."

"Murder? I don't know anything about any murder."

"Let's work backward then, shall we?" Flores said.

Flores pulled out the surveillance tape and placed the disc into the computer on the table.

Daniel gazed at the screen with a blank stare. "What does that have to do with me?" he asked.

Flores, who'd been leaning back in his chair, sat up straight and leaned forward. "Senorita Kovalenko is seen here selling your jewelry. Garnets you're passing off as rubies. We found a bag of gems hidden in the door when we searched your car this morning. The same kind of gems we found in a recent boat smuggling raid. They're being sent to Scotland for analysis. We've checked your bank accounts and spoken to the bank and the Scottish police. You've been making large deposits, tens of thousands of Euros into an account in Scotland. Our friends overseas have been monitoring your activity."

Daniel rubbed his wrists where the handcuffs had been. The red hairs on his arms stood on end. "Like I said, I don't know what you're talking about. I'm an independent businessman."

Flores laughed. "Kind of like Michael Corleone was a businessman. Where do you get your merchandise?"

Daniel spat out his response like it was poisonous venom. "Suppliers. I buy jewelry from them and sell it to my clientele."

"Who are these suppliers?" Flores asked.

"Jewelry manufacturers and dealers."

"You mean miners and smugglers illegally excavating garnets in Scotland and turning them into polished gems that look like rubies," Flores said.

Daniel's face turned a deep red, the color of one of his fake rubies. "I don't know what you're talking about."

"Why are you doing business here in Spain? Why don't you sell your jewelry in Scotland?" Flores asked.

Daniel hunched his shoulders. "It's a free country, isn't it? I like the weather here, and the market is good. Is there a law against living where you want to live?"

Flores wagged his finger at Daniel. "You've been paying Ginka Kovalenko's tuition at the University of Malaga. Ms. Kovalenko is selling your jewelry to her clients in return. You also paid Elaina's tuition before she died. It's all coming together. We questioned Dr. Rubio about it, and the next day he ends up dead, quite a coincidence, isn't it?"

Daniel shrugged.

Flores slid a grid sheet containing phone call information over to Daniel.

"We recovered a conversation on Senor Rubio's phone where he'd been threatened right before he was murdered. We traced the call to a non-existent number." Flores leaned in across the table. "The caller had a funny accent. We're also checking voice print. It won't be long before we find out who made that call."

Daniel pretended to be disinterested. He looked off into space. "Nothing to do with me."

"Oh, and we're checking the phone towers and searching your house for a gun," Flores said.

"Good luck," Daniel said.

Flores looked over at Detective DeLuca. "Smart guy, huh."

Detective DeLuca snickered.

"How do you know Ginka Kovalenko?" Flores asked.

Daniel folded his arms across his chest. "I met her through some clients of mine. Ginka and I became friends. She told me she and her friend Elaina wanted to quit dancing. They just wanted to go to school and get a degree. I felt bad for her, so I agreed to loan her the money for tuition. I said she could work for me to pay me back."

"Work for you doing what?" Flores asked.

"Selling jewelry on commission like I told you," Daniel said.

"You mean helping you pass off garnets as expensive rubies to vulnerable wealthy clients. So, you're telling me you just trust some women you hardly know to handle your expensive jewelry. Of course, maybe you trust them because you're selling cheap knockoffs," Flores said.

Daniel jerked up from his chair. The table made a booming sound when his knees hit it. DeLuca put her hand on the gun in her jacket.

"Screw you. All my jewelry is high-quality. Most of the famous people in the area are my clients."

Flores knew that the best way to get a suspect to talk was to make them angry. The best way to do that was to insult them personally. He'd used that trick on many occasions.

"I think your jewelry is junk. I think you're bringing in cheap garnets from Scotland on the smuggling boats."

Daniel's face turned the color of his freckles. "Junk! You don't know what you're talking about."

"I think you use the same boats to bring in desperate people from other countries to smuggle in your knock-off jewelry. You see, we know you're also engaged in trafficking of young Eastern European women," Flores said.

"You're crazy. I'm a legitimate businessman. I tried to help Ginka and her friend out with a few dollars."

"Were you sleeping with her?" Flores asked.

Daniel shook his head violently. "No, no way. I'm committed to my girlfriend."

"Then why would you be helping Ginka, a random woman, out if you weren't interested in her?"

"I have a big heart," Daniel said.

"Big heart? I think you figured it was a good way to get your jewelry in the country."

Flores inserted the surveillance DVD Marco had given him earlier into the laptop computer. He stopped the tape after a minute. "Who's this woman?" he asked.

Daniel stared at the film with his mouth open. "That's my girlfriend, Amira. Do you know where she is? I've been calling and texting her all night. I don't think she knows I've been arrested."

"What is she doing in this video with Senorita Kovalenko?" Flores asked.

Daniel stared down at the table. No one spoke for a time.

Flores broke the silence. "Is she involved in your smuggling enterprises, Senor Abercrombie?"

"No! She's not involved. She doesn't know anything about this. I swear on my life," Daniel said, raising his right hand.

"What was she doing at this moment?" Flores asked, pointing to Amira on the screen.

"She was doing me a favor. I asked her to drop some jewelry off to Ginka, that was all. She doesn't know anything about my business," Daniel said.

He'd backed up Marco's story, this Amira friend of his, Daniel's girlfriend hadn't been involved. It didn't lessen his anger about not knowing of the existence of the surveillance tape. What if the Chief found out? Marco's arrogance was going to be his undoing.

Daniel sat staring at the table and making circles with his fingers.

"We're going to charge you with smuggling," Flores said.

"I'm not saying anything else without my lawyer. I need to call Amira. She'll be worried."

"We're also looking into the murder of Dr. Rubio. You'll be charged with a first-degree if we think you were involved. The interview's over," Flores said and flipped off the recorder.

Detective DeLuca grabbed Daniel's arm and handcuffed his wrist. She led him down the hall to the cells. Flores heard him shouting, "I didn't murder anyone," his voice echoed as he went further into the distance.

Chapter Forty-Four

Belen called to say she wouldn't be home for another two weeks. It was her parent's thirtieth anniversary, and they'd decided to go to Italy. She invited Marco to meet them in Venice, but he told her he was too busy. He heard the disappointment in her voice. He didn't want to go partly because he felt angry. He'd been anticipating Belen's return. He needed to see her and talk to her, especially after the Amira incident and the feelings that had been stirred up.

He didn't sleep well that night. So he rose early, showered, and towel-dried his scruffy hair. He dressed for work and headed to Alvarez's. Alvarez was in a particularly good mood when Marco arrived. He whistled as he made rich, dark espresso topped with steaming milk. He even added an extra swirl, like the finishing touches of a fine painting, before handing the cup to Marco.

Marco laughed. "Why are you so happy?"

Alvarez beamed. He said, "My daughter that got married last year. You remember her, right? She's pregnant with my first grandchild."

Marco smiled. "Felicidades, I'm so happy for you."

"My wife is already overdoing everything, of course. We don't know if it's a girl or a boy, but she's already bought clothes. Alvarez said, shaking his head.

Her husband's a redhead, though, the only one in the family. I'm wondering if my grandbaby's going to have red hair?"

"How far along is she?" Marco asked.

"Three months. My daughter said we can start telling people now."

Mental note to self: Tell Eva to send Alvarez a gift when the time comes.

Marco felt genuinely happy for Alvarez. He wished he felt only joyfulness, instead he felt stressed. His main income as a consultant to the Malaga police was under threat. Flores was furious that he hadn't told him about Amira sooner. Worse, he worried Belen would never forgive him if she knew about Amira and how close he'd come to kissing her. He took the last swig of his café con leche, hoping it would lighten his mood, and hopped off the barstool. He bid the still-beaming Alvarez good day and headed off to work.

"Buen Dia, he shouted to Alvarez, who'd disappeared in the kitchen."

"Gracias, amigo, es una dia perfecta," Alvarez shouted back.

When Marco reached his office, Eva was busy at her desk. He smiled and said hello. She barely looked up from her computer as he passed by.

"Hola, Jeffe," she said, waving her hand. I sent you the links with that information on Thomas House you wanted. I'm still digging," she said.

"Thanks, great work, Eva."

Marco had asked Eva to do research on Thomas House's expansive business dealings. He wanted to follow up on the information he'd received from his friend Roberto Rios. Roberto had emailed Marco more information about House's income, which suggested that House had more business interests than they'd initially thought. House had owned a management company in New York that operated questionable nightclubs before he became Kijamba's manager. Marco clicked on links to articles that showed House posing with his spiked nineties blond hair in front of trendy clubs with pseudo-celebrities. Another article exposed how House had been charged with fraud a few years ago, but the case had been dismissed for lack of evidence. A beaming triumphant House was seen leaving a US courthouse with a team of attorneys.

As he perused the stories, something Alvarez had said struck him. Alvarez had said his son-in-law was the only redhead in the family. At Catherine's party, House had been drunk and having a loud argument on the phone with someone he called Danny, a former employee he'd said. "He'd called him a red-haired idiot." It had to be the same person, which proved that

House was involved in Daniel's illicit business.

Marco texted Belen and asked her for Catherine Taylor's number.

"What do you want with her?" Belen replied.

Marco explained that he needed to go and see her in person about his investigation. Belen forwarded him the number. He could sense her disapproval.

Then he phoned Flores and told him of his discovery. "Just want to keep you in the loop," he said.

"Good. Any more repeats of acting on your own, and you're off the case. You want us to pay for you to fly to Barcelona? Why should I authorize that?" Flores asked.

Marco tried to explain his thinking to Flores as thoroughly as possible. "So that we can get concrete proof that there's a connection between Abercrombie, the jewelry smuggler, and House. I heard House arguing on the phone with someone he called Danny when I was at Catherine Taylor's party in Barcelona. House said it was a minor dispute with a disgruntled employee. He called him a red-haired idiot. I didn't pay that much attention at the time, but now that we know what Danny Abercrombie's been up to and that they both know Catherine Taylor, it makes sense. He must have been the person House was yelling at on the phone. I need to meet with Senora Taylor to tie things together," Marco said.

Marco could hear the hesitation in Flores's voice.

"I'll authorize it, but you'd better know what you're doing, or I swear this time, you will be off the case," Flores said.

Chapter Forty-Five

When Marco phoned Catherine Taylor, she cooed over the phone like a cougar in heat. "OOOh, the hot boyfriend. I *definitely* remember you."

Marco could feel his face heating up, "Uh, yes, I hope you are doing well."

"*Sooo* good to hear from you. I was hoping you'd call sooner, but now is as good a time as any," she said.

"I need to come and see you. Belen said you wouldn't mind," Marco said.

"Mind? I can't wait."

"I need to talk to you about one of my cases."

Her voice lowered. "Oh, one of your cases? I'm not sure how I can help with that, but any reason to see you," she said.

Eva arranged a flight for Marco to Barcelona the next day. He boarded the plane early, along with businessmen in expensive suits on their way to important meetings. By midday, Marco found himself once again on the narrow streets of Las Ramblas. He checked in his hotel and let Catherine know he'd arrived. She invited him to come to her home in an hour. He wished Belen was with him.

Marco showered and combed his hair. Belen would be pleased he'd just gotten it cut so the dark layers now fell into place. He no longer looked like a scraggly dog. He took a taxi to Catherine's residence. The driver stopped in front of a Gothic structure painted a muted reddish pink. An ancient family crest painted on the building signified that the house, now divided into apartments, had once belonged to one wealthy family during the Renaissance. Marco pushed open the door, walked up the stairs to

Catherine's apartment, and rang the bell.

A woman in her forties, with her dark hair in a bun, answered the door. She wore a white pantsuit on her slim frame. She kissed Marco on the cheek. He wrinkled his nose, which was overpowered by her perfume. Her face was smooth, but her smile appeared tight, almost drawn onto her mouth. She wore a ruby and gold bracelet on her arm.

"Come in, darling. Good to see you," she said. "Still gorgeous. I see"

Her scent followed her through each room. Marco walked into the salon he recalled from the party. He sat on the blue velvet sofa at her beckoning.

"Can I offer you something, wine, tea, coffee, beer?"

"A beer would be great," Marco said.

"A beer man. I figured you were the rugged type," she said.

She returned from the kitchen and handed him a beer and a glass. She took her position on a nearby white Tangerine striped damask chair with a pattern matching the sofa.

"So, what brings you all this way? How's Belen?"

"Belen's fine. She's visiting her parents in Madrid."

She laughed. "Ahh, a free man, it seems."

Marco squirmed in his chair. "Senora Taylor, I need to speak to you about one of the guests at your party."

"Yeah, Belen told me you were a detective or something like that."

"Yes, that's right."

She furrowed her brows and snickered. "Well, how can I help? I certainly haven't murdered anyone."

"No, of course not. I'd like to get some information about Thomas House. You said he used to manage your career. How much do you know about him?"

She shrugged. "We've been friends for years."

"How much do you know about his business?"

"Like, what do you want to know?

"During your party, I heard him talking on the phone to a man he called Danny. Do you know who that man could have been?"

She twisted the ruby bracelet on her arm. "What could House have to do with your murder investigation?"

"Who said it was a murder investigation?"

Her lips seemed fixed when she talked from all of the Botox treatments. Belen had told Marco about women like that who went overboard.

"Oh, I just assumed," she said.

"I just need to get some background information. I'm assisting the police," Marco said.

Catherine got up and walked over to the table and poured herself a gin and tonic. She reminded Marco of an old glamorous Hollywood star past her prime, Norma Desmond.

She took a large gulp of her drink. The ice in her glass swooshed. "Danny… Danny, hmmm. The only Danny I know is Danny Abercrombie."

"Does he have red hair?" Marco asked.

She laughed. "Oh, yes, pure Scottish red."

"How well do you know him?" Marco asked.

"I know him through Thomas. He's a high-end jewelry dealer. I've bought some stuff from him myself."

Marco looked down at her ruby bracelet.

She held out her arm for Marco to inspect it. It was a beautiful, rich gold with a large dark red stone in the middle and a filigree design around the outside.

"This is one of Danny's pieces. Isn't it absolutely gorgeous?"

Marco nodded his head. "Yes, it's lovely?"

"I've bought several of Danny's pieces over the years. Sometimes, he comes to my annual party and brings some nice gems with him. I was disappointed when he didn't show up this year."

"How does House know him?" Marco asked.

"I think they met at a nightclub."

Marco scribbled notes in a small notepad he'd brought. "When was that?" he asked.

"I'm not sure. Listen, you can stay for dinner. I can cook us something," she said.

"Gracias, Senora, but I have plans for this evening." He really only intended to grab room service at the hotel, but he feared where a dinner invitation from Senora Taylor would lead."

"Oh well, next time. Thomas has an interest in a couple of nightclubs in Spain. I danced at one of his clubs in Puerta Bella a few years ago," Catherine said.

"Did you ever dance at the Club Azule?" Marco asked.

She nodded her head. "Yes, of course. It was one of the last places I danced. It was the hottest club around for a time. Then, the manager said I was too old, and they let me go. That's that club where the woman was murdered, right? I read about it. SAD."

"Yes, it is. Does Thomas House have an interest in that club?" Marco asked.

She sat her drink down on the side table next to her. "Oh, I don't know, he may have. He's quite the mogul. I heard it's owned by some Arab guys or some Moroccan guys or something like that. You're Moroccan, aren't you? I always thought Moroccan men were so good-looking, like film stars. We would have been good together," she said.

Marco scooted down on the sofa and took a drink of beer. "How do you know so much about House's business?"

"Thomas and I dated for a while before he met his wife."

"Oh really?" Marco asked.

"We dated for a couple of years. He's an ambitious man. That's what attracted me to him. When we met, he'd just come over from America." She twirled the ice in her glass and took a sip of her drink. "He was a dashing American," she snickered. "Which, of course, is the next best thing to a dashing Moroccan."

Marco looked at the mantel in front of him at Catherine's pictures. Pictures of her as a dancer, pictures of her with a man, and pictures of her with Kijamba, Shada, and House.

"Thomas and I clicked right away. It was an amazing time in my life. He introduced me to Kijamba, you know. It was the closest I'd ever been to a real star. We became friends. I wanted to get married, and Thomas didn't. *Asi es la vida.*" Another swirl of her drink. "I'm going to miss Kijamba. "She shifted closer to whisper in Marco's ear. "Between you and me, I know he's married, but sometimes Thomas stays a few extra days after my party. You're free to stay here tonight. What happens in Barcelona stays in Barcelona," she said, laughing at her own joke.

Marco cleared his throat. "Uhh, thanks. I've booked a really convenient hotel next to the airport. I've got to get back to Vivirrambla pretty early."

"Oh. Well, if you change your mind."

"What about Danny Abercrombie? What else can you tell me about him?" Marco asked.

She lifted her corner lip. Marco wondered how she did it, as her face seemed incapable of spontaneous movement.

"Like I said, he's a friend. I buy jewelry from him. I don't know that much about his business. Thomas told me Danny has a lot of very wealthy clients."

Marco finished the beer and declined the offer of another or 'something else' if he desired and stood to leave.

"You've been very helpful, Senora, gracias. I'll tell Belen you said hello."

She grabbed his arm with a firm grip and cooed in his ear. "You *really* don't need to leave."

Marco extricated his arm. "Please don't tell Senor House I've spoken to you."

He didn't tell her that they'd arrested Abercrombie for selling fake gems, like the ones she wore, and passing them off as rubies. Flores had instructed him not to say anything.

Marco felt relieved to be out of Catherine's clutches. He phoned Belen as soon as he reached the noisy Barcelona streets and told her of his visit.

"I never really liked her that much anyway," Belen said.

"Why did we go to her party then?" Marco asked.

"I thought it would be a good excuse to get away. Some of the other dancers that I do like were there and I thought it would be fun to see them. Barcelona is such a beautiful city. We had a good time, didn't we?" she asked.

"Except for the party, it was a wonderful trip," Marco said.

Barcelona was a beautiful city. Marco strolled through Park Gruell amidst the blue, orange, yellow, and red mosaic-tiled bridges and decorative buildings to the gardens shaped by architect Antonio Gaudi. He sat on one of the colorful park benches and typed into his iPad, making sure he made accurate, contemporaneous notes from his meeting with Catherine Taylor.

Satisfied with his notes, Marco put away the iPad and continued his trek through the park, which looked more like a fantasy land amusement center with blue and yellow objects placed in strategic places all around than a traditional park. He sat on a mosaic bench next to an elderly gentleman, wearing a grey suit and a tie, even though it was hot. His white hair was slicked back, and his white bushy eyebrows covered most of his eyes. His ear lobes were long and hung away from his face. They reminded him of Detective Flores's ears. He wore sneakers with his suit. The man pulled a jamon *bocadillo* from a bag and a bottle of water and began to eat. He looked over at Marco and nodded.

"Can I offer you some?" he asked.

"*Gracias*, no," Marco said.

"Are you un-Gitano, gypsy?" the man asked.

That question always felt more like an accusation than a question to Marco. "No, Senor, I'm half-Spanish and half-Moroccan. I was born in Spain, in Andalucía," he said.

The man nodded. Marco expected him to say something racist, like you look like one of them, which usually followed the question. Instead, the man began telling Marco of his own history. That he had nothing against Romani people. In fact, he was married to a Romani woman. They'd had thirty years of happiness together until she died of cancer a year ago. Now, he came to Park Gruell alone every day to eat lunch, as they used to eat there together when they were married. They couldn't have children. So, for all those years, they only had each other. Now, he was alone except for a nephew who lived in the States.

"I've always admired people like you and my wife. You keep going despite adversity. I suspect you had to put up with a lot of discrimination, like my wife. I miss her. I could count on her for everything. Now that she's gone, I only have my greedy nephew. He took over all my finances since I became disabled. I know he doesn't care about me. He wants the little money I've saved up when I die."

"How does someone just take over your finances? You seem very sane and rational to me," Marco asked.

The man's crinkled old eyes were moist. "He took me to court. He caught me when I was vulnerable right after my wife, Rhona, died. I had a sort of breakdown. He used my mental state to have the court give him power of attorney. I tried to notify the courts when I was better, but no one would listen to an old man. Now, I can't even write a check without his approval. He gives me a small allowance like I'm a child. That's why I like to come here to remember it like it was when life felt magical."

Marco and the genteel old soul sat and talked for some time. Eventually, Marco told him he had to leave as his flight was early the next morning.

Marco's new friend spoke as Marco rose from the bench to leave. "A piece of advice: when you get old, don't let anyone take over your finances unless you trust them completely."

He saluted Marco with a parting gesture and turned his attention to the birds eating the breadcrumbs he'd thrown from his sandwich.

Marco arrived at the airport early the next day. He was anxious to get back. During the flight, he thought about his conversation with the old man in the park, how the widower talked about someone taking over his finances. Marco noticed he often found wisdom in the words of others if he listened.

His plane landed in Malaga early in the afternoon. He went straight to Flores's office from the Airport.

He found Flores busy pouring over documents. He waved Marco in and told him to have a seat.

"How was your trip?" Flores asked.

Marco recounted his meeting with Catherine Taylor and all that he'd learned about House.

Flores admitted that Senora Taylor's information provided sufficient proof that House was tied to Danny Abercrombie. "I'll have to admit you may have been right about him. It'll be a circus when we bring in beloved Kijamba's manager. I hope this doesn't backfire on us. We could both lose our jobs over this one. Are you one hundred percent sure about this Taylor woman?"

Marco nodded. "I'm certain. She's a friend or, should I say, an acquaintance of Belen's. She's known House for years. She dated him in the past. She knows Daniel Abercrombie and has purchased jewelry from him. She was wearing a piece of his while I was there, one of his fake rubies, though I doubt she knows it's a fake."

"I agree. That's too much of a coincidence. Still, we'll need to make an airtight case," Flores said.

Chapter Forty-Six

"Spain is like a great castle that rises from the sea."
               Spain: The Root and the Flower, John A. Crow

The Chief instructed Flores to keep the investigation of House under wraps and not leak it to the media.

"I don't need that kind of press. We have enough trouble as it is," the Chief said.

Since House was an American ex-pat, Flores contacted the American Federal Bureau of Investigation (FBI). Under an agreement known as MLAT- Mutual Legal Assistance Treaty, agents in the FBI cooperated with foreign nations in securing tax returns and financial records of potential fraudsters. Flores was connected to an American attaché, Robert Benét from Mississippi, who spoke with a Southern accent. Flores explained that House was suspected of trafficking humans, money laundering, aiding in jewel smuggling, and even murder.

"Ya'll got a real live wire on your hands. I was a big fan of Kijamba, this guy was his manager you say?" Benét asked.

"Yes, he lives here in Spain," Flores said.

"Well, I'll be," Benét said.

Flores had no idea what that meant. Benét agreed to submit a formal request to obtain tax information from the US Internal Revenue Service and share the findings with the Malaga police. The FBI agent also agreed to keep the findings out of the US press.

Flores worked until late into the evenings, pouring over financial documents, text messages, and phone records. He created a flow chart of all the information. He had several more conversations with the American agent after their initial meeting. He'd begun to even understand Benét's southern drawl. He had to be available to speak to the American early in the morning or late at night because of the six-hour time difference between the two countries.

Flores barely saw his family for months. His wife supplied him with sandwiches of tuna and olive oil for lunch and a packed meal, usually croqueta and ensalada for dinner. His diligence paid off. He penetrated a web of criminality. House had established a complex flow of money from Spain to the islands. House's tax records showed that he paid taxes on and declared the income he earned from Kijamba, but no other income. He failed to report any of his "overseas investments."

In a feat of law enforcement cooperation, with the help of the Americans and the diligent efforts of his team, Flores discovered that a shell company that House had set up in the islands of Seychelles and Grenadine owned the Club Azule in Puerto Bella. House funneled money from his overseas accounts to pay for human trafficking. The trafficking of Eastern European women to work in his clubs. It was an elaborate scheme that involved various players who were all connected to one another.

Marco was right. Flores needed to secure a confession from Daniel Abercrombie, who languished in jail, unable to secure the substantial bond that had been set for him. A confession that would tie him to House. They held Abercrombie on charges of jewelry smuggling, money laundering, and wire fraud. Flores believed he'd also murdered Rubio. He wanted to connect all the dots and solve all three cases. Finally, the Chief would be satisfied. Flores arranged for an interview with Abercrombie. Marco had suggested that they put off questioning him for a while until they gathered more hard evidence.

"I understand the pressure you're under to solve these cases, but I think we should wait so we can tie in the murders and get both of them," Marco said.

"Abercrombie's been in that prison for a while now. I suspect he wants to be released. I have enough evidence to put him away for years on jewelry smuggling charges. My guess is he'll cooperate to reduce his sentence," Flores said.

"That might leave Rubio or Elaina's murder unsolved. What incentive would Abercrombie have to confess to their killings at this stage?" Marco asked.

"He knows it will add several years to his sentence if he's convicted of murder," Flores said.

"I'll bet he'd be willing to take a gamble that you can't pin murder charges on him. He has excellent, high-priced lawyers. They'll advise him not to take the deal. They'll try to get a reduced sentence and no deportation. House's lawyers will get the whole thing thrown out. It's risky," Marco said.

"Thanks for your opinion, but I think I can handle this," Flores said.

Marco threw up his hands. "Okay, if you know what you're doing," he said.

Marco's swashbuckling good looks, dark hair, piercing eyes, and charm were no match for Flores's seriousness and intellectual prowess. Flores had been a detective for years. He knew how to handle suspects. He knew how to negotiate.

"I do," Flores said.

Flores summoned Abercrombie to the interrogation room.

Abercrombie sat slouched at the table. His eyes puffy and swollen, it looked as if he hadn't slept for days. Seated next to Abercrombie was a lawyer with a moustache wearing a dark Manolo Blahnik suit.

"I told you I had nothing to say to you. You're wasting your time," Abercrombie said.

His lawyer touched his arm. "Let him speak."

Abercrombie jerked his arm away.

"You might want to listen to what I have to say. We have new information," Flores said.

Abercrombie's eyes grew wide. "What kind of information?"

"Financial information. We've obtained copies of your bank statements, all of them, including the hidden ones," Flores said.

"I don't know what you're talking about," Abercrombie said.

Flores placed a stack of papers on the table. Abercrombie's lawyer grabbed the papers and flicked through them.

"We think you're working for Senor House," Flores said.

"Who? I don't have a house," Abercrombie said, snickering at his own joke.

"Funny guy, huh? Thomas House, Kijamba's former manager, we know you work for him," Flores said.

"Don't answer that," Abercrombie's lawyer said.

Abercrombie rolled his eyes. "I'm an independent jewelry dealer. How many times do I have to tell you? I may have sold him jewelry. That doesn't mean I work for him," he said.

"I advised you not to answer," his attorney said.

Abercrombie turned up his nose and shrugged.

"Here's the bottom line, Senor Abercrombie. We've located the nine different burner cell phones you were using under different names. It's only a matter of time until we find out you've been talking to House. We have enough to charge you right now for the smuggling, which is several years in prison, then deportation. After which, you'll stand trial in Scotland. They're pretty upset about the stolen garnets. We think you were also involved in the killing of Elaina and Dr Rubio. If we tack on those charges, you're looking at your whole life behind bars. You won't be getting out except in a box. Your only hope is to confess and cooperate with us."

Abercrombie thundered. "You're crazy, I didn't kill anyone. You're talking nonsense."

Abercrombie's lawyer gestured with the index finger of a well-manicured nail, for Abercrombie to move in closer. The lawyer whispered to his client. It sounded like a fly buzzing around the room. Flores tapped his pen on the table.

When they stopped whispering, the attorney spoke. "What are you offering?" he asked.

Flores stopped tapping his pen and narrowed his eyes. "Your client must admit to his involvement in the murders and tell us everything he knows about Thomas House. We'll ask for a reduced sentence for smuggling and non-deportation. He'll only be charged as an accessory to the murders."

"Hmph, but I didn't kill anyone," said Abercrombie.

"You don't have any evidence my client was involved in any murders. It's all speculation," Abercrombie's lawyer said.

"We can tie him to Rubio since he paid the tuition for Elaina and Ginka," Flores said.

Abercrombie and the lawyer spoke to one another again.

After a few minutes, the lawyer sat straight up in the metal chair. "He admits he paid their tuition. That doesn't mean he had anything to do with murder. In fact, it shows he's a good guy. There's nothing here. You're bluffing," he said, holding up and waving the papers Flores had put on the desk. "Get back to us when you have some real evidence. My client admits to nothing. Unless you have something concrete to show us, we have nothing more to discuss," he said. The lawyer rose from the table and tripped over his chair. Abercrombie snarled at him.

Flores suppressed a laugh. At least he got a laugh out of it. They'd called his bluff. Abercrombie wouldn't confess to involvement with the murders and implicate Thomas House. It hadn't worked. "We definitely have enough evidence of smuggling, so he's going to jail either way," Flores said.

"Smuggling isn't murder. No deal," his lawyer said, his moustache twitching.

Abercrombie glowered at Flores as Detective DeLuca grabbed his arms.

She escorted Abercrombie back to his cell, followed by his lawyer, who strutted beside him.

Flores remained staring at the interrogation table. He'd have to admit that arrogant Marco was right yet again.

Chapter Forty-Seven

Marco cooked when he felt stressed, a habit he'd gotten from his grandmother, Jaddah. Cooking was a balm for the soul, she'd said. Marco's soul needed soothing. He hadn't been sleeping well. He felt tired and worried. Belen had been back for over a week from her extended holiday, but he still hadn't told her the whole story about Amira, including how many times he'd seen her while Belen was gone and how quickly Amira had to leave the country. The guilt weighed on him like a thirty-pound weight on his chest, but Belen had seemed so happy to be home. He didn't want to upset her.

He'd decided to make a special meal for them of freshly caught sea bass. The kind his dad used to catch and sell to local restaurants on the port. He smothered the fish with salt, aciete, (olive oil), and límon. He added a bit of butter in the end, a trick on a recipe he'd recently seen. He accompanied the fish with patatas Andalućian, and spinach with raisins, a dish he inherited from his grandmother and one of Belen's favorites. He opened a fresh bottle of Cava to celebrate their reunion. He'd picked up some sweet tarts for after the meal.

"You spoil me," Belen said.

"That's my aim. I don't want you to leave again," Marco said.

After dinner, they went for a walk on La Playa. They held hands on the deserted beach as tourist season had just ended. The brown sand felt warm to their toes. Across the way, the Rock of Gibraltar looked as if it floated toward them. Belen caught Marco up on events with her family. Her niece had been born while she was there, and her parents were fawning over their first grandchild. Marco told her about the case and Catherine Taylor, the lecherous cougar from Barcelona as he nicknamed her. He never got the courage to mention Amira. He just couldn't spoil things.

The next day, Marco went straight to the office and asked Eva to make coffee. He felt eager to get back to work. As Eva teetered in moments later with a steaming mug, Flores appeared in her shadow, nearly running into her.

"Detective, how can I help you?" Marco asked.

Flores fumbled and apologized for almost knocking Eva over. "Sorry, Eva. Marco, I came to tell you that you were right. I hate to admit it," he said as he wiped the sweat from his brow. It was early in the day, yet the sun was already beaming.

"What do you mean?" Marco asked, "Right about what?"

Flores explained that he hadn't been able to get Abercrombie to confess to the murders. He needed Marco's help. "I've been ordered to pull everyone in to solve these cases. The Chief is furious about these three still unsolved murders. He had to hold a press conference this morning to show the department wasn't completely incompetent," Flores said. "We've got to uncover any unturned stones, find anything we missed."

"I think we should go back to the beginning and look at some things again now that we have more information," Marco said.

He thought specifically of Idan, the smuggled immigrant who worked at Club Azule, whom they'd first detained for Elaina's murder. Now they knew Idan was a victim of Daniel and House's clandestine operation. Marco had always suspected Idan had known more than he'd told the police. Idan had recovered from his injuries and was now back working at an office building as a cleaner. "Idan, the immigrant from the club, might be more willing to open up now that he's been cleared of the charges and he's away from that club. He might talk to me," Marco said.

"It's worth a shot. You go and talk to him. In the meantime, I'm going to speak to Ginka Kovalenko again. I keep thinking she's the key to unlocking these murders," Flores said.

Chapter Forty-Eight

Marco found Idan mopping the floor at his new establishment. He rested the mop against the wall when Marco approached him. "I need to ask you a few more questions, Idan," Marco said. He spoke to him in Arabic.

"Talking to the police almost got me killed," Idan said.

"I know, and I'm sorry about that. I'm glad you're okay, but I'm not the police. If we are going to find the people who attacked you, I'm going to need your help," Marco said.

Idan picked up the mop and went back to work.

"The day Elaina died, did you see or hear anything else unusual at the club that you haven't told me or the police about?" Marco asked.

"I've told you everything I know," Idan said.

"Are you sure? It's very important," Marco said.

Idan rested the mop and thought for a moment.

"You can trust me, Idan. I'm trying to find out who killed your friend, Elaina, and who attacked you."

Idan dipped the mop into the soapy water. He stared at Marco but didn't speak for some time. Marco noticed the scars on Idan's brown arms from the attack hadn't completely healed.

"I don't want to get deported. I'm scared. I need to stay away from the police. I'm finally settled here. I can't go back to Tunisia," he said.

"I'll make sure you aren't deported. I'll protect you," Marco said, hoping he could keep his promise.

Idan slapped more suds down on the floor. He swung the mop, working in a circular motion, dissolving the suds and leaving a shiny, wet wood.

"I don't know anything else."

Marco sensed this wasn't true. "Come on. You said Elaina was your friend, wasn't she?"

Idan clutched the mop handle. "Yes, I liked her a lot. She was the only one at that club who was kind to me."

"Well then, if you cared about her, you have to tell me what you heard or saw. Her killer is still out there."

"They'll kill me too next time if they find out I talked to you again," Idan said. He squeezed the water from the mop into the bucket.

"I told you I'll do all I can to protect you. If we catch them and put them behind bars, they'll no longer be a threat to you. You won't have to pay them anymore," Marco said.

Marco hoped he had gotten to Idan with the idea that he would no longer have to pay his smuggler captors.

Idan rested his chin on the mop handle and thought. After a moment, he responded. "Okay, I did hear something that day while I was cleaning that I didn't mention. Elaina was having a big argument in the back with a man with a funny accent. I don't usually go back there to clean when the girls are there, as they may be changing. I thought one of the girls might be in trouble, so I walked back to the dressing room to see what was going on."

"What kind of accent? Did you see who it was?" Marco asked.

Idan shook his head. "I couldn't see him; he was behind the door. He was yelling at Elaina. He sounded like one of those British people but different. I couldn't understand everything he said. I heard him say something about tuition and stop worrying. He said he was dealing with the school and everything would be sorted out. That's all I heard, then I left."

"Are you sure that's all you heard?" Marco asked.

"Yes, si, that was all. I hurried back to my cleaning before anyone saw me. You will protect me, right?"

"I'll do all I can for you, Idan. Gracias for the information."

Idan looked down and continued to mop. "Okay, I hope so," he said.

Chapter Forty-Nine

Walking along the paseo of Puerto Bella, Marco watched the yachts swaying in unison in the blue-green water. He stopped and looked over at the Ellington bar. The bar, which had outside seating that faced the sea, was a popular spot, the first stop for many, before going on to nightclubs like Club Azule that stayed open all night. Marco wondered if anyone from the bar could shed any new light. He decided to go in and speak to the staff. The bar was empty on the inside as most patrons sat outside enjoying the sun. He ordered a beer, spoke to the bar staff, and asked if anyone recalled seeing a red-haired Scottish man at the bar on the day of the murder at Club Azule.

One of the waiters, a young British man, answered. "Yeah, I told the police about an incident we had that day. We had a couple of unruly patrons that we had to throw out of the bar. It was early in the afternoon. The ringleader was a red-headed guy with an Irish or Scottish accent. He got real loud and belligerent, which was odd, because he didn't seem that drunk. Then he started yelling at the women in the bar, calling them all hookers and whores. That's when I had to ask him to leave," the waiter said.

"Did you see where he went after you asked him to leave?" Marco asked.

The waiter pointed towards the paseo. "He headed down the pier. I watched to make sure he didn't come back here. I didn't want him offending my customers."

"Do you remember what time that was?"

"It was sometime in the late afternoon because I had just started my shift. I start at four," the waiter said.

Chapter Fifty

Flores banged on the door of Ginka Kovalenko's apartment. One of the other women who lived there answered. She wore a white bathrobe and slippers. Her robe was partially opened, exposing her ample breasts. Flores looked down and took her cue to enter the apartment. He walked to the center of the living room and waited.

"Ginka!" she yelled. "Someone's here to talk to you."

"Who is it?" Ginka asked.

"Some man," the woman said. The woman walked away unconcerned about her exposure to a stranger.

Ginka emerged moments later. She gestured for Flores to sit down. "What is it now, Detective? I'm starting to think you have a crush."

Flores blushed. "I need you to tell me everything you know about Daniel Abercrombie."

"I've told you everything," she said.

Flores shook his head. "No, not everything. I know Daniel's connected to the club. He's more than a mere patron. If you help me now, I may be able to help keep you from being charged as an accessory."

"Accessory? What are you talking about?" she asked.

"I'm talking about murder. If we find out you knew anything you're not telling us and we charge Daniel with murder, you'll be charged as an accessory," Flores said.

"I didn't murder anyone."

Flores shrugged his shoulders. "You were an accessory if you helped him. If you tell me everything. I'll speak to the prosecutor and recommend that you not be charged."

Ginka sighed. "Will I be deported?"

"I can't answer that. It depends on the prosecutor. If you don't cooperate, you'll go to prison and then be deported for sure. This way, you have a chance at least."

Her face fell. "I'm dead either way. I guess I don't have a choice," she said.

"No, not really. Tell me how Daniel Abercrombie is tied to the Club Azule?" Flores asked.

Ginka slumped onto the couch. "He runs the club. Hassan did the schedule and managed everything, but Daniel ran the place behind the scenes."

"What do you mean he ran the club?"

"I mean, he was in charge. All the money we made, including tips, went to him. He'd started demanding more money from us, and he started making us see more private clients. He said we had to start paying back our tuition," she said.

Ginka said that Elaina had started to rebel. She and Hassan fought about it. "I told her not to argue with him. That he was dangerous. I told her we could come up with a plan."

One day, Elaina confessed to Ginka that she and Dr. Rubio, the university administrator, were in love. She said they were going to get married, but Daniel objected. They'd decided to run away together."

"Elaina was engaged to Dr. Rubio?"

"Yeah, he bought her a big ring, three karats. She was sad she couldn't wear it in public."

"How did Abercrombie find out about Elaina and Dr. Rubio?" Flores asked.

"I don't know, for sure." She spoke in a low voice as if she was afraid of being overheard. "I think our other roommate may have heard her on the phone talking to Rubio and told Abercrombie. We're not really friends with her, and I don't trust her."

"Were you jealous of Elaina since she was about to get out?" Flores asked.

"No, I was happy for her. She said she'd find someone to introduce me to, one of Senor Rubio's friends," she said.

"Did you ever hear Abercrombie threaten Elaina?" Flores asked.

"Daniel came to the club one day. I heard him yelling at Elaina. He was furious. He said Dr. Rubio was taking his money away, and the boss wouldn't tolerate it. He told Elaina that she and Dr. Rubio had better stop what they were doing or else."

"Who's the boss, and why didn't you tell us this before?" Flores asked.

"I don't know who he was talking about. Danny said he'd kill me if I told you about him."

"It was Danny that was here that day I came to see you, not Paco, wasn't it?"

She picked up the cushion on the couch and clutched it in her arms. "Yeah, he wanted to know what I knew. He told me I'd better not say anything to the police, or I'd end up like Elaina. That's why I said it was Paco when you asked," she said.

Chapter Fifty-One

Admitting one's mistakes can lead to spiritual cleansing, Flores told himself. He'd made a mistake. It'd been too soon to pressure Abercrombie. Now, the time felt right. Ginka had tied him to the murders. He summoned Abercrombie. This time, he invited Marco to participate. When Abercrombie entered the small gray interrogation room, he smelled as if he hadn't bathed for weeks. The entire room took on a musty odor.

His lawyer sat beside him, this time wearing a blue suit. "We told you last time my client doesn't agree to anything," his lawyer said.

"We've got some new information you'll be interested in," Flores said.

The lawyer shifted in his chair. "What kind of new information?"

"A witness has come forth who heard your client arguing with Elaina that day?"

Abercrombie twiddled his thumbs and stared at the table.

"A server at the Ellington Bar also remembers him coming in drunk and yelling at women that day. The server says Daniel had to be escorted out of the bar and that he saw him walk towards the Club Azule. That places him at the scene. It wouldn't take a genius to put it all together," Flores said.

"These witnesses appeared suddenly like magic?" the lawyer asked.

"They came to our attention through the investigation," Flores said.

Abercrombie looked across the table and glared at Marco. "Where's Amira? She still hasn't been to see me?"

"She's gone," Marco said. "You won't be seeing her again."

Flores interrupted. "Our witness says you were upset about Elaina's engagement to Dr. Rubio. That you yelled at her and threatened her if she didn't do what you wanted."

"I never threatened that hooker," he scowled.

"Our witness says you did."

Flores turned his attention to Daniel's lawyer.

The lawyer leaned over to speak to Abercrombie. Flores snapped off the recording device. Marco and Flores played with their respective pens while Daniel and his lawyer conferred.

"We don't have much time," Flores said, pointing at his watch.

The lawyer rustled the papers in front of him. "My client will consider giving you information. What are you prepared to offer?" Abercrombie's lawyer asked.

"I'll talk to the prosecutor about 20 years instead of the customary thirty-year sentence permanente, for the smuggling, and second-degree murder for Elaina and Dr. Rubio," Flores said.

"What about extradition?" his lawyer asked.

"We can't guarantee what the Scottish government will do, but we'll talk to them to negotiate if he pleas."

Flores turned his attention to Abercrombie. "Senior, we need to know everything about your relationship with Thomas House."

Abercrombie slumped back in his chair as if defeated. He and his lawyer whispered again. Flores tapped on the table.

"Perhaps we can negotiate," the lawyer said.

Abercrombie rolled his eyes. "Fine, what do you want to know?" He mumbled under his breath, "I hate you bastards."

"Shhh, just tell them what you know," his lawyer said.

"I ran into financial problems in my business. I met Thomas House at the Club Azule when I came over from Scotland on a golf trip. At first, it fascinated me to meet the manager of the famous Kijamba. House and I became friends, and he bailed me out of debt. I owed him. House told me there was a lot of money to be made selling my Scottish gems overseas. That I could pay him back by making him a partner in my business. He said he had a friend who could polish the jewels, so they looked like pigeon blood rubies. He already had a whole operation going with Hassan, smuggling in Eastern European women to dance at the club. We worked it so I'd manage the women, pay their tuition so they'd look legit, and I'd get them to sell my jewelry to their clients, and we'd split the profits," Abercrombie said.

Flores tsked. "Money off the backs of women like Ginka and Elaina," he said.

"It worked okay until Elaina threatened to ruin everything, saying she intended to marry Dr. Rubio," Abercrombie said.

"Elaina threatened to turn you in to the police, didn't she?" Marco asked.

Abercrombie shifted in his chair. "Yes, that bitch was going to ruin everything. She threatened to tell Amira I was having an affair with Ginka, if I didn't leave her alone and let her marry Dr. Rubio."

"Were you having an affair with Senorita Kovalenko?" Marco asked.

"I slept with that hooker, so what. It didn't mean anything. Amira would've been mad, though."

Flores shook his head in disgust. He hated men who showed no respect for women. Thinking of women only as objects to sell like property was the lowest form of life he could think of. He hoped Abercrombie would be put away for many years. He glanced over at Marco, who seethed. He looked as if he wanted to nail Abercrombie to the wall. "You went to the club to threaten her, didn't you?" Flores asked.

Abercrombie nodded his head. "I tried to be reasonable. I tried to tell her it was too dangerous for her to marry him. She refused to listen. She said Rubio was paying off her debt to the smugglers and paying for her schooling. She was going to start a new life."

"You couldn't have that," Marco said.

Abercrombie wriggled in his chair. As criminals often did when Marco focused his piercing eyes on them. "It was an accident. The gun just went off. The next thing I knew, she was lying there surrounded by all that blood. All I could think was to get out of there."

"What did you do with the gun?" Flores asked.

"I tossed it in the sea. What else could I do?"

"And Dr. Rubio, was that another *accident*?" Flores asked.

"House handled that himself. I tried to warn Rubio. I called him that night. He said he'd serve his time, then retire and make a fresh start with Elaina. The next day I heard on the news that he was dead." Abercrombie turned to Marco. "Where's Amira? I was going to ask her to marry me before all of this," he said, raising his hands to display the handcuffs. "I love her. She's the reason I did all this, so she'd have everything. I can't believe she left me."

Marco squinted his eyes and stared at Abercrombie. "You did it because you were greedy and wanted money. You tried to bring Amira down with you. It was *you* sending me threatening notes, wasn't it?"

Abercrombie nodded his head. "I knew you'd been seeing Amira."

Flores looked at them both, puzzled. "You also attacked that young immigrant in the club, didn't you, Senor Abercrombie?"

"That was Ahmed," Abercrombie said

"Then you killed Ahmed," Marco said.

Abercrombie sat with his head in his hands and didn't answer.

Chapter Fifty-Two

As day broke, the sky appeared purple and blue like an impressionist watercolor painting. Ninja-looking figures dressed in black with the red berets surrounded the parameters of one of the most opulent villas in La Cala de Mijas, a quiet little town a few miles from Vivirrambla. Flores, dressed like the rest of the Malaga police in all black with a bulletproof vest, accompanied the team. Marco stood close by in civilian clothes. The house was still. Everyone was sleeping. When the sun broke, the team of police first awakened House's wife when they burst through the front door, pointing guns. House tried to escape through an open window. He ran towards the woods behind his Olympic-sized pool. He was no match for the stealthy police, who tackled him and handcuffed him on the patio. The metal from the cuffs reflected in the crystal blue chlorine water.

House stood in his pajama bottoms at the base of his elaborate pool. "You're making a big mistake. "I'll see to it you're off the police force before we get downtown," he shouted.

Two junior officers jerked his arms behind his back and advised him not to try to escape again. House instructed his wife to call their family lawyer, pronto. The noise woke up his children, who stood by the pool, gaping, as the Malaga police carted their father away. They didn't utter a word at the sight of their dad's head being pushed into the back of the car, which took off with blaring sirens.

Flores worried how Shada would react to finding out that the man she'd trusted after the tragic death of her husband was a criminal and a smuggler.

He wished he could've warned her beforehand, but to avoid leakage, the operation demanded secrecy.

After the raid, Flores went home to shower, tell his wife what had happened, and that he'd be gone the rest of the day. She said she'd been worried when she'd awakened in the middle of the night, and he wasn't in bed. She made him a full breakfast and a cup of steaming café con leche while he showered and changed. He returned to the kitchen with wet hair, his cowlick sticking up, and turned on the television while he ate. The Chief was fielding questions from reporters about the arrest of music legend, Kijamba's manager. Flores appeared on camera directing his officers as they stuffed a scared-looking House into the police car.

When he got to the station, it was chaos. Reporters surrounded the building, trying to get a story. Flores instructed his men to keep them out.

Later that afternoon, officers brought House to the same interrogation room where Abercrombie had been questioned. He looked pale and shriveled in his prison garb, like a middle-aged old man trying to hang on to his youth; he was the "Picture of Dorian Gray." A short, middle-aged fancy-dressed lawyer accompanied him. Flores explained to House the nature of the interrogation involving several alleged crimes, including murder. House's lawyer protested the arrest, demanding his immediate release, claiming that he was being falsely imprisoned.

"Do you know who this is? We'll sue you for millions. You'll never work again; Senor House is a very important person," the lawyer shouted.

Once House's lawyer finished his screed, Flores placed papers on the table in front of them, which House's lawyer snatched off the table.

"Senior House, we have evidence you are involved in the international smuggling of jewels, selling fake jewels as rubies in Spain, and human trafficking. We also believe that you are complicit in the murder of Dr. Miguel Rubio," Flores said.

The lawyer rested a gold prince-nez on the bridge of his nose and examined the paperwork. "You've got nothing here. This is just a bunch of speculation," the lawyer said.

"We've already spoken to Daniel Abercrombie; he's confessed and implicated your client," Flores said.

"My client doesn't know who that is," his lawyer said.

"I've never heard of him," House said.

"Abercrombie informed us you are the true owner of Club Azule. He accused you of being responsible for everything, including the illegal trafficking of women from Eastern Europe. He claims that you killed Dr. Rubio," Flores said.

"This Abercrombie person has confused me with someone else. Maybe he's crazy."

Flores pulled out more papers from a manila folder and spread them out on the table.

House's lawyer frowned and peeped over the top of his glasses at the new documents. "This is all speculation," the attorney said after he rifled through them.

"Our prosecutors say these documents show evidence of continued criminal activity by your client," Flores said.

"These documents merely show he had a lot of business interests, just like a lot of wealthy people," his lawyer said.

"I'm afraid they show more than that. They show tax avoidance and hidden money on the islands and around the world," Flores said. He directed the lawyer to a specific set of papers. "These documents prove your client is the owner of the nightclub Club Azule. Did Kijamba find out about all your crooked dealings? Is that why you killed him?" Flores asked.

Dropping all pretense of the class and elegance he'd worked so hard to show, House raised his arm and lunged forward across the table. A skirmish followed, which nearly got out of hand until the prison guards and Detective Deluca subdued House.

"If you try that again, Senor House, we'll send you immediately to solitary confinement," Detective DeLuca said.

House jerked his arm away from Detective DeLuca. "How dare you talk to me like that? I would never have killed Kijamba. He was my friend. I wasn't even in Vivirrambla that day."

CHAPTER FIFTY-TWO

"Oh yeah. Where were you? Flores asked.

House ran his fingers through his hair and settled back onto his chair. "I was out of town looking at new homes."

"I see," Flores said.

"My family wants to move. We've been looking at houses. They like Fuengirola. Look, you can ask my real estate agent. I was with her the whole day. I told Kijamba I couldn't make the video shoot. I rushed back to Vivirrambla as soon as I heard the news on the radio."

Flores pulled out his notebook. "Who is this real estate agent?"

"Her name is Isabel Boer," House said.

"Isabel, who?" Flores asked.

"Isabel Boer," House said. "She's Dutch."

"As you can see, my client was nowhere near the bullring when Kijamba was killed," said the lawyer.

"What about Dr. Rubio? I know you murdered Dr. Rubio because he threatened to turn you in and confess to the human trafficking operation," Flores said.

"My client doesn't admit to anything," his lawyer said.

Chapter Fifty-Three

The town of Fuengirola sparkled with the glow of the Christmas season. White lights wrapped around the trees that lined the streets. Colorful ornaments hung from lampposts and buildings. Marco always liked the town this time of year. He parked in a lot near the train station, which stood on the edge of town, and walked past pastry shops with Three Kings statutes and holiday treats in the window. He considered buying a pastry, but decided he needed to watch his intake. His stomach was becoming flabby. Marco searched for the address of Isabel Boer's real estate office. He stopped in front of what looked like a home. A young woman with thick long, curly, raven-colored hair and porcelain skin greeted him when he opened the door.

"Come in," she said.

"Thank you for agreeing to meet with me," Marco said.

She wore a light blue flowing shirt and black pants set against black heels. Her large brown eyes were lively and danced. She gestured for Marco to sit in the chair by her desk. The room, filled with pamphlets and pictures of houses, smelled of pine from the Christmas tree in the corner.

"Would you like something to drink?" Isabel asked.

"No thanks, I won't take up much of your time," Marco said.

"How can I help you?" she asked.

Marco pulled up the calendar on his iPad with some dates circled and showed it to her.

"I need to know if you showed Senor Thomas House, an American businessman, any properties on any of these dates."

She perused the calendar. "Yes, I spent two days showing him properties. He was a demanding customer. I had to show him everything in town. His wife wanted a certain kitchen. He wanted tennis courts and a pool, the bedrooms had to be large enough, and the master bedroom had to have a walk-in closet. He just recently put a bid in on a house near Simon Cowell's estate."

"How did you meet Senor House?" Marco asked. "I'm sorry to have to ask you this but, were you only his real estate agent?"

She blushed and tossed her great mass of hair over her shoulders. "Oh yes, he came on to me, but I told him I'm in a relationship and I wasn't interested. I thought he was going to take away the listing. I didn't feel comfortable with him at first, but it was too big of a commission to give up. We saw several houses in one day. The next day I had to get up early to show him more houses. I was *ex...hausted*. We didn't finish until late in the evening. I was going to contact him tomorrow to follow up on his bid," she said.

"He's tied up right now," Marco said. "He won't be buying any property in the near future.

Isabel scrunched her face. "Oh, so I should re-list the property?" she asked.

"Yes, he won't be available anytime soon," Marco said.

Chapter Fifty-Four

Public pressure to solve Kijamba's murder, already intense, had increased with the arrest of House. Newspapers ran stories each day that talked about the ineptness of the Malaga police force. They should send the case to Madrid, one editorial said. The Chief told Flores that if the cases weren't solved in the next two weeks, he'd hand them over to another officer.

"We've gone over everything several times and re-examined all the evidence," Flores said.

"I think we need to take another look at the murder weapon to see if there's a clue we missed or anything. I don't think we really looked at it. I'll go talk to the coroner," Marco said.

"Fine, whatever you think might help. I'm desperate to do anything," Flores said.

The coroner, Javier Bortello, sat on a black stool, as stark as the room, reading a pamphlet. When Marco approached, Bortello pulled his glasses up over the bald spot on the top of his head and greeted Marco with his usual contempt. "What can I do for you now?" Bortello asked.

"It's about Kijamba's murder."

"Yeah, I figured. The police are getting some bad press for not solving that one," Bortello said.

"You told me that the murder weapon was a small dart in Kijamba's ear. Do you still have that dart?" Marco asked.

"I think so. I gave it to the police, but they sent it back," Bortello said.

Bortello got up and walked over to a long metal structure and opened one of the drawers, containing bodies. He pulled out a plastic bag labeled T. Smith and handed it to Marco.

"This is it."

"Can I borrow this?" Marco asked.

"I guess if you make sure you return it to me. I can't have evidence getting lost. I'd get all the blame for it. I need Flores to sign off on it. By the way, we examined that residue you found on the bed when we first found Kijamba. It was Botox. We didn't pay any attention at first because all the stars use Botox, but I thought I'd let you know."

Marco grabbed the bag from the coroner. "Hmmm, that's interesting. Thanks for the information. I'll make sure this is returned intact. Gracias, Javier."

Bortello grunted. He pulled his reading glasses down over his eyes and went back to what he'd been doing. Marco scuttled out of the room. He always hurried to escape the smells of death and chemicals. No wonder Bortello was always grumpy. Anyone would be if they had to smell that all day.

Marco walked back from the hospital to his office. He put on a pair of latex gloves and opened the baggie he'd gotten from Bortello. It contained a silver dart. He held it up to the light. He marveled that such a small object could have killed such a big presence in the world. A tiny bit of residue of poison remained on the dart, which was labeled EVIDENCE DO NOT TOUCH. Marco examined the bag closely, turning it back and forth, careful not to touch the poison. He noticed small markings etched onto the dart. He pulled a magnifying glass that he occasionally used from a closet in his office. He deciphered the name Cabela's in tiny letters on the head of the object.

He typed Cabela's in his search engine. The results revealed an American company that sold darts, dart guns, and other hiking and hunting materials.

Marco had used a blowgun once or twice when he and his father took trips to the mountains of Carmena, so he wasn't unfamiliar with them. Marco's father would sometimes shoot rabbits, which he'd offer for sale as a special, along with his daily catch of fish to the local restaurants. Marco walked over to the Ayuntamiento, a few blocks away in the Casca Antiqua, Old Town, and spoke to his contact in records, an older woman who wore thick glasses. She always assisted him when he needed information. He asked her how to obtain import and export records of shipments to Spain from the Cabela's company within the last year. She directed him to the Registrar of the Secretariat of Commerce. Marco spoke to the manager of international shipping, who was surprisingly cooperative once he learned it related to Kijamba's death.

"That pop singer's death hit everyone hard. I hope you find the killer," the manager said.

The Registrar said that most of the imports from Cabela's were to companies that sponsored gaming competitions, though a few gun and dart sets had been sold to individual customers. He handed Marco a printout depicting imports and exports of products over the past year. Marco thanked the manager and took the list into a private room where he could review it. Halfway through, he noticed that one of the individual purchasers of the products listed was named Jacobs, C Jacobs…Bingo. Cipriano Jacobs, the blues singer, Kijamba's best friend.

Chapter Fifty-Five

Flores arose at four o'clock in the morning and grabbed a thermos of coffee. His short brown hair stood on end. He didn't have time to use his usual gels for the unruly cowlicks. They were bringing Cipriano Jacobs in for questioning. Flores was anxious to hear what he had to say. He hoped he'd finally found Kijamba's murderer. Flores finished dressing and rendezvoused with his team. At daybreak, as the moon disappeared to take her nap, they banged on Cipriano's door. Cipi appeared wearing shorts and flip-flops as if he'd been sleeping on a beach in Jamaica. His partially opened pajama top revealed gray chest hair.

He sounded groggy. "Who is it? What is it? What do you want?" he asked.

Flores shouted through the door. "Police, Senor Jacobs, open the door."

When Jacobs finally let them in, Flores and his officers stormed into the living room.

"Get dressed. You need to come with us," Flores said.

Cipi's eyes widened, and he panted for breath. "Why? Am I under arrest?" he asked.

"Not yet, but we strongly suggest you come and talk to us," Flores said.

A few minutes later, Cipi emerged from the bedroom in jeans and a bright floral shirt. He accompanied Flores to the station, where he was taken straight to the interrogation room.

When everyone was assembled, Flores clicked on the recording. "I'll get to the point. We have information that you purchased darts and shooting equipment from a company in America called Cabela's," he said.

Cipi grimaced as if in pain. "Yes, I've shopped at Cabela's for years. What's this about? You brought me here because I shop at Cabela's?"

"Why do you need these items? What exactly do you do with these darts and guns?" Flores asked.

"I shoot as a hobby. I belong to a shooting club here in Vivirrambla. We have a big competition once a year. I've won the trophy three times. Is there a problem? I still don't know why I'm here," Cipi said.

"Are you aware Kijamba was killed with a small dart, a dart that contained poison?" Flores asked.

Cipriano stared dumbfounded at Flores. "He what? I assure you it wasn't from one of my guns. Why would I want to kill Kijamba? He was one of my best friends."

Flores hunched his shoulders. "You tell us."

"I haven't even touched my guns since the last competition over a year ago. I keep them under lock and key unless I'm using them," Cipi said.

"My men are searching your house as we speak. Where do you keep the guns and darts?" Flores asked.

"I keep them locked up in the closet in front of a bedroom. Like I said I only use them for competition or practice," Jacobs said.

"We'll see," Flores said.

"You think I'd use one of my competition darts to kill, Kijamba? You're crazy," Cipi said.

"It's starting to look like you did," Flores said.

After more questioning, Detective DeLuca ushered Jacobs out of the room.

Flores was back in his office when he got the news. Officers had searched Jacobs's house. They'd found a blowgun and several boxes containing darts and other equipment organized in a cabinet near the bedroom. They were bringing it all back to the station to be marked as evidence.

Chapter Fifty-Six

Marco parked in front of Shada's manicured lawn. The air smelled of freshly cut grass. The grass was lush and green, even though it hadn't rained for months. Pink bougainvillea danced with roses and lilies in the front garden. Marco greeted the gardener working in the yard with a nod and knocked on the front door. A pretty maid, who blushed when she saw him, let Marco in and escorted him to the now-familiar sitting room. Shada greeted him. Her eyes were lined with black liner, and her eyelashes were long, yet none of these make-up attempts masked the look of weariness on her face. She invited Marco to take a seat.

"Can I get you anything? I've been so upset ever since Thomas was arrested. I haven't been eating. Kijamba trusted him for all those years, and he was running all these businesses right under our noses. I can't believe it," she said, shaking her head.

"You didn't know anything about his other businesses at all?" Marco asked.

Shada shook her head. "No of course not, we paid him enough to be quite well-off. It never occurred to me or Kijamba that he'd be doing anything illegal."

"Kijamba never mentioned any suspicions at all to you about House before he died?

"Nothing. I don't know if you know, but today's the twentieth anniversary of Kijamba's first hit record."

"I heard it on the radio," Marco said.

"I still can't get used to him being gone. I cry myself to sleep at night. I let House comfort me. I feel like a fool. You don't think he killed my husband, do you?"

"The police are doing all they can to find out who killed Kijamba. I need to ask you about Cipriano Jacobs. What was your husband's relationship to him?"

She fell back in her chair and flopped her arms beside her. Cipi? Why do you ask? They were close. He was like a brother to my husband. He taught Kijamba a lot about music. Cipi was trained by BB King and other greats. He plays classical blues and contemporary. He showed Kijamba how to appreciate the classical sound and to incorporate it into his songs. The critics said Kijamba's music became much more sophisticated because of Cipi. Don't tell me he's involved. I don't know how much more of this I can take."

"Do you think Cipi could have resented Kijamba for getting all the attention after all these years? Maybe he was upset his career wasn't going where he wanted?"

"No way. He was 1000% supportive of Kijamba," Shada said.

Did you ever hear of Cipi threatening anyone? Did he have a bad temper?" Marco asked.

"Cipi? No. He's a teddy bear."

"I'll be truthful. We've discovered that he purchased the type of dart that killed your husband from a company in America," Marco said.

She gasped. "This must be some kind of mistake. I don't care what you found. Cipi loved my husband. He'd *never* kill Kijamba."

"Did you take any pictures on your phone that day of the video shoot at the bull ring?" Marco asked.

"I took pictures, mostly of Kijamba," Shada said.

"Do you mind if I take your phone?" Marco asked.

"Sure. I gave it to the police when this first happened, but they sent it back to me."

Shada got up and went over to a modern glass coffee table and pulled a cell phone out of the drawer. She handed it to Marco. "Here's the phone I used that day. These are the last pictures of my husband."

"Thanks, I'll take good care of it. One more thing, did you see anyone pass anything to Kijamba during the video shoot?" Marco asked.

She paused for a moment, "No, I don't think so. What's going to happen to House? Will he go to prison? What about Cipi?"

"House is going to prison for a long time. At this point, we just have some questions for Cipi." Marco said. "Don't worry, we'll get to the bottom of it, Senora. If you think of anything else, please give me a call. I'll give you my card again," Marco said, handing her the card.

He felt sorry for Shada. He genuinely liked her. He hoped for her sake that Cipi was innocent.

"No one can come and claim ownership of my work. I am the creator of it, and it lives within me."

Prince

Chapter Fifty-Seven

arco believed Cipi's arrest was premature. He told Flores that he doubted that Cipi could have slipped a dart into Kijamba's ear as they knew the killer had to be in proximity to Kijamba. Cipi was a big man with large hands. The person who stuck the poisonous dart into Kijamba's ear that day had to be nimble and quick, neither of which described Cipi.

Flores remained unconvinced. "It was a good arrest. It was his dart gun, and he had motive. The prosecutor agrees with me. I'm going to bring him in again."

"I don't think he did it," Marco said.

"I go where the evidence takes me," Flores said.

They called in Cipi, who'd been booked on charges of murder, for questioning. The scene at the station was surreal. The uniformed officers in the building seemed torn between treating Cipi like a rockstar or a common criminal.

The guard sat him down in front of Marco and Flores. He looked even bigger in his prison attire. His braids hung to his shoulders. This time, Cipi had hired a lawyer.

Flores spoke into the recording device on the table beside him. "Senor Jacobs, we are here to talk to you about the murder of singer Kijamba, aka Terrence Smith, Jr."

Cipi pulled his chair up to the table. His eyes seemed to plead. "You've got the wrong person. I would never have killed Kijamba."

"During our investigation of you, we've discovered evidence that you owed some money, quite a lot of money, over thirty thousand Euros to Thomas House," Flores said.

Cipi looked down at the papers that had been put in front of him. He nodded. "I'm ashamed to say I have a gambling problem. I'm a recovering addict. I lost my wife and everything I own due to gambling. I've been clean for five years. I admit I still had some debt, but I've been paying it down."

"House financed your gambling debt, didn't he?" Flores asked.

Cipi nodded. "Yes, he gave me the money to pay it off. I've been paying the interest on that loan. I paid the loan off ages ago, but House charged me sixty percent interest on it. It'll take years to pay that back."

"Why didn't you get the money from Kijamba?" Flores asked.

Cipi looked down at the table. "I was too ashamed, and I didn't want Kijamba to know that I was in that much debt. That's why House charged so much interest. He threatened to tell Kijamba what a loser I was if I didn't pay him his exorbitant fee."

"House had been threatening to tell Kijamba about the money, hadn't he?" Flores asked.

Cipi looked down at the table. His voice sounded muffled, and he mumbled. "Yeah. He told me I'd better have his money in thirty days, or he'd tell Kijamba about my problem and make sure Kijamba got rid of me."

"Speak up, Senor Jacobs. We need to hear your voice on the recording. So, you'd have done anything to keep Kijamba from finding out," Flores said.

Marco looked over and rolled his eyes.

Cipi's counsel thundered, "Now, you wait one minute. He didn't say that."

Flores ignored the lawyer and kept going. "If Kijamba cut you off, you'd have no means of support. You'd be in debt and alone. You'd lose everything, wouldn't you?"

Cipi stared at Flores through his old, lined eyes, creased from too much partying and too much grief. "Kijamba would never do that to me. He'd have understood. I should have told him in the first place instead of going to House."

"The darts and dart gun in your closet implicate you in murder, Senor Jacobs," Flores said.

"I told you already. I play darts for recreation."

"Would anyone else have access to the closet where you kept the dart equipment?" Marco asked.

Cipi sighed and shook his head no. "I live alone."

"Does anyone visit you on a regular basis?" Marco asked.

Cipi thought for a moment. "Catherine was in town from Barcelona. We've been dating on and off for many years."

"Catherine Taylor?" Marco asked.

"Yeah, she came down a week before to celebrate Kijamba's video with me. We get together about once a month."

"You're dating her?" Marco asked.

Cipi looked at Marco and frowned. "We started seeing each other when I was having a tough time. I'd just gotten divorced. I was having some health problems. I had bad tinnitus, you know, and she sent me to a doctor who treated me with some Botox treatments in my ear. It helped a lot. We've been seeing each other since then. She comes down from Barcelona for the weekends, then she leaves. Neither of us wants more."

"Did she have access to your gun cabinet?" Marco asked.

"Yeah, I guess so, but Catherine, there's no way," Cipi said, shaking his head. "She'd never go near that closet. She hates weapons."

Marco and the police had all assumed Catherine had been in Barcelona. Now they knew she'd been in town when Kijamba was killed.

After the guards escorted Cipi back to his cell, Marco turned to Flores. "I wonder what Catherine Taylor was doing the day of the shoot?"

Marco walked back to his car and called Shada on his car phone. "I apologize for bothering you again, Senora. I need to ask you a question. How well do you know Catherine Taylor?"

"Catherine? She's a friend of ours. I've known her for a few years. Why?"

"Did she visit you the week Kijamba was killed?" Marco asked.

"Yes. She stayed with us for a few days. She went back and forth to Cipi's. She helped me with a party we had for Kijamba. Then after the party she went to Cipi's, they've been dating for years, although I don't think it's going anywhere. I told her she needs to stop waiting for him."

"Did she attend Kijamba's filming at the bullring?" Marco asked. He didn't remember seeing her, but then again, he had no reason to know who she was at the time.

"Of course," Shada said.

"Did she have any disagreements with you or Kijamba?" Marco asked.

Shada was silent for a time. "Now that I think about it, she had a few words with Kijamba a while back about the video, if I remember correctly. She'd been angry because Kijamba hadn't asked her to be one of the dancers. Kijamba told her he needed younger dancers. At first, she seemed upset. Then, after she talked to him, she told me she understood."

Marco wondered if she really understood.

Shada broke his train of thought. "By the way, I was going through my things and separating Kijamba's things to give away."

She paused.

"I know that it must be hard for you," Marco said.

"It is. Anyway, I was looking through my jewelry, and I noticed one of my bracelets was missing."

"Bracelet? Did you report it to the police?" Marco asked.

"No, I just noticed it. I guess I could've misplaced it with all that's going on. I have been a little absent-minded. Kijamba gave it to me for our anniversary."

"Do you know where Kijamba brought the bracelet?" Marco asked.

"Kijamba told me House had gotten it for him from a friend who sold jewelry. I rarely wore it."

"Can you describe the bracelet?" Marco asked.

"It has designs around the bracelet and a really nice ruby in the center."

Marco's ears perked. "Did you say the bracelet had a ruby in the center?"

"Yes, a gorgeous ruby, deep red color. Why do you ask?"

"Did you have it appraised?" Marco asked.

"We hadn't gotten around to it, but House said it was worth over one hundred thousand U.S. dollars. We insured it for a million," Shada said.

Marco didn't want to upset her further, but he felt he had to tell her the truth about Abercrombie and how the ruby was most likely a garnet worth considerably less than Kijamba had paid.

Her voice shook. Fake? My ruby is a fake?"

"Most likely. Hopefully, your husband only paid what it was worth," Marco said.

"That's it. I hope Thomas gets life. Why did you want to know about Catherine Taylor? Was she involved in all this? I don't have anyone I can trust."

"I know it seems that way, and I'm sorry. Regular procedure, the police are following up on all leads," Marco said.

Chapter Fifty-Eight

Seasons had passed, winter clematis bloomed, and time had moved on; yet they still had no suspect in jail for Kijamba's murder. Flores shook his head in disbelief when Marco told him the latest about the stolen bracelet.

"Catherine Taylor's name keeps coming up. Did you know she'd referred Cipi to a doctor for Botox treatments for tinnitus?" Marco asked.

"What does that have to do with anything?" Flores asked.

"I think it has everything to do with it. I'll talk to you later," Marco said, disconnecting the FaceTime call.

Marco had FaceTimed Flores to tell him about the bracelet while going for a walk. He hurried back to his office, turned on his computer, and began a search for more information on Botox.

Eva popped her head into his doorway. "Jefe, there's someone on the phone for you. I can barely hear them, but it sounds urgent."

Marco picked up the landline on his desk. He tried to decipher the whispered voice.

"Is this Marco?" The voice asked.

"Si, soy Marco? Dime. A quien es?"

The voice whispered lower so that it was barely audible. "It's me, Shada. You need to come over right away. Catherine Taylor is here, and she has a gun. She's holding one of my servants."

"Did you call the police?" Marco asked. He could hear her voice quiver.

"No, I called you first. I heard the noise from the bedroom and locked myself in the closet. I'm really scared," she said.

"You did the right thing, don't move. We'll be right there, don't unlock the door for anyone, and stay away from the windows."

"Hurry!"

Within minutes, police cars roared towards the Spanish Beverly Hills home. They pulled up in front of Shada's with a fanfare of noise and blazing lights. They surrounded the home and climbed to the roof of the building, guns aimed and ready. A woman with her hair pulled back tightly and in a bun pulled open the curtains. Flores directed the men and women to stand down unless he gave the order.

The woman showed herself through the window holding a long knife to another terrified-looking woman's throat. Then she dragged her hostage to the front door and opened it.

"Don't come in. If you do, Shada's dead," she said.

Marco whispered to Flores that it was Catherine Taylor and that the woman being held hostage wasn't Shada. She was one of the servants.

"Why is she saying it's Shada?" Flores asked.

"Leverage. She thinks we'll give in to her demands more if we think it's Shada. I talked to Shada. She's hiding upstairs in a closet. Don't let on that we know, or she might get angry and harm the hostage," Marco said.

The police commanded the woman to put the knife down and give herself up. There was no way she could get out of this, they told her. She dragged the woman back inside and slammed the door. She seemed confused as she told the police her demands. Flores popped one Altoid after another as they tried to negotiate. Soon, more law enforcement appeared, and Flores was handed a megaphone to demand that the woman surrender. Catherine continued to pace the floor, peering out of the curtains periodically with the hostage.

They reached a standstill after an hour. Flores handed the megaphone to Marco. "You try. You know her. Maybe she'll listen to you," he said.

Marco aimed the megaphone towards the window. "Catherine, this is Marco. You have to give up. There is no way out. The police aren't going to leave. If you want to tell your side of the story, you must come out and let her go."

"Marco, that good-looking gypsy detective?" she asked.

"Yes, it's me," Marco said.

"You shouldn't be here."

"Come out, I'll make sure you're taken care of and treated fairly. You can't hide in there forever. You can't hurt any more people."

Marco could feel the tension in the air as the officers looked through telescoping lenses with their fingers on the trigger. "Catherine, listen to me. You're surrounded. If you don't surrender, you won't come out of this alive. No one will ever know your side."

"I've done some bad things. No one will want to know my side," she said.

"I want to hear your side if you come out of there with your hands up. I promise I'll listen to you," Marco said.

"Do you promise to listen to me?" Catherine asked.

"Yes," Marco said. "But you must come out and let the hostage go."

The front door opened slowly, and the woman being held hostage was thrown into the street. Catherine emerged with her hands up. The scene moved rapidly as police rushed the house. Catherine Taylor, wearing navy blue linen pants and heels and a ruby and gold bracelet, was tackled to the ground by the officers. Marco entered the house and found Shada hiding upstairs in the closet in her bedroom. Black mascara ran down her face, and she was shaking. Marco took her hand and pulled her from the closet. She walked onto the front lawn, and just as they led, Catherine led away. She hugged Marco and cried.

Chapter Fifty-Nine

Once Catherine had been checked into the Malaga woman's security prison, Flores and Marco set up a time to speak to her. She glared at Marco when she entered the interrogation room. "You tricked me. You don't care about my side of the story."

"I'm here to listen. When I visited you in Barcelona, you were wearing Shada's bracelet, weren't you? You stole it from her house when you were there for the party," Marco said.

She shrugged. "So, what? I stole a bracelet. Big deal. That slut had Kijamba and everything she wanted in the world. Thomas bought that bracelet for me. He told me Kijamba saw it and loved it. So, he sold it to him to give to Shada. She was wearing my bracelet; can you believe it?"

"You pretended to be her friend, but you hated her, didn't you?" Marco asked.

Catherine sneered. "Why shouldn't I? She had it all: the money and the fame. She had Thomas wrapped around her little finger. He'd do anything she said. You see the way he fawned all over her. Did you know I tried to sell Kijamba one of my songs, and that witch intervened?"

"You write music?" Marco asked.

"Are you surprised? You thought all I could do was show my body and dance? I wrote one of the songs on his new video. Stupid me. I gave it to Cipi. Cipi was like Kijamba's dog. He obeyed Kijamba's every demand." She gestured with her hands in the shape of paws. "He gave Kijamba my song and said it was his."

"Did you kill Kijamba because of that?" Marco asked.

She looked over at the empty white concrete walls. "I didn't kill him," she said.

"I think you did," Marco said.

"I think you did, too," Flores said.

She sneered at Flores. "Who cares what you think?"

Catherine volunteered little in the two-hour interview. She'd been sedated and seemed dazed. Flores requested that the prison psychiatrist evaluate her.

"You may be right about this one. She's got some issues," Flores told Marco once the tape had been turned off. "If she's guilty, we'll need to tie her to the murder weapon."

"She must have stolen a dart from Cipi's apartment during the week she stayed with him. We have to find out where she got the poison and how she was able to shoot a dart in his ear without anyone seeing," Marco said.

The next day, Flores had good news for Marco. "The Barcelona police found some medical books in her house. They shipped them over to us. They also found several boxes of Botox, Clostridium Botulinum. The boxes have been sent to the lab for analysis," Flores said.

Flores and his team had also tracked down Catherine's doctor, who conveniently had offices in Vivirrambla. A man with a reputation for passing out Botox like a dentist handing out lollipops to children.

Chapter Sixty

Marco turned on more light as his office had gotten dark over the last few minutes. He made himself a decaf coffee. He'd been drinking too much coffee, and it kept him up at night. He opened his laptop and pushed the CD into it. He decided to re-review Kijamba's video shoot. He'd retrieved a copy of the raw cut from police evidence. The video showed Belen and the other dancers getting ready and lining up behind the singer. Marco smiled as he watched Belen, the grace of her movements and the passion in her eyes as she danced flamenco to hip/hop. The videographer then panned over to the bull ring entrance, where the famous bullfighter, Ricardo Ortiz, waited in the wings for his cue to enter to fight an imaginary bull.

Marco paused the CD. He noticed something; the image was faint. Marco zoomed in on it. A young Spanish boy handed an envelope to Kijamba. Kijamba opened it, read its contents, and threw it to the ground. Marco zoomed in further, he paused the video, and jotted down the name of a courier company, *"Delivery Espanol."*

He clicked off the video and contacted the company. He decided to go in person as it was near his office. When he got to the store and asked for the manager, everyone remembered the day because of Kijamba. The manager referred him to the courier who'd delivered the envelope to the bull ring that day, a young man in his early twenties.

"Oh, definitely, I remember it. Are you kidding me? I got to see Kijamba in person making a video," the animated courier told Marco. "It was one of the greatest days of my life."

"Do you remember who asked you to deliver the envelope?" Marco asked.

"Sure, a woman, one of those classy types. She looked about forty. I thought she must have been a friend of Kijamba's. She paid cash and gave me a big tip."

"Did she ask you to deliver it directly to Kijamba?" Marco asked.

"Yep, she said it was urgent and that Kijamba needed it for the video. So, I went right away and handed it right to him. Still can't believe I saw him up close."

"You went to the bull ring while the video was being shot?" Marco asked.

The courier nodded. "Yeah. I had a hard time getting in, too."

Marco thanked the courier. He returned to his office to resume watching the video shoot.

Right after the courier scene, a dark-haired woman stood in the background, shadowed by the bullfighter. He was glad that was still a part of the raw footage. The woman was slim with dark features, which were hard to distinguish. The same woman appeared again at the end of the video when everyone hugged and congratulated Kijamba. The woman hugged him and seemed to quickly whisper in his ear, at which point Kijamba swatted something away from his ear like flitting away an annoying fly. The exchange happened in a few seconds. Kijamba moved on to speak to other dancers. Marco was sure the woman was Catherine Taylor. She fit the profile, among the women at the video shoot.

Catherine Taylor had put Botox into a dart she'd stolen from Cipi's cabinet and stuck it into Kijamba's ear as she congratulated him. By the time Kijamba got ready for bed that evening, the Botox poison, which had been saturated on the dart, had spread through him until, finally, he suffered cardiac arrest.

They brought Catherine back into the interrogation room. Her elegant bun, which had been pinned to her head, now appeared as a black mass of wild hair. Her eyes had deep dark circles. The long lashes were gone. Without her makeup, she looked like an aging prune that had been in the sun too long. Marco did a double take as she entered the windowless room.

"What does the dynamic duo want now?" She asked once she was seated across from Marco and Flores. Detective DeLuca lurked over her, ready to pounce at any moment should Catherine make one false move.

"We want to know what happened, Catherine," Flores said.

"Here's your chance to tell your side of the story," Marco said.

Catherine shifted in her chair.

"You had a note delivered to Kijamba during the taping," Marco said. "What was in that note?"

Catherine looked down at the table.

"What was in that note, Ms. Taylor? I'm not in the mood for games," Flores said.

She folded her arms and stared at Flores. "I told Kijamba that I loved Thomas and that I wouldn't let Kijamba ruin his life."

"What did you mean by that? How was he going to ruin his life?" Flores asked.

Catherine leaned forward. "I found out he intended to turn House over to the police," she said.

Flores and Marco stared at her.

"Kijamba knew about House's activities?" Flores asked.

"Kijamba had found out about House's jewelry smuggling activities, hadn't he?" Marco asked.

Catherine said nothing. She chewed on her nails.

"How did Kijamba find out?" Marco asked.

"I don't know how he found out. I stayed with them over the weekend before the video shooting. I overheard him on the phone. I'd gone to Kijamba's study to ask him if he wanted something to drink. He didn't know I was there; he was telling someone that he knew all about House, but that he was waiting for the right moment after his video had finished to go to the police. He said he didn't need any distractions while he was filming. He didn't even want Shada to know. When it was all over, he'd fire House and go to the police," Catherine said.

Catherine looked up from the table. Her eyes seemed far away, as if she'd entered another solar system. "I couldn't let him do that."

"You were angry at Kijamba, weren't you?" Marco asked.

Flores stuck the raw footage CD Marco had examined that had now been wheeled into the interrogation room, into the player. He fast-forwarded to the place where the figure stood behind the bull-fighter Ortiz. "That's you behind Senor Ortiz, isn't it, Senora Taylor?"

Catherine didn't speak.

Flores took the video to forensics to enhance the film's quality. It now showed the woman quickly jabbing something in Kijamba's ear as she hugged him. He froze the CD, then he went over and pointed to the screen. "Here you are, sticking something in Kijamba's ear."

She looked away from the screen. "Yeah, I stuck it in his ear. I was furious with him. He stole one of my songs for his new tract. He changed the words slightly, but it was my song. He stole my song, and he wanted to put Thomas away. When I asked him about it. He called me a hanger-on leech. Creep," she said.

"What exactly was in the note?" Marco asked.

Catherine snarled. "It was a contract for royalties and the copyright to me of the song I wrote. I wanted him to agree to sign everything over to me."

"Why did you deliver it during the video shoot?" Marco asked.

"I wanted him to know that this was his last chance. When he threw it on the ground. I saw red. I told him before the shoot that I knew what he intended to do about Thomas. I told him I wouldn't let him turn Thomas in. He called me a desperate, washed-up old hag."

Marco leaned into the table. "I talked to Cipi. You didn't write that song. Cipi wrote it, and he freely gave it to Kijamba. They had an agreement that Cipi would receive a generous percentage of the royalties," Marco said.

She growled like a tangled feline in a net. DeLuca touched her hip where her gun rested.

"Let me tell you something. Cipi was a forgotten, tired, old blues singer whom no one cared about until I came into his life. When I met him, he was depressed. He'd gambled away everything. He told me I inspired him to stop gambling and write again. I convinced House to pay off his bets. I did everything for him. I listened to every boring version of that song and told him how to make it better. Cipi owed everything to me."

"So, you wanted to frame him for murder," Marco said.

Catherine shrugged.

"You killed Kijamba over a song?" Flores asked.

"If I had the copyright on that song, I'd have gotten millions in royalties. Then I could take care of Thomas, and he could get a divorce. He wouldn't need to rely on Kijamba. I could have taken care of both of us with that money."

"Thomas House was a married man with a family," Flores said.

"He had planned to leave her. We'd started making plans to move to another country and start again. I told him I'd have enough money to support us."

Marco and Flores snickered. Catherine stared at them, startled.

"You believed him that he intended to leave his wife for you, a washed-up dancer?" Flores asked.

"Thomas House has money stashed away all over the world. He didn't need you. If he divorced his wife, it wouldn't have been for you," Marco said.

Catherine glared at them. "You don't know what you're talking about. Thomas loved me. He told me he did. That spoiled brat, Kijamba, wanted to deny me what was mine, and he wanted to ruin Thomas. I couldn't let him. I did what I had to do for the man I loved."

Flores raised his eyebrows. "You're under arrest for murder, Senora Taylor."

Detective DeLuca escorted her back to her cell.

When she'd gone, Flores turned to Marco. He beamed. "We did it," he said.

Marco smiled. "Yep, we did."

The lab results came back shortly thereafter, showing Catherine's fingerprints on the poison dart. Her lawyer advised her she had no way out. That she should avoid a trial. She gave a full statement.

The Chief was ecstatic. The papers called him a hero. He congratulated both Flores and Marco. They were both recognized in the papers and given a commendation by the new Mayor of Vivirrambla.

Alvarez patted Marco on the back when Marco went for his usual coffee and introduced him to the restaurant as his favorite customer. Marco's friends called and texted their congratulations.

Once Flores and Marco wrapped up all the details, Belen and Marco went out to celebrate. Belen told Marco she was stunned that Catherine, someone she knew, had killed Kijamba, a legend of music beloved all over the world.

She looked at Marco over her wine. "We definitely won't be going to any more of her parties," she said.

About the Author

Paula B. Mays is a Native of Washington, D.C. She is the Current President of Sisters in Crime (SINC) Chesapeake Chapter, a Trademark attorney, a former USPTO (US Patent and Trademark Office) attorney, and has a Master of Public Health (MPH) degree from George Washington University. *Murder in La Plaza De Toros* is the first in a new series of mysteries set in a fictional town in Southern Spain. Paula has also published articles in the Huffington Post and has written other trademark-related articles. She lives in Arlington, Virginia.

AUTHOR WEBSITE:

Home | P Mays Mysteries (paulabmays.wixsite.com)

SOCIAL MEDIA HANDLES:

Paula Mays | LinkedIn

https://twitter.com/msmarbella

paulamays179 (@paulamays179) | TikTok

Also by Paula B. Mays

Murder In The Parador

Mystery Short Story: The Muffin Lady | Kings River Life Magazine